"Spill it, McKay. You [...] up your sleeve."

"Shame signs."

The hard cross of her arms over her midsection went slack. "Go on."

"The bet is simple. If I don't change your mind about men, I'll wear a shame sign and post it to social media. You get to decide what it says. Heck, I'll even let you make the sign."

The exact moment when she got interested in this idea played out in a very subtle head tilt. A lesser man might have missed it, particularly one who paid a lot of attention to driving. But Heath had stayed alive in Afghanistan by honing his ability to read everything about his surroundings.

And she was frothing at the mouth to watch him lose. Game on.

"You're serious."

"As an undertaker at a hanging."

Dear Reader,

Welcome back to Hidden Creek Ranch! This is the second book in the series starring sisters who inherit their grandfather's former stud farm in east Texas, near Gun Barrel City (which is still the best name for a Western town ever). Charli and Sophia Lang are remaking the place into a resort where guests can pretend to be a cowboy for a day.

Except the ranch is overrun with lots of "ologists" as Charli calls them, all of whom are getting in the way. No one gets in Charli's way as much as Heath McKay, though. The former SEAL is her official bodyguard, and she lives to give him the slip...until he strikes a most unusual bet with her. The wager is designed to help Heath do his job, not put him in such close proximity to Charli that she starts to intrigue him. They definitely weren't supposed to fall in love, and the archaeologists weren't supposed to find solid gold statues worth millions of dollars hidden in the woods. How is Heath supposed to keep Charli safe when he's started to care about her, and the threats are coming at them from all sides?

Thank you for joining me on this adventure. I can't wait for you to dive into the pages and discover the allure of treasure hunting alongside Charli and Heath. Happy reading!

Kacy

PS: I love to connect with readers. Find me at kacycross.com.

BODYGUARD RANCHER

KACY CROSS

ROMANTIC SUSPENSE

Harlequin®
ROMANTIC
SUSPENSE™

Recycling programs
for this product may
not exist in your area.

ISBN-13: 978-1-335-50262-9

Bodyguard Rancher

Copyright © 2024 by Kacy Cross

Harlequin Enterprises ULC
22 Adelaide St. West, 41st Floor
Toronto, Ontario M5H 4E3, Canada
www.Harlequin.com

Printed in Lithuania

MIX
Paper | Supporting
responsible forestry
FSC® C021394

USA TODAY bestselling author **Kacy Cross** writes romance novels starring swoonworthy heroes and smart heroines. She lives in Texas, where she's seen bobcats and beavers near her house but sadly not one cowboy. She's raising two mini-ninjas alongside the love of her life, who cooks while she writes, which is her definition of a true hero. Come for the romance, stay for the happily-ever-after. She promises her books "will make you laugh, cry and swoon—cross my heart."

Books by Kacy Cross

Harlequin Romantic Suspense

The Secrets of Hidden Creek Ranch

Undercover Cowboy Protector
Bodyguard Rancher

The Coltons of Owl Creek

Colton's Secret Past

The Coltons of New York

Colton's Yuletide Manhunt

Visit the Author Profile page
at Harlequin.com for more titles.

To my firstborn—It means the world to me that you're still the most enthusiastic supporter of my books. This one is for you.

Chapter 1

Charli could feel the ranch hand watching her. Not in the I'm-being-paid-to-keep-you-safe way, like she'd expect given the fact that he'd been employed to do exactly that. But in the way a man watched a woman when he wanted her to know he was interested.

Well, *she* wasn't interested.

She refused to so much as glance in his direction as she strolled from the back door of the house to the barn. Heath McKay was the opposite of easy on the eyes. The man was so hot he could burn a woman's retinas if she stared directly at him.

He knew it too. He was in that category of male who could charm a nun out of her habit. Who always had the next woman waiting in the wings—or maybe even right on stage at the same time as his current woman. How did Charli know? Because Heath McKay was Exactly Her Type in huge ten-foot-tall letters and she had crappy taste in men.

Her sister, Sophia, whom Charli secretly called Super Sophia, had hired him to make sure no one kidnapped any other Lang women from the ranch. After Sophia's harrowing experience of being taken from their home at gunpoint, she'd laid down some serious cash to ensure there were no repeats. Charli could have saved her the trouble. No one paid enough attention to The Other Lang Sister to bother kidnapping her.

She was about to change things, though. She had a plan. A good one. She was going to rise from the ashes of her old life and be the superhero of her new life. Maybe not Super Sophia, because her sister already had that locked. But someone else just as good, like Black Widow.

That was it. Charli could be Black Widow, eater of men, completely and utterly fearsome to the opposite sex. Black Widow was also awesome at her job and beautiful.

She could dye her hair red and buy some black outfits. It could work. She'd been telling herself to have a goal, hadn't she?

Now she just needed the right man to complete this picture.

"Paxton," she trilled as Heath's partner, the lean computer whiz, exited the new barn directly in her path. Lucky break. "Exactly who I was looking for."

Or rather, he was good enough.

"Me?" Paxton Pierce pointed at himself, a thin sheen of panic glazing his eyes that could be considered offensive if she let herself stop and think about it. "I was just...uh, Jonas is expecting me to move the horses from the south pasture with some of the other guys."

"You still have to do cowboy stuff even though you're technically doing security now?" she asked innocently, despite knowing that Paxton, Heath and Sophia's boyfriend, Ace Madden, were still working undercover as ranch hands. The fewer people who were aware of their real jobs, the better. "What if I have a security emergency? I might need you to subdue an intruder."

Heath was still watching her. She could feel his gaze between her shoulder blades, and it set off something inside that she could only describe as *delicious*. But she'd take that to her grave.

Charli let her fingertips graze Paxton's arm the way Black Widow might when she was being coy and flirty. It wasn't a chore. He was so cute with his clean looks and even cleaner Stetson, which looked like it had never hit the dirt. When she'd decided to move to the ranch and find a nice cowboy, Paxton Pierce was exactly what she'd pictured in her head.

Paxton could be the one to break her streak of cheating SOBs. He was clearly a great guy, one who called his mother every Sunday and had likely never seen the inside of a jail cell. Probably. This was her fantasy, and he could totally star in it.

Paxton's Adam's apple bobbed as he stepped just out of her reach. "If you have a security emergency, that's what McKay is for."

Yeah. Heath McKay was the problem, with his square jaw sporting a perpetual five o'clock shadow, and hooded gaze with even more shadows, and biceps that could make a woman drool. There was not one lick of *nice* anywhere in that man's body.

"Can't I switch babysitters midstream if I want to? Ask Ace to assign you to me instead?"

Man, there was an idea. Why hadn't she thought of that before now?

"Because—well, actually…" Poor guy swallowed so fast that he almost choked. "I'm what you call the brains. McKay is the brawn. Not that he's not smart, but his talents are definitely in the physical realm."

Oh, there was absolutely no question about the validity of that statement. But seriously. They'd caught the guy who had been terrorizing Sophia. The university people had squirreled away the gold coin she and Ace had found. What was there, really, to protect Charli from?

"I like a man with brains," she said with a little laugh.

Paxton did not seem bowled over by her charm. That was deflating. Maybe she should reel it back a little. Come at this from another angle. What would Black Widow do? She wouldn't sit around and wait for a man to figure out how awesome she was.

"Maybe you could find some time to ride with me out to the west pasture?" Charli fluttered her lashes. "I need to do a practice trail ride run before the guests start arriving next week."

That's when she'd start being taken seriously around the ranch. When people would see her as the other Ms. Lang instead of Charli, the screwup sister of the boss. As soon as she and Sophia welcomed the first guests, this place would stop being an inheritance and start being a dude ranch.

The Cowboy Experience. It had been her idea, one that she was secretly so proud of that she sometimes danced around in a circle of glee that Sophia had taken the suggestion.

Soon, she'd be able to forget she'd gotten fired from her last job at a pet store. A *pet store* for crying out loud. Where she'd been in charge of cleaning birdcages.

"Uh." Paxton glanced around feverishly. "I'd love to go on a trail ride but I, uh, I have to go do a thing with Jonas?"

"Are you sure? You don't sound sure."

Paxton edged away, pulling at his shirt collar as he practically tripped over his own two cowboy boots. "I'm sure. Ask McKay to ride with you on your trail ride, uh…thing."

She watched him go, the sun beating down on her back, vaguely disappointed Black Widow channeling had not gone well. But what did she expect? That she'd magically figure out in the course of two minutes how to not be a train wreck when it came to her love life? More practice needed, stat.

But when she turned around, Heath was standing a scant two feet away.

Not the sun on her back, then. *Him.* It was always him, right there, leaning against the fence, arms crossed in that insolent slouch that screamed Lock Up Your Daughters. His battered hat had seen more than its share of action, as had the very lived-in body underneath it. A scar ran along the base of his neck as if someone had tried to slice his throat but then abruptly stopped.

The man reeked of promise and next-level decadence.

Heath tipped his chin, his heated blue eyes tracking her with a lazy, practiced sweep. "Maybe you should try on someone your own size."

"Like who? You?"

She crossed her arms and stared him down in kind, but she had a feeling her own sweep of his cut torso and legs that went on forever had a lot more intensity in it than she'd like. It wasn't fair. No human should be that perfectly put together.

"Yeah. You could do worse."

"I have," she informed him sweetly. "That's how I know exactly what I'd find inside your box of chocolates. No interest in a repeat, thanks. You can toddle off and go do whatever undercover security agents do when they're pretending to be cowboys. I'm sure you're bored out of your mind watching me anyway."

"Bored is not the word I'd use."

Nonchalance rolled from him in waves, as if nothing bothered him, which pushed every single one of her buttons. A man this hot must have a volcano under his skin and she'd pay money to see it erupt. It would serve him right for harassing her.

"Well, when you think of the right word, don't come find me," she shot back and pivoted to walk away, speaking to him over her shoulder. "I'm going back to the house. Where I'll be doing very boring things that don't need your attention."

"Pierce is all wrong for you," he called, and she could almost hear his mouth tipping up in that amused smile that fooled no one. "You need someone you can't run roughshod over."

"I'll keep that in mind."

She escaped into the house, shutting the door of the blue Victorian behind her, then leaned on it, her lungs curiously unable to drag in air all at once. That man drove her bananas. But that didn't stop the frappé mode activating on her insides whenever he was around.

There had to be a cure for that. She'd tried going out with him once, just to see if she could burn off the attraction by feeding it. No dice. She'd spent the whole time with a heightened awareness that it wouldn't take Heath McKay more than about five minutes to break her heart. And she'd yet to patch it back together after the last loser had finished with it.

Careful to stay away from the windows in case *he* was peering through one, Charli skirted the kitchen island and dashed for the front door. Her babysitter was likely still stationed near the back door, his gaze trained on it in the event she made a reappearance.

Joke was on him. She lived to give him the slip.

No one put Charli in the corner. Well, except for the times she did it to herself. Which was most times. But that was the beauty of her brand-new plan. She was reinventing herself. No more screwing up. The time for that had long passed.

Skipping out the front door was a piece of cake. She had a lot of practice exiting a building without making a sound. She'd done it as a teenager plenty of times—it was easier to sneak out than it was to upset her single mother who was doing the best she could to raise three daughters after Charli's deadbeat dad had taken off.

Then there was the time she'd had to back up quickly after coming home to her apartment early to find Toby in bed with a very enthusiastic woman who was not Charli. Definitely not the time to hit a squeaky floor joist.

Better to stay off that subject before she forgot she was over Toby's cheating hide.

Back outside, Charli rounded the house near the long drive and headed for the woods. She really did have to scout the area for her trail ride, but she'd skip the horse this time. Too visible. Heath would insist on coming along and she wasn't about to fall for that trap. The more time they spent together, the harder it would be to convince herself she wasn't attracted to him.

This circular path to the woods meant she had to veer close to the encampment where all the university people lived. They had said it would be temporary, but it was starting to feel like they'd never leave. Over two dozen tents lined the south pasture, most of them housing archaeologists or anthropologists or some other kinds of *ologists* with names that were largely unpronounceable by regular humans. There were some museum people thrown into the mix too, or at least that was her understanding, after they'd found the jade beads from some dead guy's tomb in Mexico. Pakal the Great.

Apparently, her deadbeat father had actually found some

kind of treasure during his frequent jaunts to the Yucatan. The whole time he'd been busy ignoring his family, he'd scored some priceless artifacts and then buried them in various places around his father's ranch.

Grandpa Lang had died, then left the ranch to Sophia, Charli and their baby sister, Veronica, who had yet to check out her inheritance. Ergo, they now owned the treasure too, for whatever good that did when Sophia had unilaterally decided all the stuff should go back to Mexico.

As long as the *ologists* left before the guests got here, they could have the dead guy's tomb decorations.

And then Heath would be free to leave the ranch. No more laser beams between her shoulder blades. No more lying awake at night fantasizing about threading her fingers through his almost shoulder-length thick, curly hair, mussed from a day of hat-wearing, cowboy things.

"Hello, luv," a silky voice said from behind her.

Charli glanced over her shoulder to see one of the university guys with his eyes glued to her butt. He wore a Harvard T-shirt and a smirk that he'd likely developed around the silver spoon in his mouth.

"Hey. My eyes are up here." She pointed with two fingers to her face. "And it's Ms. Lang."

"Ah. You're one of the sisters." His gaze traveled up her front to land on her face as instructed, but his attention still felt a tad…off. "I'm Trevor Longley. Which Ms. Lang are you, Sophia or Charlotte?"

"Neither one." Not that she owed him any sort of explanation, but she couldn't stand it when someone called her Charlotte. "I'm Charli. Charlotte is a spider or a princess, take your pick, but don't address me that way if you expect an answer."

"Charli, then," he adapted smoothly, catching her hand

in his and bringing it to his mouth in some kind of weird eighteenth-century mannerism that she'd seen a dozen times on *Bridgerton*.

In real life, it wasn't so charming. It was kind of creepy. Plus, this guy wasn't British. He did have that moneyed New England look about him, though, so maybe he thought that counted for some reason?

"Well, see you around, Trevor," she said in hopes he would take the hint.

He didn't. He fell into step beside her, hooking their elbows together as if they were old pals and she'd invited him along on her trail ride scouting trip. This was getting a little tiresome and a lot out of hand.

She disentangled their arms and scowled at him, which obviously didn't mean the same thing to Harvard guys as it did to everyone else, since he just laughed.

"That's no way to be," he said with what felt like forced cheerfulness. "We're going to be good friends, I can tell."

"Because I'm giving you all sorts of come-on-to-me vibes?" she asked witheringly. "Maybe you need your vision checked."

Trevor's smile got a little less friendly and developed an edge she didn't like. "That's no way to speak to a guest."

No, it wasn't. Should she reel it back? Practice being a little more friendly? She kind of sucked at that. But there was something off about Trevor that tripped her radar.

"You're not a guest, Trevor," she emphasized. "You're a grad student who is quickly wearing out his welcome."

Where was everyone else? There were supposed to be approximately nine trillion dig nerds around here. Every time she left the house, she tripped over more than her share, yet there was no movement from the temporary campground. The woods behind her felt eerily quiet.

Why hadn't she thought to scout for a trail in the front part of ranch land where the grad students usually didn't go? Because she'd been thinking about Heath, not anything that mattered.

"You're going to want to watch your mouth, Charlotte," he said sharply and that's when he grabbed her.

His fingers bit into her arm as she yelped. What was this guy's problem?

She couldn't get free. No amount of yanking pulled her arm loose and the last tug wrenched her shoulder. "You're hurting me."

And if she didn't figure this out, he could do a lot more than that. Genuine fear coated her throat.

"Good," he snarled, all traces of his previous cheer gone. "I'm trying to be nice to you but you're obviously a bi—"

"Take your hand off Ms. Lang."

Heath. His voice saturated the tense atmosphere, flooding her with relief.

His expression as hard as his body, Heath materialized at her side, towering over her. And Trevor. Who didn't seem to be aware of the fact that Heath McKay stood a head taller and outweighed him by fifty pounds of muscle.

"Find your own amusement, friend," Trevor tossed out, his fingernails cutting into her skin. Also known as not following orders.

Heath cracked his neck, his gaze lethally honed into Trevor's face. "Looks like I have."

Chapter 2

Heath didn't like most people. He liked them even less when they came with a big sign on their forehead that read *I'm Entitled*.

This Harvard guy was going for some kind of prize, though, with a how-fast-can-I-die vibe, putting his hands on Charli like he had every right to, even as she was telling him no. Freaking dig nerds. They'd scurried into every nook and cranny on the ranch, causing problems and creating security nightmares.

Now this.

"Looks like you have? What's that supposed to mean?" Harvard snarled. "You think I'm going to share?"

Heath leveled his gaze, boring straight into the dude, giving him a giant opportunity to do the right thing so everyone could walk away. "I think you're going to provide me with about fourteen seconds of very satisfying entertainment. And then I'm going to deposit you in the back of a squad car to face assault charges. Or you can reassess the situation and make your own course adjustment."

Harvard glanced at Charli and then back at Heath and laughed. *Laughed*, like Heath habitually walked around issuing empty threats.

Just because he'd made a vow to stop solving things with

his fists didn't mean he couldn't take a brief hiatus from his new, calmer persona. In fact, it would be his pleasure.

No. No punching the idiot. That wasn't how this should go down. Heath wasn't that guy anymore.

Okay, deep breath. He could do this without resorting to violence. There were other ways to handle handsy jerkoffs. Even when Heath had a signed contract that said he was responsible for keeping Charli safe and had unwritten latitude to do that however he saw fit.

"You're going to want to take a step back, *friend*," Heath informed Harvard with as much venom in his voice as he could muster.

"Or what?"

That was the million-dollar question, wasn't it? Old Heath would have put this guy in traction and enjoyed every second of it. But Margo's exact words when she'd dumped him zinged through his head 24/7, leaving no room for his temper to make an appearance. If he wanted to prove to her that he wasn't the hothead brawler she'd labeled him as, he had to stop acting like one.

He *wanted* to stop. He wasn't a SEAL any longer. Reacting with a cooler head worked much better for civilian life.

Another deep breath didn't soothe the seething mass of anger simmering under Heath's skin. Dark edges crowded his vision.

And Harvard's hand was still clamped around Charli's arm. She didn't look quite as terrified as she had, but she was still in distress and Heath needed to fix that.

"Or I'll help you take a step back," Heath said silkily without specifying how he'd accomplish that. "How do you think your bosses would feel about you manhandling the owner of the ranch where you've been invited to dig?"

Harvard tossed his head. "My father's lawyers will handle any trouble you stir up."

Of course they would. His father probably paid a retainer fee specifically for this jerk-wad, much of which would have likely been spent erasing previous assault charges. It wouldn't shock him to discover Harvard had the rap sheet of a choir boy working on his Eagle Scout.

Now Heath was good and righteously pissed. Some trash deserved to be taken out, ex-girlfriends' opinions aside. "Then this is for both Charli and all the other women who have been standing in her shoes."

He popped the guy right in the nose. A good, hard, wholly satisfying jab that broke a lot of stuff that held his face together. The dark edges around Heath's vision dissolved. The dig nerd screamed and finally released Charli in favor of cupping his nose, which was currently pouring blood into his palm.

Nice. Heath took the opportunity to shuffle Charli behind him, where he could feel the heat of her warming his back. She clutched his arm, peering around it at her former assailant, clearly quite happy to have the wall of Heath between them.

It made him happy, too.

"I'll have you arrested for this!" Harvard announced, his bravado still in full force even after being treated to what amounted to the opening volley. "Do you know who my parents are?"

"Equally entitled brats?" he hazarded a guess, rolling up on the balls of his feet in case Harvard got some kind of idea that whatever dozen or so boxing classes he'd taken last semester would in fact help him here. This guy was the type who seemed incapable of taking a hint. Or a hit.

"My father—"

"Is not here," he finished for him. "And I would ask myself how hard it will be to dial him up after I break every single one of your fingers."

Finally, Harvard developed a slight glint of panic somewhere in the vast unreached places of his brain. "You can't do that."

"Well, let's deconstruct that, shall we?" Heath offered, crossing his arms lazily as if he had all the time in the world for a chat. Which he did, since Charli was his only job, but he'd already broken his vow once, and he'd rather not do it a second time. With his fists tucked away, it might be easier to remember to use his words instead. "If by 'can't' you mean I'm incapable, try me. Happy to give you a demonstration. If by 'can't', you mean you're going to stop me, thanks. I needed that laugh today. Or maybe you meant 'can't' as in it's a reprehensible thing to do and my moral fiber will prevent me from taking such a heinous step? Which is it?"

Harvard looked confused. Not a surprise. Most people didn't expect a guy they called the Enforcer in the Teams to have a vocabulary too. His ability to spit out twenty-dollar words was what had first won over Margo. She'd often told him how sexy the combo of muscles and a mouth was. Until he used the muscles. That, she wasn't so fond of.

"Heath, it's okay," Charli murmured from behind him, her palm still wrapped around his arm. "I'm fine. We can go."

"It's not okay," he growled, his gaze still boring into the dig nerd. "Because Harvard here isn't quite convinced that he should be taking a new path in life, one that leads him away from the wages of sin and toward the kingdom of righteousness where he respects women and fully understands the meaning of the word no."

He could practically hear Charli's eye roll. "I don't think you're going to convert him in the space of five minutes."

"I definitely won't if you don't let me continue."

Harvard tipped his head back, presumably to help with the blood flow issues his broken nose was causing him. "I need to go to the hospital."

Reluctantly, Heath nodded. "That you do. I'll let you live on one condition. That you swear never to touch another woman unless she asks you to. Square?"

"Whatever, dude. I'm walking away. Leave me alone."

"That is also up to you. I would be thrilled to never look at your face again," Heath informed him pleasantly. "You come near Charli, you get to find out what broken fingers feel like. You stay away from her, we never speak again. Your choice."

In what amounted to the smartest decision he'd made thus far, Harvard marched away, blood dripping from his fingers. Which left Heath with an even bigger problem—Charli. The thorn in his side. The Lang sister Madden had dubbed a loose cannon.

Heath just called her trouble. She even smelled like it, a infuriatingly indecipherable combo scent that was both feminine and dangerous at the same time. Probably because every time he caught wind of it, his body tensed for what followed: a punch of arousal to his gut and an unsettled certainty that she was about to piss him off.

"You're something else, McKay," Charli said, her voice a lot stronger now that Harvard wasn't around. "I thought you were going to talk him to death. Breaking his fingers would have been a lot more satisfying."

For him too. But he'd reeled it back, letting the dragon inside sleep. Maybe he could do this after all. Wouldn't it be something when he could show Margo that she'd called it wrong? That he was capable of being husband material.

But what would be more awesome—Charli not putting him in a position to have to break anyone's bones. He spun. "On that note, Ms. Lang, let's talk about why you went out the front door, like that was going to stop me from knowing you'd left the house?"

Charli had the grace to look embarrassed. "You have freakish stealth senses. It's infuriating."

"That's not an answer." He didn't uncross his arms, mostly because he hadn't lost the urge to break something and the only things around were a large rock or a tree, and he'd grown attached to the skin on his knuckles. "You can't give me the slip, so it's baffling to me that you keep trying. Maybe stop?"

"Maybe quit following me around?" she suggested sweetly, lifting her brown hair off her neck in an unpracticed way that would make a lesser man salivate.

Yeah, it was hot outside. Which was why he'd much rather be sitting in the shade doing surveillance with Charli safe in the house. "Talk to Sophia and Madden if you don't like it."

"Maybe I will. Paxton would be a much better choice to play bodyguard."

No. He wouldn't. Charli terrified him, which was amusing. But it was also not a good mix when trying to handle the difficult task of keeping her safe. Especially since she seemed determined to increase the complexity by refusing to cooperate.

"Good luck with that," he told her. "In the meantime, I need you to help me do my job. Go back to the house and stay there."

That way, he could circle back with their mutual friend

Harvard and make sure the dude understood he'd made an ironclad promise that Heath would be helping him keep for the foreseeable future. It would be best if the dig nerd went back to New England and saved everyone some grief, but odds of that happening were slim, unless Heath encouraged him to further consider the idea.

"I have things to do." Charli's crossed arms mirrored his.

He fought the urge to uncross them for her. Touching her would open up a whole can of worms he'd rather leave sealed tight, and he'd already pushed the limits of his restraint by not breaking more of Harvard's face than he had.

"I'm a fan of things," he told her with feigned nonchalance that he wished would magically calm down all the stuff writhing to get out. "I can do things, too."

"I bet you can," she muttered. "I should have qualified that with *solo* things."

"There is no solo at Hidden Creek Ranch. Not for you." He left off the implied bit, namely that she caused her own problems by not trusting him to do his job.

"I'll just sneak out again," she told him pertly. "So there's really no point in insisting that I go back to the house."

"Then I'll just come inside with you," he insisted through gritted teeth, willing his tone back into the realm of tranquil and collected. "You can't win this, Charli."

She stared at him, the air crackling between them with tension and a lot of other stuff that he'd refused to examine too hard. The whole point of New Heath was to show Margo what he was capable of in a relationship. Margo was it for him. He just needed to figure out how to get her back. He had zero interest in Charli Lang. The weird sparks between them didn't count.

"Fine. I'll go back to the house but only because I have a headache," she conceded. To her credit, she didn't protest nearly as much as he'd expected her to when he proceeded to escort her back the way she'd come, restricting herself to only a bit of jostling and thrown elbows.

Once he clicked the door shut—with her on the right side of it this time—he texted Madden to double up on rounds to ensure someone had eyes on all sides of the house while Heath made a short side trip to help the dig nerd pack up and leave.

Okay, and maybe to give himself some time to cool off. Because he was not cool. At all.

Replaying the scene in his head where the jerk-wad put his hands on Charli wasn't helping. Neither was reliving the feel of her standing behind him as he faced down the threat. He liked protecting those who couldn't do it for themselves. It was in his blood.

What he did not like was the sheer difficulty of stuffing his feelings into a tight container. It should be easier to handle a simple thing like reining in his temper. Granted, he'd made the vow to give up Old Heath before being assigned to watch over a champion button-pusher like Charli Lang.

But still. He'd done a lot of hard things in his life, not the least of which was earning his Trident after BUD/S training. Lots of guys rang out. But Heath had persevered, then spent a decade serving Uncle Sam overseas, ridding the world of filth one deployment at a time.

The loose-cannon Lang sister was not going to beat him.

Determined to ride off his anger, Heath saddled a horse and rode out to the university encampment. His mood didn't improve. Instead of tempting himself twice in one day, he found Harvard's project manager and had a civil word about reassigning the jerk-wad to another dig. The less people put him in a situation that required him to reel it back, the better.

Then he did a perimeter sweep along the east fence line at a full gallop that put enough endorphins in his bloodstream to take the edge off. Who knew that horseback riding would be the magic ticket to getting his sanity back?

Slowing to a walk to allow his mount—both of them, really—a chance to breathe, Heath focused on his surroundings, gradually aware of a prickle along the back of his neck. It was a warning sign he'd learned never to ignore, which was the reason he'd come home from Afghanistan alive.

Something wasn't right. What?

There. A circular patch of grass lay in the wrong direction from the surrounding area.

Heath cantered over to it, peering down at the green someone had stomped flat. No question it was a human, because in the center lay a couple of cigarette butts.

No ranch hand would have left behind something like that, not if they wanted to keep their job and their hide, because Jonas would have both if he caught one of his guys littering where the horses grazed. Not to mention how harmful a cigarette butt would be to a horse if one accidentally ingested it.

One of the university or museum people, then?

Or two of them… Heath homed in on the second circle, not as obvious as the first. It had been a meeting. One orchestrated outside of security camera range. For Heath's money, he'd say because one or both weren't supposed to be on site, or they would have just chatted anywhere on the property.

It was hard to tell from the evidence how long ago this meeting had taken place, but Heath recalled it had rained about a week ago, so probably since then. But the horses had been in this pasture two days ago, and several of them liked to eat the grass on the other side of the fence. Odds were, they would have trod all over these circles, destroying them.

So within the last two days. At least one, maybe even both these people weren't supposed to be here, which made them a threat to Charli and Sophia.

Oh, no. Not on his watch.

Adrenaline poured into his system, priming him for battle. A haze clouded his vision. He kicked the horse into gear, a warrior on the warpath.

Just as the horse hit a full gallop, he remembered. Forced a breath, like he'd been training himself to do. He wasn't the Enforcer anymore. He couldn't be. But then what did that make him? Who was this post-SEAL Heath McKay if he wasn't that guy?

Heath pulled the horse back into a trot and then stopped, rubbing the back of his neck as the sun baked his shirt into his sweat-soaked skin. What could New Heath do to handle this situation calmly and without violence?

Inform. Madden and Pierce needed to be updated on the situation.

Track. Heath could follow the trail and see where it led. Nothing more. And then he'd see what was what.

Chapter 3

"Earth to Charli."

Charli blinked and focused on Sophia's face across the desk that they were sharing for the moment. "Sorry. Did you say something?"

Sophia set her pen down on the pad that held her written to-do list, the one that she regularly vetted to see if the task would make it to the real to-do list on her phone. It was exhausting even thinking about having a tryout to-do list, as if one list wasn't good enough—the tasks actually had to *audition* for a spot.

"I said, is everything on track for the decorator to finish tomorrow?" her sister told her. "For the third time. I guess I don't have to ask what's taking all your attention after that big production Heath made to escort you into the house."

The wry twist of Sophia's lips set off a lick of guilt in Charli's gut and she glanced away, toward the wall of the office. "It's not what you think."

Nor did Charli think telling Sophia exactly what had happened with Trevor the Handsy Harvard grad student would be a great plan either. She'd side with Heath and that would make it twice as hard for Charli to leave the house without her bodyguard in tow.

"I get it. I have a hard time concentrating sometimes too,

when I know there's just a couple of walls between me and Ace." Sophia's voice took on this dreamy quality that she didn't have to explain at all.

Or rather, Charli would prefer that she didn't. Everyone knew Sophia and Ace were gaga over each other and they'd happily rub it in everyone's faces if given half a chance. It was both nauseating and jealousy-inducing.

"Yeah, you don't actually get it," she grumbled. "McKay is a pain in my butt, that's all."

"I thought you guys were dating."

There was a glint in Sophia's eye that Charli didn't like. It was part *I'm about to interfere* and part *what in the world is wrong with Ace's partner?*

"It didn't work out."

"Oh."

She could see Sophia trying to reason out in her head what the issue could have possibly been, and odds were high that telling her Heath was *exactly* Charli's type wouldn't actually explain anything. Neither did Charli feel like spelling out why Heath being her type wasn't a good thing. Sophia never made bad choices or screwed up anything.

This ranch—the Cowboy Experience—was Charli's chance to change her fate. Falling back into the same old same old traps wasn't happening. Except that meant she had to focus and stop making Sophia repeat herself.

More to the point, she had to stop daydreaming about Heath's biceps. And his unexpected chivalrous streak. Really, what woman could resist a man who *defended* her, and then threatened the loser who'd cornered her?

She'd never felt so feminine and important and protected in her life. Because of *Heath*.

It was messing with her.

Charli squared her shoulders. "The decorator will be

done tomorrow. Guaranteed. I paid a little extra for a rush job."

"You did what?" Sophia set down the pen she'd just picked up. "Char, you can't do that without talking to me. We have a budget."

"Yeah, but I'm an equal partner," she argued, thrilled to have that leg to stand on. "I have to make decisions sometimes without consulting you due to time constraints. I'm trying to get a job done on schedule and did what I deemed best in that moment. Doing this together means you have to trust me."

Spoken like a true Black Widow in the making. Black Widow wouldn't flinch when faced with questions about her choices.

Sophia blew out a breath and nodded. "Okay. You're right."

She was? Charli stared at Sophia, convinced she'd misheard. "Okay? As in…okay? You're fine that I spent the extra money?"

This was a test. A trap. Something. Sophia never thought Charli was right about much of anything.

Shrugging, Sophia gave her a look. "I'm trying to do as suggested. Trust you. I don't like it, but I can't be in control of everything or there's no point in doing this together. So, yes. You're right."

Well. Charli crossed her arms and sank down a little bit in her chair as something light and fluttery beat at her heart. "That was a lovely apology."

Sophia rolled her eyes. "Don't get used to it. Switching gears after a lifetime of being a control freak isn't something I'm going to accomplish with a lot of grace."

A grin tugged at Charli's mouth. "I can give you a lot more chances to practice."

"Please—" Sophia cut off whatever she was about to say when someone knocked at the door.

Ace poked his head in without waiting for Sophia to call out to him, his trademark cowboy hat the color of beach sand set low on his forehead. "We have a situation."

Her sister's boyfriend had two modes: mushy in love with Sophia and all business. This was definitely the latter. He bristled with authority, looking like he could handle anything thrown at him with efficiency and expertise. And he had. He'd gone searching for Sophia with righteous fury when she'd been kidnapped, yet still managed to give off the impression he'd invented cold calculation. He was attractive, if you liked the clean-cut all-American type.

In short, he was the opposite of his partners. An iceberg to Heath's volcano and Paxton's computer brain. Charli often wondered how in the world they'd become friends.

Sophia sat up straighter, her expression alert. "What's going on?"

Ace stepped inside the office, his hat automatically in his hand because he was that kind of guy. "McKay found evidence in the south pasture that we might have some unwelcome company on the property."

"There are a lot of people on the ranch who are unwelcome," Charli said with an arched brow. "You're going to have to be more specific."

Ace glanced at her. "It was a meeting between at least two people, conducted out of range of the security cameras. That means at least one of them isn't on the official roster of those authorized to be on site as part of the excavation team. In the digital age, we assume that a face-to-face conversation means someone didn't want their association tracked and also has a good handle on the ranch routine since they picked a time with low risk of being seen together by a staff member. All of that adds up to a problem."

Sophia's expression flattened. "An associate of Cortez?"

That was the name of the guy who had kidnapped her sister, but he was in jail with no chance of bail. Charli recalled that he'd given the authorities a very limited amount of information about his associates, but the one name he'd offered up had landed like a bomb: Karl Davenport. Her father's treasure hunting partner.

"It's possible," Ace admitted.

"Cortez only had one associate who matters." Sophia and Ace both looked at Charli. "It's true. I'm just saying it. It's Karl, right? That's who you think it is. Isn't that why Ace is here having this chat with us?"

The implications of that—she couldn't even wrap her brain around it. But she did know one thing. It meant there was a lot of Heath in her future unless she figured out something else superfast.

"My liaison at the sheriff's office confirmed that Karl Davenport is still at large, yes," Ace said. "And most certainly dangerous, given that he hired Cortez to rough up Sophia and scare her away from the ranch."

"Oh, man, this is not good." Sophia tapped her pen against her paper to-do list, her mind obviously on the hundreds of things that they still had to do to get the ranch ready to open its doors to guests in less than a week. What she did not look like was scared. Nothing scared Sophia. It was a skill Charli would like to learn.

"Maybe it's someone else," Charli suggested with a confidence she wasn't sure she felt.

This was the last thing they needed. The guests would be here soon, and it was already going to be hard enough to navigate around all the dig nerds. Throwing another threat into the mix didn't help.

Sophia stared at her. "Like who? Dad?"

"Well, maybe." That had honestly never occurred to her, but she latched onto the alternative with gusto. "Why isn't that possible? Just because we haven't seen him in years doesn't mean he won't make an appearance now that the university people are digging up his cache. Maybe he wants it back."

"That's also a possibility," Ace said with zero inflection, giving away nothing of what he was thinking. "Which doesn't mean David Lang isn't a threat to either of you. You'll forgive me if I wait to pass judgment on his paternal instincts until I have a reason to trust him."

"That's fair," Sophia said, and Charli nodded. "You'll certainly not get an argument from either of us on that front."

"Yeah, I'm happy to pass full judgment of his father skills right here and now," Charli said with a scowl. "David Lang is a name on my birth certificate. That's it."

Honestly, the idea of their father roaming around the ranch that he'd never bothered to claim as his birthright might sit worse with Charli than knowing it was Karl Davenport out there plotting harm to people she loved. David Lang was a parasite on humanity. The kind of man who dumped his responsibilities at the drop of a hat, who thought nothing of donating sperm and skipping town in favor of gold over his family.

"We're assuming nothing at this point," Ace told them. "Other than the fact that whoever it is doesn't intend to march up to us with identification and his hands raised. So we have a security issue that my team is handling. Needs to be allowed to handle."

And that was the real reason he was here. Charli could see it plastered all over his face. "You came to make sure I'm properly chastised about ditching my shadow earlier."

Sophia glared at her. "Charli. We talked about this. You can't roam around without Heath. That's the whole reason he's here. To keep you safe."

"I know," she grumbled as the reality crashed over her. If she wanted to cross the finish line with the Cowboy Experience, she had to give a little—and that meant agreeing to be babysat. "I hear everyone loud and clear. I solemnly swear I will drag McKay around with me everywhere I go, including the shower and to bed."

And that was precisely where she assumed he'd end up if given half an inch of latitude. She could see it now, the way he'd disarm her with the perfectly logical excuse that he could protect her much better if he never left her side and wouldn't it be handy to have someone to wash her hair while he was there and already naked?

Yeah. She could see it. Her brain seemed pretty set on looping that scene through her mind's eye over and over again. She nearly groaned as she pictured exactly how much of her bed Heath would take up.

Ace's expression, to his credit, didn't budge an inch. "The logistics of how he protects you are between you and him. I'm only asking that you don't leave the house unless you're in the company of the man tasked with ensuring you don't end up on the wrong end of a nine millimeter."

"Do you think we need to consider delaying the opening of the ranch?" Sophia asked Ace in all seriousness, like that was an option she was considering.

"Hold on," Charli protested as it felt an awful lot like the office floor had turned into quicksand. "I said I wouldn't go anywhere without Heath. You have Ace watching out for you. The guests will be fine. No one cares about them."

"Well, we don't know what these new intruders might want," Ace said, hesitating. "We can't be sure they aren't unknown threats with unknown motives. They could be after the treasure themselves, hoping to beat Davenport and the university people to the punch. Pierce ran a lot of analyses, but we don't have enough evidence to be certain about anything."

"We should consider delaying the opening, then," Sophia said with a nod, her mouth tight.

"No, we can't consider that." Charli pinched the bridge of her nose, as her plan started circling the drain. "Just give it a few days. Ace and his team will be stepping up surveillance and stuff, right?"

Ace confirmed that with a nod, tapping his hat against his wrist. "I'm hiring a couple of guys to start doing perimeter sweeps in rotation. We're not leaving anything to chance. The more information we can get, the better prepared we'll be to handle whoever these guys are."

"We don't have a couple of days," Sophia countered. "We have one day. If we're going to delay the opening, we have to give people enough notice to cancel flights and rebook."

Charli's temples started throbbing. "We're not telling people to cancel flights. The opening is happening."

Otherwise, her stake in this would slip away. This was the only thing she'd ever had in her life that she could point to and say, *This is mine. The Cowboy Experience is happening because of me.*

"Give it a day, Soph," Ace told her, and something passed between them that made Charli's throat hurt. They had something special that most people would never get to experience, herself included. Why couldn't she get interested in a straight arrow like Ace? Surely there were more guys like him out there.

Heath McKay wasn't one of them, though. That fact presented itself to her loud and clear when she texted him that she had to go to the store later, like a good girl who did what she was told.

She stepped out of the house and into the maelstrom of testosterone and biceps on her porch. "Punctual. I like that in a man."

Heath reset his hat on his head, the new angle highlighting his amazing cheekbones. "Agreeable. I like that in a woman."

She made a face at him. "Don't get used to it. As soon as you figure out who had the clandestine meeting in the south pasture, I'm back to inventing creative ways to frustrate you."

"Pretty sure that's still going on," he muttered as he opened the passenger door to his truck, an ancient flatbed that she'd always assumed he'd procured from somewhere as part of his cover. It didn't fit him in the slightest. A sleek Jaguar was more his speed, with a deep, throaty engine, ready to pounce or sprint away pending his mood.

"I'm here. In the truck with you," she pointed out when he slid into the driver's seat, then nearly swallowed her tongue as the cab filled with Heath.

It was more than a physical presence. She could feel him along her skin even though both of his hands were on the wheel. Delicious. And then some. But she had no intention of feeding his ego by letting him see her reaction.

"You in here is what's frustrating," he commented mildly as he backed out of the circular drive in front of the main house. "What store are we going to?"

"Whatever one in town carries tampons," she said and

grinned as he shot her a look. "What? You wanted to spend twenty-four seven following around a woman, congrats. This is part of life."

"Do you hate all men or am I just special?"

"Men are generally the spawn of Satan, but I will admit a particular pleasure at riling you specifically," she informed him with genuine cheer, a minor miracle given the way her day had gone thus far.

Heath rolled to a stop at a red light and turned his head to treat her to a once-over that wiped the smile right off her face. It was the first time she'd registered him really *looking* at her, and she suddenly had the worst feeling she'd turned to glass. As if he could see everything, even the things she didn't want him to.

"What?" she croaked out defensively. "Is my shirt backward?"

"Not all men are evil," he countered. "Though before too long, I'm going to be asking for the name of the one who left you with that impression."

Oh, man, he'd definitely walked right in and helped himself to a whole heap of Charli's vulnerabilities without her consent. That was not okay.

What would Black Widow do?

She'd kick the man on her way to the curb. "Beg to differ. You can ask for a name, but you're not going to get it. And for your information, more than one man has given me my set-in-stone viewpoint about the origins of the male species, so the odds of you changing my mind are zero."

"Wanna bet?"

Chapter 4

*W*anna bet?

A throwaway phrase. One Heath hadn't necessarily meant for her to take literally. But Charli's brows lifted as she contemplated Heath, and dang if he didn't like being the subject of her perusal. Even if she was looking at him as though he'd started spouting sonnets. And yes, he did know what a sonnet was, but he wasn't planning on reciting any to her.

What had just instantly scrolled through his mind was way better.

"Do I want to bet what?" she asked.

"Whether I can change your mind. About men," he clarified because she was totally the type to misread this very specific offer, which definitely needed about a hundred guardrails to keep it from going south. "You've obviously got an ex in your rearview mirror who treated you like a disposable wipe. I'm saying I can prove to you that not all men are like that. I'm not like that."

Charli threw back her head and laughed, a silvery sound that shouldn't be coaxing ripples along his skin, especially not when he was reasonably sure he was the source of her amusement.

"It's not funny," he growled.

"It is on so many levels that I can't fully address each one fast enough." She held up a finger. "But really, I only need the one point. You have nothing I want, so there's nothing to bet."

Now she was talking his language. There was nothing on this earth Heath liked more than a challenge, and she'd just dropped one right in his lap. Never mind that he'd come up with this idea strictly because they had to spend every minute in each other's company. Why not be productive at the same time? Practice being New Heath a little.

Except she'd turned it on its head because that's what Charli did—disrupt things.

"Darling, you are such a liar. I have plenty you want," he drawled and grinned when a telltale flush rose up high on her cheekbones. "But I wasn't talking about that kind of bet. As much as I am thinking about some very interesting images you've kindly put into my head, I'm suggesting totally different stakes that I am positive even you will appreciate."

Heath kept his gaze trained on the road ahead, giving Charli plenty of space to work up a healthy curiosity. He could practically hear her teeth grinding from here, which put a nice little kick in his chest to know he'd managed to get her worked up. Finally, she crossed her arms.

"Spill it, McKay. You clearly have something up your sleeve. The sooner you lay it out, the sooner I can shoot it down."

"Shame signs."

The hard cross of her arms over her midsection went slack. "Go on."

"The bet is simple. If I don't change your mind about men, I'll wear a shame sign and post it to social media.

You get to decide what it says. Heck, I'll even let you make the sign."

The exact moment when she got interested in this idea played out in a very subtle head tilt. A lesser man might have missed it, particularly one who paid a lot of attention to driving. But Heath had stayed alive in Afghanistan by honing his ability to read everything about his surroundings.

And she was frothing at the mouth to watch him lose. Game on.

"You're serious."

"As an undertaker at a hanging."

Her mouth twitched. "You're something else, my guy. I'm assuming that the reverse is true. If you somehow pull a rabbit out of that Stetson and hit whatever criteria I come up with that proves you've changed my mind about men, I have to wear your shame sign."

"Of course." He reset his hat on his head, already contemplating the sheer number of bunnies that he'd be forced to conjure before too long. Because she was going to say yes. He could feel it. "I already have the wording picked out. 'I was wrong, and Heath was right.'"

"You know my problem with men is that they're all horn dogs who can't keep their pants on around other women, right?"

Yeah, he wasn't confused. Trying not to be too stung by her tone, he glanced at her as he parked in the lot at the Walmart in Gun Barrel City. "What exactly happened with the former Mr. Charli that gave you the idea that's difficult?"

Her expression iced over. "There's no former Mr. Charli. And that's not part of the deal. No history lesson included. Take it or leave it. And note that my idea of faithful is extremely stringent. You'll get zero freebies like a random woman's number in your phone who's 'just a friend.'"

She accompanied this with exaggerated air quotes and a sneer that hooked him in a place he was pretty sure she hadn't been trying to reach. He stared at her, trying to figure out why the rock she'd stuck in her chest to replace her heart bothered him so much.

Charli meant nothing to him. What did he care if she'd been burned so badly by her crappy ex?

"For the record, I'm not a player," he murmured. That had never been Margo's problem. "But I'm game for leaving our history out of the mix."

He was more than happy to keep his motivation for all this to himself, though he would have explained it if pressed. Probably. Maybe not all of it. Actually, he wasn't even sure he could fully express why this bet had become such a big deal so quickly, but it was.

Because if he could prove to Charli that he was different than her cheating ex-boyfriend, that he had what it took to treat a woman like a queen, then he could prove to Margo that he was husband material. Right? Charli would get to see a man who knew how to toe the line. One who could be more righteous than a choirboy on Easter Sunday with zero passionate outbursts to his name.

And Heath got a free pass to practice for the real thing. No one would get hurt. Everyone wins.

It was the most brilliant plan in the universe.

"How is this even going to work, McKay?" Charli asked, the thread of incredulity lifting the ends of her words past the point where it sounded like she was still on board. "To prove you're not a serial cheater, we'd have to get married and be together until the day we die. And you and I would probably kill each other before we hit our one-week anniversary."

He had to laugh because yeah. "That's what makes this such a great deal for you. You get the Heath McKay special and don't even have to worry about whether you can do your part long-term."

"Wait. What?" He had her attention now.

People streamed by his flatbed on their way into the store, but neither of them got out of the truck. With one hand draped over the steering wheel, he lifted a shoulder as if it was obvious. "This is a bet. You have to do something for me in exchange. This is not just a one-way street."

Though if this worked, he would get the most benefit. Old Heath would be laid to rest forever. New Heath would emerge as a man worthy of an elegant, classy woman like Margo.

"You're saying you don't think I can do my part?" she ground out and then seemed to think better of doing her own digging in. "What are you even talking about? Is there more to this than you bringing me flowers or whatever passes in your head as a lame attempt to change my opinion about men?"

"Yeah. You have to give me a fair shot. Unlike the last time."

Clearly stymied by the direction of the conversation, Charli stared out the front windshield as if she hoped to glimpse whatever had captured his interest on the other side of the glass. Ha. Little did she know that every iota of his focus was on her. The shift of her leg against the seat. The way her index finger tapped against her elbow. A restless energy that his own recognized. It was part of what fascinated him about her, that she could be so magnetically alluring without a power suit or a pair of ice pick stilettos in sight.

And he didn't have any better handle on her this time than he had last time.

Nor had he realized that her previous rejection still prickled a little. Maybe that had snuck a few tendrils into the roots of this deal. She didn't have to know that.

"For your information, I gave you a fair shot last time," she informed him loftily.

Also known as the one and only time he'd tried to breach her defenses with the atrocious crime of taking her to dinner at the steak place one street over. He still wasn't sure what had spooked her, but since his heart belonged to Margo, the way it had ended—with her fleeing from his truck the moment he'd pulled up at the ranch—was for the best.

He'd only been trying to move on with the one woman who had sparked his interest in the months since Margo had kicked him to the curb. See if he did that again. This bet wasn't about that.

"We have different definitions of what constitutes a fair shot," he countered mildly. "So different that I'm making it part of the terms of the bet. For this to work, you have to commit. Three weeks. No arguments. No weaseling out of it because you have a headache."

Suspicion narrowed her eyes as she swung her gaze to meet his. "What do you get out of this?"

The million-dollar question. Suddenly he wasn't so keen to lay all of his cards on the table, after all. "An opportunity to do my job without having to hunt you down for one. We have to spend time together, whether you like it or not. This at least gives us both a chance to relax a bit."

Truth. Or as much of it as he planned to give her.

Her chuckle caught him off guard. "You're the least relaxing person I've ever met and you're the liar if you don't say the same about me."

"I meant relax in the knowledge that we're stuck together," he shot back with a smirk. "You can't ditch me for three weeks. During that time, you treat it like we're in a relationship. I'm betting you can't do it."

Man, she was good. Not a muscle in her body twitched. He would know. He was so dialed into her that he might be able to detect if she so much as moved a hair. That's the only reason the slow smile that spread across her face punched him so hard in the gut.

"You're one more stipulation away from a straitjacket," she said and that's when he knew he had her. "Counter term. You have to take me on official dates. One a week for every single week of the three. You're paying. And no cop-outs. McDonald's doesn't count."

Shocked that she'd fallen right into his trap like that, he contemplated her, his own suspicions raising one of his brows. "You'd agree to that?"

She lifted her hands. "What, to letting a man turn himself inside out to impress me with his imaginative ability to conjure new and noteworthy date locales week after week? Yeah. I'd sign up for that in a heartbeat."

"Then we have a deal." He stuck out his hand, wondering if she even realized he'd already won.

Because whatever number her ex had done on her, the creep had done him a huge favor. Heath McKay knew how to treat a woman. Where she'd gotten the idea that he couldn't keep it in his pants, he had no clue, but commitment was his middle name.

Where he struggled was tamping back his tendency to be over the top with it. Margo wanted refinement—that's what he'd give her. After he spent the next three weeks getting his technique honed. New Heath had free rein from here on out. No letting his emotions off the leash. Should be easy. This was Charli after all.

Charli stuck her hand in his and the jolt sang up his arm. She'd felt it too, judging by the way she snatched her hand back and turned to look out the passenger window. "You're going to a lot of trouble just to get me to stop ditching you."

"I'm a workaholic. Sue me," he commented with a grin. "Besides, I like to win."

"Same goes."

Oh, he had no doubt. There was only a certain kind of woman who would take a deal like this one, and it wasn't the sort who looked forward to having a man pick up the check. Odds were, she'd go hard in the direction of trying to trip him up, stringing women across his path in hopes of goading him into violating the terms.

On that note—since he hadn't been born yesterday—they needed to put a few things in blood before he'd ever agree that he'd lost this bet at the end of the three weeks. Which he already knew she'd try to claim regardless. "When we get back to the ranch, we're each going to write down our criteria for how we judge who wins. It goes in a sealed envelope. Mine to Sophia, yours to Ace."

"What good is that going to do?" she complained, instantly dismissing it with a curt slice of her hand. "I'm just going to write down something that will stack the deck toward me, and you'll write down the same for you and we'll argue about it till the cows come home."

"I mean we'll write it down for each other. And then if it's sealed, no one can argue that the criteria wasn't met."

For who knew what reason, that was the thing that got a reaction from her. And it was the strangest mix of slightly dazzled and a whole lot unhappy about it. "You're a lot slicker than I give you credit for."

"I'll take that as a compliment."

And the bet as a challenge. In more ways than one. He certainly hadn't climbed into this truck with the intention of using Charli's shenanigans as a way to practice being New Heath. But if this was what it took to get Margo back, great. He could do his job keeping Charli safe at the same time. Brilliant.

That's when she slid out of the truck and sashayed into Walmart without so much as a by-your-leave, forcing him to scramble after her. As she walked, she tossed a smirk over her shoulder.

His chest iced over. She was planning something.

What, he had no idea. He'd missed that crucial point during the negotiations, too set on his own agenda to realize she had one of her own. Of course she did. No woman with the personality of a bottle rocket about to explode agreed to a bet that a mere man could change her opinion about much of anything, let alone whether he could change her mind about men as a whole.

Too late. She hadn't fallen into his trap. He'd fallen into hers.

Chapter 5

For better or worse, Charli had a new boyfriend. The best kind—one that would vanish in three weeks. Or sooner.

Not that she thought for a millisecond that any of this nonsense meant anything to Heath, which was most of the reason she'd agreed to the bet. Okay, maybe more like fifty percent, the other fifty percent being the absolute need to win. Not just because of the shame sign potential, though that had sweet bonus written all over it.

But because Heath McKay needed to be taken down a peg or twelve. He thought he could change her mind about *men*? Heath—who defined everything that was wrong with men and then tacked on a few more of his own unique surprises. That guy thought his moves would be smooth enough to make Charli forget that the whole time, he was trying to win a bet. And would do anything to get there.

That alone put her blood on boil.

Besides, Heath didn't know that Black Widow's superpowers lay in driving men away.

Nor did she have any plans to inform him. He had three weeks to do his best to resist her natural man repellent, but in the end, Charli would prevail. She always did.

Even her own father hadn't bothered sticking around. Sometimes late at night, she relived that early childhood trauma of lying awake, straining for the sound of her dad coming back home. She'd wanted to be the first one to hear him, to realize that all her prayers had been answered. Eventually, she'd grown into an adult who'd gotten used to disappointments and a silent God.

This bet would be no different. She'd put Heath in his place and move on.

Except when she came out of her room, she practically tripped over her new boyfriend, who was waiting for her outside her door in a casual lean that made it seem like he was holding up the wall with his sheer physical presence, instead of the other way around.

Gah, how did he look so good in the morning? Any woman with naturally curly hair like his would have to spend hours taming it. Not Heath McKay. No, he stuck his chocolate brown hat over it and instantly turned into a cowboy supermodel, complete with the rugged five o'clock shadow that would make any breathing female wonder what it felt like against her skin.

"Do you ever shave?" she grumbled by way of greeting because pre-coffee, that was the best he was going to get. Better to get used to it now.

Heath rubbed his chin absently. "Only if I remember. Why, are you worried about beard burn when I kiss you?"

Gravity ceased to exist and nearly threw Charli to the ground, but of course, he was right there, grasping her arm the moment she faltered. Annoyed at his quick reflexes and even quicker grin, she scowled at him. "You never said anything about kissing."

"I never said anything about not kissing. Besides, if I have to be monogamous for the next three weeks, who else am I going to kiss?"

"A pig that flies by?" she suggested sweetly. "Because you'd have a better shot, frankly."

He just squeezed her arm with a slight thumb caress, which set off a flurry of tingles that she didn't hate. But she wasn't about to let Heath know that.

Only the look on his face shut down her throat, freezing it.

"Trust me, Charlotte," he murmured. "There will be kissing. We're supposed to be acting like we're in a relationship. It's a natural progression considering how much time we're going to be spending together. You're eventually going to realize you actually like me."

That was enough to get a laugh out of her icy throat. And make her forget to spit out a reminder at how much she hated being called Charlotte. "You keep right on dreaming, McKay. With an imagination like that, you should go work for Disney."

"Fine. No kissing. Unless you start it," he said, crossing his arms to show off his biceps, which she suspected he did to remind people that he could deadlift a half-grown horse if he had a mind to. "In the meantime, I have a job. Two jobs. Charli's babysitter and eventual Bet Winner. How smart of me to combine the two."

Yeah, she'd gotten the message yesterday. This whole bet was a scheme he'd cooked up to amuse himself while he did his job. That was another reason to lean into smearing him all over the pavement. Driving him into the arms of another woman would be oh-so-satisfying for a multitude of reasons.

Even though part of her wished it wouldn't be so easy. A small part. Tiny—way in the back.

Most of her just couldn't wait to shove his face in the fact that he'd done nothing but solidify her place in the world as a woman who had his number. It was zero. He had as much of a shot at changing her mind about men as she did of stumbling over one who could.

Which reminded her of the ground rules she'd come up with last night. She turned toward him to lay them out and misjudged the distance, smacking straight into his solid torso. His hands snaked around her waist instantly, holding her steady. Holding her against the magnificence that lay under his shirt, which she'd thought she'd already cataloged pretty well visually. Oh, she so had not.

"Are we starting the kissing already?" he murmured, his smoky gaze locked on hers with enough intensity to steal her breath. "Or are you just demonstrating your willingness to stick by my side? I'll admit, I didn't think you'd be so into that aspect of this deal."

"I'm not." She lifted her hands and slapped them onto his chest, fully intending to shove him back a healthy step, but kind of got lost along the way when the feel of him fully permeated her fingers.

The good Lord had definitely been in a mood when He'd built this one. Then Heath had added additional texture, like the scar along the base of this throat, highlighted by the sun-bronzed skin around it. There was so much to see and do and explore that he should sell tickets to the wonderland of his torso. There might be drool in her future.

"Charli." She slid her gaze to his face, which was this delightful combo of leashed and struggling with it. "Unless you're planning to spend the next three weeks with me in your room with the door shut, you're going to want to stop looking at me like that."

That was enough to put a fire under her feet, propelling her backward.

And enough to allow her brain to jump-start itself.

Plus give Heath the opportunity to let a dangerous smile spread across his chiseled jaw. "Miz Lang, I do believe you've already moved on to third date territory."

"Oh, don't be ridiculous," she snapped, completely aware that she'd just handed him a lot of ammunition that she'd likely be sorry for later. "I never said I wasn't attracted to you. I'd have to be blind and maybe from another planet not to realize you look like a movie poster for a *Magic Mike/ Yellowstone* crossover."

Instead of laughing like she'd expected—like any other man would have—Heath cocked his head and gave her another one of those deep perusals, as if her skin had vanished, leaving her thoughts and dreams exposed for him to read. "Why does it bother you so much? That you're attracted to me?"

"Because it makes it harder for me to win the bet. Duh." She tossed her hair, terrified he'd see right through her lie.

If he found out he was exactly her type, no telling what he'd do with that knowledge. Plus, she didn't *like* that she naturally drove men into the arms of other women. It hurt. And allowing herself to admit an attraction to him gave him the power to do that.

"Maybe instead of pushing me away, you should try sliding into this," he suggested. "It's a freebie. No harm, no foul. Practice being in a healthy, long-term relationship with no strings."

The concept was so mind-boggling she could only stare at him for a hot second. "What is this nonsense you're babbling about?"

He shrugged. "It only makes logical sense. If we're in this bet and I have to shadow you in the first place, why not drop all this animosity and just enjoy spending time with me? I'm not a monster. A lot of women find me a pretty good guy to have around."

"I just bet," she mumbled before realizing that she already had, which slammed a scowl onto her face. "You've proven how handy you are in a crunch. I get it. You're the bestest bodyguard in East Texas. What you are not is boyfriend material."

The temperature in the hall dropped twenty degrees, along with his expression. Ice cubes might start forming at any minute. "One of the stipulations of the bet is that you have to give me a chance. Which you've so far failed to do. You have no idea what I'm made of. That's the point of the bet, isn't it? Besides, you act like I'm planning on losing. Nothing could be further from the truth. This is your chance too, to be wined and dined within an inch of your life, doted on by a man who knows a thing or two about it."

With that impassioned speech hanging in the air between them, he spun and stalked toward the stairs.

Well. Mr. Temper Tantrum had a long three weeks ahead of him if he couldn't take a hit.

"I'll be downstairs," Heath called over his shoulder. "Not getting in your space. But you can't leave the house without me, so don't bother."

Charli had been on her way downstairs, but changed her mind, since broody cowboys with hooded expressions might be even more her type than the flirty, troublemaking kind. Her room sounded like a lot more fun.

But the moment she shut the door, the four walls mocked her. No, she hadn't given Heath a fair shot. Nor did she intend to. That would be a very quick way to lose the bet, especially if she forgot for a minute that none of this was for real. It would be easy to get caught up in it. Begin to believe some of his rhetoric.

How did she know? He'd gotten a pretty good head start during their one and only date.

The only way to handle the next three weeks and arrive on the other side unscathed was to stay in the zone. Show him that Charli on the offensive was a force to be reckoned with, the kind of hurricane that spit men out on her way to wreak more destruction.

Basically, standard operating procedure. Instead of Black Widow, she'd embrace Hurricane Charlotte. Best part—she already knew how to destroy everything.

Because that had gotten her exactly what she wanted in the past? Charli flopped onto the bed.

Her eyes squeezed shut automatically as the sight of Toby with that waitress from Applebee's spilled into her brain uninvited. It happened less and less now, but there was a time when the image sat front and center any time she was awake. She'd recognized the waitress immediately because the tramp had flirted with Toby shamelessly, right in front of Charli. As if she hadn't been sitting there, or worse, provided absolutely zero threat to the woman's agenda.

It had messed with her head. She'd unleashed on him the moment they'd hit the threshold of their apartment, accusing him of exactly what she'd later walked in on. Only with distance had she started to question if he'd been unfaithful from the start—or if she'd driven him to it.

What if *she* was the problem? What if she turned men into cheaters, solely because they were looking for a scrap of affection and warmth, only to seek it elsewhere?

Ugh, no. She couldn't think like that. She was not the problem. *They* were.

And Heath McKay was exactly the man to prove it. All she had to do was exactly what he'd laid out—give him a fair shot.

Resolute, she stormed downstairs to find him, determined to get this bet rolling so she could win. As expected, he wasn't far away, standing in the kitchen chatting up Sophia, an easy smile on his face. Not the kind he ever gave Charli.

And the second he saw her at the entrance to the kitchen, underneath the arch that led to the dining room, his smile slipped into the self-satisfied smirk she'd long grown used to.

"Come to apologize?" he asked, crossing his arms, which she immediately realized was his way of putting a barrier between them.

He did that a lot.

Because he was always expecting Hurricane Charlotte to hit him full force in the chest?

Yeah, she needed to take a step back and reassess. Big-time.

Like Heath had said, this was her one and only golden ticket to see what might happen if she didn't act like a banshee on the loose in a relationship. What would better solidify to her that she wasn't the problem than to take him up on what he was offering? She could ease into this bet. See what it was like to be in a relationship where she already knew the score, with a clear end in sight. It could be like…training.

Besides, the moment she caught Heath's eye wandering, which it would, she'd win. She could smugly start doodling some signs and call him a dog, content in the knowledge that she'd been right all along. It wouldn't be her fault and she wouldn't be the one to blame for whatever happened.

And in the event she ever found a man somewhere who could actually be faithful, she'd have some intel to use. No one had to know she was using this fake relationship as a proving ground for what happened if she just relaxed and had fun while waiting for Heath's true colors to eventually show.

"Yeah, I did," she said with a nod, more convinced than ever that this was the right track—especially since it would knock him off his. "Come to apologize."

Heath's eyes goggled so hard that she almost laughed. Men were so easy. Sophia glanced between the two of them and shook her head.

"Not getting in the middle of this," she said and held up her hands, backing away slowly.

Neither Charli nor Heath watched her go. His gaze was locked firmly on her, slightly squinty, as if he couldn't quite figure out what had happened.

"Are you feeling all right?" he asked.

"You can cut the sarcasm," she said with less venom than normal and didn't even choke on it. "Especially since you know you hit the nail on the head. I had no intention of giving you a fair shot. And it occurs to me that you probably put that down as your criteria for what I need to do to win, so I'm essentially beating you at your own game by apologizing."

"Which you have yet to do," he reminded her, his smirk softening into enough of a smile that it didn't hurt nearly as much to return it as she'd have assumed.

"I'm getting there. I'm sorry I was so prickly earlier. I'm done. Where are you taking me on our first date?"

That's when someone banged on the back door hard enough to rattle the frame.

Heath's entire demeanor shifted from casual to red alert, his shoulders thrown back as he expertly slid in front of her, angling his body as a shield. Just like he'd done when putting himself between her and the dig nerd. He rippled with authority and promise, as if advertising to the world that nothing would get through him.

It was his Protect Charli mode, and it was so affecting that her mouth went dry.

"Stay behind me," he murmured, and she didn't mistake it for a request.

Besides, where would she go? She was exactly where she wanted to be. Well, almost. There was still a lot of space between them, and the heat pumping from his body would feel delicious against her skin, she had no doubt.

She followed him as he took two steps toward the door and opened it only a crack so she couldn't see who it was through the solid male torso blocking her view.

"I need Miss Lang," a male voice rang out, high-pitched with excitement and urgency. "We found something."

"Who are you?" Heath demanded as Charli tried to peer under his arm. "What do you need her for? I'll give her the message."

"Oh, I'm one of the grad students. Ben Fuentes. But that's not important. Dr. Low sent me to get Miss Lang. She needs to come to the Harvard trailer so we can show her."

He meant Sophia. But guess what? Charli's last name was Lang too and she was standing right here.

"Show me what?" Charli called out, muscling her way around Heath's growling form, pretty sure any grad student named Ben wasn't carrying a gun under his T-shirt.

Ben turned out to be a scrawny, earnest kid who might outweigh her by five pounds. "The statue we found. It's solid gold. Dr. Low is conservatively estimating its worth at five million dollars."

Chapter 6

Chaos erupted at Hidden Creek Ranch after the Harvard find, and Heath wanted to punch whoever had unearthed the statue.

He shouldn't. But it was hard to remember why. None of the university people stood still long enough for him to wind up a fist anyway, another logistics nightmare that had become his reality in the four hours since Dr. Low's assistant had broken the news. Apparently, everyone on the ranch proper had heard about the artifact, and all of them wanted to see it.

Strangers milled around the Harvard trailer constantly, which wouldn't have normally hit his radar since Madden had made sure Heath knew Charli's safety was his number one priority, but the ranch operation had spiraled out of control more quickly than any of them could get a handle on.

No more undercover security. It was *all* out in the open now. Nice because Heath didn't have to help round up horses any longer, but that didn't make any of this easy.

With Charli safely in the house—for now—Heath tried to concentrate on his temporarily assigned task. There were too many people to account for. Anyone could slip into a crowd this size, and no one would know a threat had joined their ranks because they were all basically kids with academic degrees in stuff he could barely spell.

There should be lines. Check-ins. ID requirements.

That's why Heath was here. To instill order. Except the really smart ones were giving him a wide berth, clearly recognizing that the former SEAL with the glower might be the biggest threat around. The dumber ones stood in easy-to-pick-off circles, laughing and pushing up their glasses as they waited their turn to view the hunk of metal that had turned his life into a three-ring circus.

Madden stalked into his field of vision, likely from the house, but Heath wouldn't know because he'd completely lost his focus. And his cool.

"What?" Heath snapped. "Do you have a third job to hand me?"

Ace Madden, his oldest friend, didn't even blink at his tone, which was one of many reasons they jelled. "If I did, you'd handle it."

Yeah, like he was handling the first two so well? For all he knew, Charli had bolted out the front door like a prison escapee thirty seconds before the floodlights spilled into the yard. This would be the one and only time he'd be unable to follow her, which might account for at least half of the reason his skin felt so itchy.

The inability to punch something was the other fifty percent.

All he needed was an excuse, like another one of the dig nerds putting his hands on Charli. Of course, given Heath's current circumstances, someone could be dragging her off into the woods right now and he'd never know.

It was killing him.

And the longer he went without unleashing his frustration, the tighter his fists clenched.

"We need more guys, Madden," he muttered at about half the volume he'd like, but there were too many of the people they were here to keep safe milling around. And that was still his job, even if he didn't like the fact that he'd been temporarily reassigned.

"We do," Madden agreed. "Especially when Sophia is currently having a meltdown and I can't be there to provide the shoulder she needs."

Heath rolled his eyes. "Sure, and Sophia's version of a meltdown probably looks like a lesser woman having a bad hair day. I'm sure she's fine."

But Madden just gave him a look. "Let's have this conversation again when someone you love is kidnapped and held at gunpoint, which took about ten years off my life, by the way, then add in a complete monkey wrench like a priceless ancient artifact showing up at the ranch you're tasked with ensuring is secure while she's crying in the kitchen."

Aw, man. If it was anyone else, Heath wouldn't care how broken up about it the guy sounded, but it was Madden. He blew off some of his mad and breathed. Or tried to, anyway.

"Is Charli with her?" he asked. "Is she okay?"

"She's the one talking Sophia down right now." Clearly at his limit, Madden took off his hat and ran stiff fingers through his hair with the other hand. "I need these people in a line, McKay. I need to know everyone on this ranch at all times, where they are, what they're doing. How do I do that with a six-hundred acre ranch?"

Heath lifted his hands, mostly to cover the wash of relief that coursed through him to hear that Charli was still where he'd left her. "I'm the brawn. Shouldn't Pierce be running some numbers or something?"

"He is. He's holed up in Sophia's study throwing together

a heat map that's supposed to cross-reference unique sig-natures with satellite imagery, but there are a lot of trees on the property, so it's taking a while for everything to do the whatever thing he calls it. Execute the code."

Heath nodded, focusing on breathing in hopes it would calm him down. Everyone was doing their part, but it didn't help his state of mind to hear that Sophia was upset. Was Charli upset too? What if she was crying and Madden hadn't even realized because he was too worried about Sophia? No one was there to pay attention to the other Lang sister.

Since he was the only one who seemed to be concerned about that, the only way for him to get back to his real as-signment would be to fix the mess in front of him. At least the part he could control. And *should*, because his friend needed him to.

"All right, everyone," Heath bellowed over the chatter to the entire field full of grad students. They all froze and looked at him. Excellent. "We're going to play a game called help me do my job. Line up if you want to see the jaguar head or whatever it is. If you don't want to stand in line, go back to your designated area. No exceptions."

"What if we've already seen it?" one of the dig nerds asked, with a nervous glance at Madden, as if trying to as-sess whether the two of them would enforce the rule. "Can't we hang out and discuss? I mean, this is *our* job."

"Oh, I'm sorry, you must have mistaken me for some-one who cares," Heath shot back with saccharine sweet-ness. "That statue thing has been exactly the same for a thousand years, give or take. I'm pretty sure you can talk about it tomorrow without losing anything important in your analysis."

The dig nerd licked his lips, apparently contemplating

whether arguing would get him anywhere, but finally nodded and slunk off, his cell phone already in hand to switch his commentary to text messaging, most likely.

A dozen or more people followed him, shooting Heath the kind of dirty looks normally reserved for authority figures who broke up keg parties. Fine. He'd take that. Though when he'd turned into the guy on the other side of that equation, he had no clue.

An eternity later, some semblance of a line had formed, and Heath presided over it with his fists mostly by his side. There were a couple of dicey moments when a newcomer didn't realize how strictly enforceable "single file" was meant to be.

And he still didn't see any sort of opening that would allow him to peel off and check on Charli.

Madden had stalked off to oversee some other area of security that Heath didn't want to know about. Presumably to ride the back forty looking for intruders or possibly to check on Pierce's progress with his computer program. Not that Madden had any better of a shot at understanding that man's brain than anyone else did.

At seven o'clock, Heath's stomach had already started eating itself in protest for being so empty and the line had dwindled, so he cut it off, ordering everyone to go back to their campsites. He personally watched Dr. Low as she locked the jaguar head into the safe bolted to the trailer floor. Someone could drive off with the whole trailer, but it wasn't currently attached to a vehicle, and the ancillary security contractors they'd hired had showed up an hour ago to run perimeter sweeps overnight. Madden would probably put at least two of them on stationary sentry duty outside the trailer.

Word may have already gotten out to the world at large

that the trailer held something worth five million dollars. It was Madden's job to make sure the quality of security matched the value. Heath had done his part. And now he needed to turn his focus to his slightly less relaxing second job—Charli. Assuming she'd stuck around this long.

An eternity later, he found her in the kitchen, leaning against the sink, phone in one hand and a beer in the other that she sipped absently. A couple of drops of condensation slid down the longneck, which meant it was cold, and he'd never seen anything he wanted more in his life.

Only he couldn't pick out whether it was the woman or the beer that had struck something inside him.

Until Charli glanced up, her gaze snapping onto his with…something. Not animosity. Not her usual trouble. Something else, which he had no vocabulary to explain, but wanted to.

"Hey, stranger," she called. "You look like you need this way more than I do."

She crossed and pressed the bottle into his hand, which was indeed chilled enough to cool him down a few blessed degrees. Without hesitation, he guzzled the sweet nectar of a wheat beer he'd have never touched otherwise, but thoroughly enjoyed after a hard day of herding nerds.

Maybe because the glass against his lips had been against hers not moments before. He tried not to think about that too hard.

"Thanks," he rasped, wholly unsettled at this dynamic between them that didn't seem to be veering toward a knock-down-drag-out, which he'd been braced for.

"Have you eaten?" she asked, peering up at him critically as if she might glean the answer for herself.

"Not since a million years ago," he admitted, hard pressed to even recall the last time he'd put food in his mouth, especially since his gut was currently registering the intensity of Charli's gaze instead of its lack of food.

She shook her head, lips pursed, and snagged his wrist, leading him to the table. "Sit. I'll warm up some of the leftovers from dinner. It's hamburger helper, but with ground turkey, and it's not too bad if you don't think about it too much. Green beans or no?"

"Uh, yes, I guess?" Was there a right and wrong answer?

Charli's smile made him think there probably was, and he'd managed to find it. "You're a better man than Ace. He wouldn't touch a single green bean and Sophia threw one at him."

Before he could fully wrap his head around what was happening, she'd heated a plate of leftovers and slid it onto the table in front of him, adding a fork and a napkin. Then she plopped down on the bench seat next to him with a fresh bottle of beer, stuck her elbow on the table and leaned her face into her hand, her brown eyes huge and beautiful.

"What is going on here?" he blurted before realizing how accusatory it sounded.

But Charli's grin just widened. "If you have to ask, I must not be doing it right. Eat your dinner, McKay. You look like you're about to pass out."

From shock, yeah. "You're being nice to me. It's weird."

That made her laugh. "You've had a hard day handling university people. You deserve a break from Hurricane Charlotte. Don't get used to it."

No danger of that. No one had ever taken care of him, not like this. Well, maybe his mom back when he'd been a kid. But this was different. Completely. He took another sip of his beer that had previously been Charli's, unable to stop being dazzled by the entire scene.

Only he was too hungry to think about it too much. The

hamburger helper wasn't terrible, even with the healthier option of ground turkey. As his arteries weren't getting any younger, it was a nice touch. The green beans crunched instead of turning to mush in his mouth, a surprise.

"Sophia is a good cook," he announced as he wolfed down the rest of it.

"I'd pass on your compliments, but I'm the one who made it," she countered wryly. "I can understand your confusion, though. Sophia reeks of the kind of woman who knows her way around a pot and a stove."

"It's definitely the best thing I've eaten in a while," he said and elbowed her. "Don't think I didn't notice that you kept your role as the chef a secret until you heard my opinion."

She made a face. "Not an accident. Tell me what's happening outside."

"You didn't poke your head out?" he asked. The hits, they kept on coming. "Frankly, I'm not even sure why you're still in the house. I expected you to be long gone."

The pause grew some teeth as she stared at him, and it took a lot to keep from fidgeting. Heath didn't fidget. But she'd always managed to get under his skin without much effort. Coupled with all the strange vibes running between them, he scarcely knew which end was up.

"This is me behaving," she finally said. "I told you I would. It's not your fault there's so much going on with the stupid statue."

This was such a revelation that Heath didn't bother to hide his reaction—which was caution and confusion and not a little disbelief. He put his fork down on the table and fully turned on the bench to peruse her without a barrier between them.

"I didn't believe you," he told her honestly. "Earlier,

when I asked you to stay in the house and you said okay. I thought it was a throwaway line, one you'd immediately invalidate by climbing out the second-story window or something."

Her brief flash of a smile caught him in the gut. "It's too high. I broke my arm doing that when I was ten, by the way."

"Not a shock," he advised her and lifted his chin. "Madden said Sophia was crying earlier. It would be like him not to notice whether you were too. Are you okay?"

"Why, Heath McKay." She clutched a hand to her heart and gasped theatrically but not before he saw the emotional glint in her eyes that he suspected she was trying to cover. "Points for sincerity and since you went to the trouble to ask, I'll be honest. This jaguar head is a big problem. For more reasons than one. Let's just say I'm not a crier, but that doesn't make me okay."

Nodding, he didn't think. Just reached out and snagged her hand, squeezing it tight. Silently telling her that he got it. "If it makes you feel better, I'm not a crier either, but I almost made an exception when this one UT kid called me sir. Who did he think he was talking to? I'm barely old enough to be his...somewhat older brother."

That made her laugh and upped the emotion quotient in her eyes. Which he strangely liked a lot.

"You're being nice to me, too," she sniffed. "It's not as weird as I want it to be."

"I told you, most women think I'm a pretty good guy. It's not my fault you didn't believe me."

"Oh, I see." She did this thing where she rearranged their fingers in a fluid motion so they were interlaced. Like they were holding hands. On purpose. "This is you pretending we're in a relationship. I get it now."

Actually, he'd forgotten all about pretending. But he nodded anyway, as if she'd hit the nail on the head, and tried to conjure up an image of Margo. "Since you brought it up, I never did get around to setting a time for our first date."

She shot him a saucy grin that immediately drained Margo from his mind. "I hate to break it to you, but I think this is it."

Sharing a beer over the kitchen table while exhausted after a day of standing around in the sun? No. Not even a little bit. "This is *not* a date. Trust me, you'll know when it happens and it's going to be way better than this."

Tomorrow night. Maybe. If Madden could get all his security issues sorted by then. Actually, Heath would make sure he did. Because he suddenly didn't feel like waiting to flip this script and be the one to dazzle *her*.

Strictly for the bet. This time he'd remember it was practice.

Chapter 7

Charli poured coffee into an extra-large Yeti cup she'd found in the back of the cupboard. It was probably meant for someone who had planned a long morning of riding clear out to the south end of the property, or maybe someone like Super Sophia, who needed the extra caffeine hit to mow through her gargantuan to-do list.

Well, Charli wasn't either of those, but she was a woman who couldn't get Heath McKay's blue eyes out of her head long enough to sleep. That counted. Especially when Sophia called a meeting at 8:00. In the morning! Like, who had meetings that early? Corporate weirdos and politicians probably. Not ranch owners.

Except this one, she thought. Her sister had no respect for how difficult it was to be an independent woman who didn't need a man but kind of wanted the one that had been dropped in her lap. Charli couldn't figure out how to admit that to herself, let alone out loud where it would become a quick path to losing the bet.

That was probably the most painful part—having to temper the stuff inside that Heath had stirred up last night with all his gentle consideration over how she was doing. This was what she got for agreeing to give him a fair shot. It was a quandary. Because, yes, she got it. He was actually not a bad guy. No news flash there. They *all* started out that way. They ended up the same, too—heartbreakers.

Charli eyed her coffee mug that suddenly didn't feel large enough to hold the amount of caffeine technically needed this morning. So, she gulped down a quarter of it, sticking her tongue out to cool it as she topped off the cup to the brim, then stirred in hazelnut creamer, the only way to fly.

Smug that she'd beaten Sophia to the office, she settled into the chair on the guest side of the desk, content to let her sister have the business side. Sure, they were equal partners, or at least Charli liked to think they both considered that the case, but that didn't change which Lang sister was good at organization and numbers and other stuff that crossed her eyes.

Sophia bustled in at eight o'clock on the dot, making it feel like a virtue to be precisely on time. And now Charli felt like an overeager golden retriever who couldn't wait for someone to play fetch with her.

"Good morning," Sophia said, her tone that of a well-rested woman who knew exactly her place in life. "I appreciate you being here bright and early. I know you're not a morning person."

"No one is a morning person," she grumbled. "Some people are just better at hiding it than others."

Sophia slid into her chair and set her own coffee mug, a regular-sized earthenware one with a blue rim, onto the desk, then steepled her fingers around it as if warming them. "I like mornings. Especially when it's quiet. I can actually think. Which is why I got up at five a.m. and sat on the porch."

The thought made Charli's head hurt. "What did you think about?"

"Whether we should start canceling bookings."

"What? No."

With that gauntlet thrown down, the meeting got serious. Charli's spine stiffened, driving her to the edge of the chair. This was definitely not enough coffee.

"Char." Sophia rubbed at one eye and that's when Charli noticed that her sister didn't look all that well-rested and it was probably the ranch that had kept her up, not Ace. "We talked about this. The jaguar statue is the last straw. You saw what it took to keep everyone in some semblance of order yesterday."

So she'd peeked out the window a time or twelve to watch Heath corral all the dig nerds. So what? It wasn't a crime, and the scenery had a lot to recommend it.

"Heath handled it," she countered. "With style. And they hired all those other guys too."

Who had come heavily armed, she'd noted. Every single one of the new security guards carried a semiautomatic rifle along with an expression that suggested he would not appreciate being tangled with. The ranch was in good hands.

Sophia stared at her as if she'd just suggested that they coat the new security guys in honey and stake them on an anthill. "You think the guests will consider armed guards a good addition to the staff? Think again. We have to depend on word of mouth for the first six months to generate new business. I don't think 'they have people with really impressive guns' is the kind of review we're going for."

Slouching down in her seat, Charli stalled with a big show of drinking her coffee. Yeah, of course she'd thought of that. Kind of. It felt like a plus to have extra security on staff because that meant Heath would have the capacity to take her on a date sooner rather than later. Which she was looking forward to—strictly because he'd piqued her curiosity, no other reason.

What she should be focused on was the ranch. And the guests. Which she was, right now, and it totally counted. "I get the point. But they're moving the jaguar thingy at the end of the week. Dr. Low promised."

That news had been the one thing to get Sophia to stop crying yesterday. It had put a lump in Charli's throat to see her sister so upset, but it was just a minor setback. Everything would work out.

"You think that's the extent of what there is to find here?" Rubbing her eye again, Sophia blew out a breath and picked up her coffee mug but didn't drink it. "I'm afraid it's the tip of the iceberg. This place is going to be crawling with additional search teams and new experts. I don't think we have a choice but to cancel bookings and delay the opening of the ranch."

The fatigue in her sister's face poked at Charli. "This is because you think you have to do this by yourself."

"What, run the ranch?"

"Yeah." She rolled a hand in the general direction of the window. "And make decisions. You don't trust me with the really heavy lifting. Just the decorating and such."

"I'm not… Char, this is a conversation. A meeting. If I was going to make all the decisions, I would have done that at five thirty, when my brain got to the end of a very long list of pros and cons for delaying."

Sure. Her sister had every intention of listening to Charli's point of view. That's why she'd framed the whole thing as "we don't have a choice."

"Fine. Let's talk. Tell me when you think we can open if we delay."

"I don't know."

"Exactly. Because there's always going to be one more thing they might possibly find if we let the university people keep looking." This was where Charli could shine—laying down the law. "So we tell them they're done. Take your jaguar head and go. Don't come back. Your welcome is officially worn out."

"We can't—"

"This is *our* ranch, Soph. We can." Warming to her subject, Charli jumped to her feet, scarcely registering the slosh of coffee in her cup. "We don't have to cater to the university people. Maybe we introduce a treasure hunt element for guests. Like the diamond field in Arkansas where you can sift through sand yourself in search of one. I read that a woman found one worth millions of dollars not too long ago. We'll advertise that you too can find valuable stuff on our land if you just come pay us a lot of money."

This idea had huge profits written all over it. The publication of the jaguar head find would fuel that fire. It was free publicity. All they had to do was get everyone with university or museum affiliations gone—and boot the security detail—then work out the new plan.

No more Cowboy Experience. This was all about gold, baby.

But Sophia's dubious look sent her suddenly jubilant mood back down to earth.

"What?" Charli spread her hands. "You don't love this idea? It's perfect."

"We already have a ton of work into the first idea," Sophia said wryly. "Expensive graphics on our website. Signage. No plan for security when a guest finds the other five-million-dollar jaguar head, the female one."

Wait, what? Charli's mouth dropped open. "There's a female one? Why didn't you mention this earlier?"

"I've been trying to get there but you keep shooting off in another direction," Sophia supplied unhelpfully. "Dr. Low mentioned it when she came by last night. You were busy."

With Heath. And she wasn't even a little sorry. That scene in the kitchen last night had stirred up something inside her that she wasn't sure how to handle. But wanted to figure out.

It had felt like something real. How other people might interact in an adult relationship. She was starting to think she hadn't had one of those yet.

Sophia continued. "One of the people on her team authenticated the head they found as part of a cache of treasure cataloged in some cave drawings in Central Mexico. There are supposed to be two. Whoever hid the male head on the ranch property may not have possessed the second one. Or they might have and it's still here."

The weight of this information pulled at Charli's shoulders. Why did there have to be two? One priceless giant jaguar head couldn't be enough for the Pakal guy or whoever had commissioned the statues?

"That just means more publicity for us, right?" she suggested feebly, guessing that Sophia's implacable expression meant the treasure hunting idea wasn't happening. "Okay, fine. I get that we don't have the right kind of plan to manage a crap ton of people searching for something worth that much money. We stick with Cowboy Experience. But delaying the opening, dealing with cancellations, that's bad business, too."

Sophia was already shaking her head. "I'm trying to do the right thing here, Char. I don't want to screw up the Cowboy Experience before it starts. But we've got a lot of dominoes stacked up here that I don't know how to stop from falling and wiping us out permanently."

Yeah, that was the problem. Sophia didn't know. And that meant Charli couldn't know either. It didn't matter if she had four hundred and eighty-seven good ideas for how to manage these obstacles, no one in this room wanted to hear them.

She resisted crossing her arms and sinking down in her chair for a good long pout. Barely.

This was par for the course, though. Her sister didn't think she had a single thing to contribute, so that was that. They weren't opening the Cowboy Experience next week. Instead, they'd spend their time cleaning up after a bunch of grad students and wincing every time one of them scared the horses with their ridiculously loud videos they played on their phones, but never watched with earphones.

"I'm calling it," Sophia said. "Permanent delay of the opening."

"Compromise," Charli said and stood, willing it to come across as a position of power. "Delay the opening but set a deadline for the university people. Two weeks. If they don't find the female in that length of time, odds are it's not here. That'll have to be good enough."

Sophia blew out a breath. "Two weeks? That's so soon. Why not two months?"

Because that was too long. "Three weeks, final offer. And they have to publish the fact that the female head is lost forever on their way off our land."

Three weeks fit the terms of her bet with Heath, too. Then he could wear his shame sign and be gone from her life, taking all his confusing vibes with him.

Her sister nodded, but it didn't feel like a victory. "Okay."

Great. Three more weeks until Charli could point to

the Cowboy Experience and say she'd done that. Until she could claim that she'd truly found her niche in the world. It was better than nothing, and meanwhile, she'd have Heath to entertain her.

Somehow, looking on the bright side hadn't fixed her frustration. Sophia had still driven a hard bargain and a compromise wasn't the same thing as trusting Charli. She had this. But her sister didn't have a single drop of faith.

Fuming and itching for a place to unleash her mood, she stalked out of Sophia's office. She found exactly who she was looking for outside, climbing from the driver's seat of one of the off-road UTVs that he and the other guys had started using in place of horses to ride the fence line.

"McKay," she called, and he swung around to face her, a grimace her reward for getting his attention.

Good. He was in a mood too. She could tell by the faint lines of annoyance around his mouth and eyes. Neither made him look happy to see her.

"You're not supposed to be outside," he said by way of greeting, his attention clearly split between her and whatever he'd been about to do when he'd arrived in the yard. "Go back to the house, Charli."

She crossed her arms. "You owe me a date. You can't keep using work as an excuse."

And here he thought she'd be the one trying to ditch their prescribed time together. But with the delay of the opening, everything was upside down and she did not do idle well at all.

No reason not to get this bet on the road. Especially since in her current state of mind, she'd be driving him away sooner rather than later. Men wisely steered clear of Hurricane Charlotte when she got a full head of steam.

Except Heath didn't cross his arms and glare at her in

kind. He shut his eyes and sucked in a breath through his nose, then took off his hat to run a hand through his damp hair, which should look ridiculous after being squashed by a Stetson for hours. But nothing looked ridiculous on him. This might as well be a commercial for something masculine and expensive that no one could remember the name of but sold out instantly.

"I'm sorry," he murmured, his eyes locking onto hers, the glacial color in complete opposition to the warmth there.

She couldn't look away all at once. "You're not allowed to apologize. I'm mad."

His gaze bored through her, and the rest of the yard fell away. It could have been full of circus monkeys instead of grad students and she'd never hear a single chirp.

What did he see when he looked at her like that?

"Not at me, you're not," he countered mildly and then unexpectedly lifted two fingers to her face, sweeping hair from her eyes in what was obviously a clear ploy to touch her, but she didn't mind so much. His fingertips lingered, sliding down her cheek in a wholly delicious way. "It's okay, though. You can yell at me as long as you want. I can take it."

The man scrambled her brain. "You can't do that. You have to fight back."

His smile was nothing short of diabolical. "You can count on that. Later. Seven o'clock. Dinner. No excuses."

Mollified in more ways than she cared to admit, she cocked out a hip. "What if I'm busy tonight?"

"You're not." His gaze swept down to her toes, curling them without anything more than the heat he always generated. "Wear something pretty."

Oh, man. She'd have to raid Sophia's closet. The black Dolce & Gabbana Charli had been eyeing would do nicely.

Sophia's shoes lacked even an ounce of personality, but that was fine. She'd pull out her red stilettos and maybe have a shot at being able to whisper in Heath's ear if the mood struck.

She blinked. Speaking of moods, Heath had completely changed hers. It was a neat trick that had certainly never been in the arsenal of any man she'd ever dated before. Er, any man she'd *wagered* with before. The more she reminded herself this wasn't real, the better.

That didn't stop her from thinking about their date the rest of the day.

Chapter 8

The stairs in the Victorian house that had belonged to Charli's grandpa did not mix well with five-inch heels. Side note: halfway down the flight was not a good time to discover this.

Fingers digging into the handrail, she clomped down two more steps cautiously. If she ended up in a heap at the bottom, she'd be spending date night in the hospital instead of giving Heath grief over his choice of locales.

Because there was no way he'd come up with anything that would impress her. She'd lived in Dallas her whole life basically, and there was very little she didn't have access to from Cirque du Soleil to Taylor Swift to high-end restaurants to world-class shopping.

What she did not have was a lot of practice wearing these shoes on a ranch. Lesson learned for next time. There was no way on God's green earth she'd change now—this dress fit her like a glove and the in-your-face red of the shoes gave her confidence.

She'd need it to spend more than five minutes with a man like Heath who oozed masculinity and authority.

By the time she hit the ground floor, one ankle twinged, but she ignored it and strode across the hardwood like a supermodel, grateful all at once for the flat surface to practice. She was doing that a lot lately.

Practice. It shouldn't sound like such a bad thing. Was there a point in life when you got to stop practicing and start *doing*, though? That was the crux of why Sophia forcing the Cowboy Experience delay still stuck in her craw.

She wanted action. Hurricane Charlotte was in the house and that persona suited her to the ground, way better than Black Widow had. It was past time for her to move forward with the plan that would fix her life.

She made it to the kitchen without stumbling once. Small wins. Now she could get on with her practice date. The thought almost didn't curl her lip.

What did she want, though? A real date and a real chance with Heath? She'd had that. No, thank you. Practice was far better. She'd go into this with her eyes wide open, category five gale force winds ready to blow his cheating hide from here to eternity.

Except when she answered the back door at precisely seven o'clock, most of her brain function shut down.

Heath McKay knew how to clean up.

Hatless, he'd obviously washed his hair with angel's wings. Nothing earthly could make his curls look so soft and so perfectly tousled around his face. He wore a pair of khaki pants with an impressive crease likely courtesy of a dry cleaner, but the fact that he'd ranked her as worth both the cost and effort struck an odd nerve.

When had that become a bar that men couldn't hit? And how dare Heath be the one to leap over it with ease and grace?

"You're wearing date clothes," she said and yes, it sounded every bit as accusatory out loud as it did in her head. He'd worn jeans the one and only time they'd done this before.

"You're not," he growled, his gaze heating as he swept her from head to toe, lingering on the shoes. "You don't listen very well. That dress is the exact opposite of pretty."

She scowled to cover the wave of goose bumps rising on her skin along the path of his scorching sweeps. "What's wrong with this dress? It looks fantastic on me."

"That it does," he agreed, but he didn't sound pleased about it at all. Then he twirled a finger. "Go on and let's get the torture out of the way. Give me all of it. I'm pretty sure I can handle it."

"I'm not playing fashion model for your enjoyment," she said primly and almost crossed her arms over her chest but that would only highlight the V of the dress.

"Too late." His grin bordered on wolfish as he hustled her backward and shut the door, leaning against it. "You can't pretend you didn't wear that outfit for me. I already know you did. And Charli? I am enjoying the daylights out of it."

Well, that was something. The heated appreciation glimmering from his gaze worked its way beneath her skin and she almost shivered. Okay, he wasn't wrong. She had pictured his reaction a time or two as she'd gotten dressed. Was she really going to balk because he'd come out of the gate with an attitude?

It was Heath. Torture sounded like a good punishment for his dictatorial arrogance.

Good thing she'd practiced. Without the slightest wobble, she did a slow spin and relished the almost inaudible sound of him sucking in a breath. Ha. Take that.

Her spin screeched to a halt, courtesy of Heath's arms. Which he'd just hauled her into.

Breathless all at once, she lifted her gaze to his, registering all at once that the stilettos did indeed put her at a much different height that worked extremely well with his.

"I wasn't done with my pirouette," she grumbled even as her entire body sang with some otherworldly chorus that hopefully only she could hear.

"Yeah, you were."

His voice had gone hoarse and the catch in it prickled her skin. She'd done that to him. She'd affected him. It was heady stuff. His hot hands at her waist didn't feel all that fake. Probably because the rest of her had made itself at home up against the hard planes of his body. Heath definitely didn't have an ounce of fat on him anywhere. Except maybe between his ears.

"You can unhand me," she informed him loftily, proud that their proximity hadn't affected *her* voice. "You'll wrinkle this dress and then I'll look like I just rolled out of bed for the rest of the evening."

Bad choice of words. Or good, pending how she was supposed to take the fact that his fingers spread across her back, nipping in deliciously. What he did not do was let her go.

"That happens to be my favorite look on a woman."

Of course it was. She nearly rolled her eyes. "If you're trying to lose the bet, you're well on your way."

"Funny, I don't see any other women around here," he countered. "Just you."

His gaze burned through her, and she had a bad moment when she realized she might have miscalculated with this dress. If her goal had been to keep all his attention on her, it would have been a brilliant move judging by his reaction thus far.

But that wasn't her goal, exactly. It didn't seem too likely that his eye would be wandering any time soon. In fact, he might not have peeled his gaze from her once from the moment she'd opened the door. It was...not a terrible feeling.

That's when it occurred to her that if she lost the bet, she might end up with a whole lot more than she'd bargained for. Because losing meant that he'd changed her mind. That she had to concede Heath wasn't like other men. It meant he was one of a kind. Special.

And she already knew that was true.

Her heart pounding, she stared up at him, terrified all at once that he'd read the things racing around in her heart. Dang it, even in the heels she hadn't gained enough of a height advantage to feel close to being on a level playing field. Which might have more to do with the vulnerabilities she'd only just started to uncover.

Being off-kilter pushed her into a dangerous mood.

"Seems like we're doing an awful lot of standing around on this date you promised me," she said snippily.

"I also promised you I'd fight back," he reminded her with a lethal grin. "How'm I doing?"

Oh.

She had to laugh, and it released a lot of the tension that had bunched her shoulders. This whole scene was a setup. He was practicing *and* making good on his promise from earlier.

"Better than I thought. You're a lot more diabolical than I'd bargained for."

"That's what happens when you make a deal with the devil."

That she had and she wasn't even a little sorry. Heath wasn't a simpering idiot like Toby. This whole thing wasn't real. How great was it that she could be completely herself, no holds barred, and Heath would just brush it off? He wasn't going anywhere, no matter what category strength Hurricane Charlotte reached.

Plus, he smelled divine.

Feeling a lot more solid, she made the mistake of relaxing, only to discover it nestled her deeper into his embrace, which he did not miss. The atmosphere around them fairly crackled and if there was ever a time in the history of the world for a first kiss, this was it.

Strictly in the name of practicing.

When her gaze dropped to his mouth, the corners lifted as if he knew exactly what she was thinking about. What she was considering.

Only odds were high he had no clue. Because what she was actually turning over in her head was how quickly they'd both dropped into this place where they were so easy with each other. It was slightly fascinating and wholly terrifying. But she didn't have the urge to flee. Not even a little bit.

"You're looking at me that way again," he murmured and lifted a lock of her hair away from her face. "I like your hair down."

"Yeah? I was going for a little less tomboy and a lot more 'I look like I belong on the arm of Heath McKay.' Did it work?"

"And then some."

He shoved his fingers through her loose hair, somehow making it feel like a caress. Suddenly dinner was the furthest thing from her mind. He'd given her all the latitude. He wouldn't kiss her—*she* had to make the move.

Would she? *Could* she?

That's when someone banged on the door behind Heath, startling them both.

He whirled instantly, reminiscent of the time when Ben

the grad student had brought news of the jaguar statue. Charli's pulse tripled as everything warm and lovely and languid inside froze.

Heath bristled as he yanked open the door. "What?"

This time, she had five inches on her past self and could partially see around Heath's shoulder. It was Dr. Low and a couple of the higher up university people. No grad students in sight.

Foreboding settled into Charli's stomach. She knew before Dr. Low opened her mouth that her date was ruined.

"Someone broke into our research trailer," Dr. Low explained, her faint Southern accent more pronounced as she pushed her salt-and-pepper hair back from her ears.

"What?" Charli shoved at the steel shoulder blocking her way and it was only because Heath let her that she succeeded in ducking under his arm. "We have armed security agents guarding all the trailers. Is the jaguar head missing? How is that possible?"

The guys Ace had hired had all looked so formidable that Charli herself had tiptoed around them, and she was paying their salaries. If someone had gotten around *them*, none of this was going to work.

Dr. Low shook her head. "No, not the trailer with the safe. That's our admin trailer. I'm talking about the research trailer we moved to the east pasture where we found the head."

Pieces of Charli's vision started going gray, which didn't help her focus on the trailer under discussion. They had more than one trailer, she knew that, but she couldn't have told anyone the difference for a million dollars. And she vaguely recalled that the trailers used to be sitting at a right angle in the grassy area near the barn, but so many people had started milling around the yard in hopes of peeking at the gold statue, they'd moved one somewhere else. The south pasture apparently.

And she really needed a better handle on the things happening on her own property. This was her job now.

She squared her shoulders. "What happened? Was anything taken?"

One of the other PhDs spoke up, a man wearing a sport coat with elbow patches so ancient that they'd half worn away. "It doesn't seem like it. A lot of the equipment is destroyed, though. It was a very expensive break-in for nothing being taken."

"We'll call the police," Heath said, his jaw clenched so tight it was a wonder he hadn't cracked a few teeth. "Start cataloging what you can with pictures."

"We're already doing that for insurance purposes," Dr. Low said. "But this is unacceptable. This kind of thing can't happen again. It's set us back weeks."

The gray in Charli's vision went black as this uncontrollable urge to break something swelled through her fingers. "You make it sound like it's our fault. What exactly are you accusing *us* of?"

"Can you excuse us a moment?" Heath said and it wasn't a question. He tugged Charli backward with a hand around her waist and shut the door in the faces of the university people.

And then he turned her in his arms and hauled her close. That's when she realized she was shaking. The solid lines of Heath soothed her instantly, though the gentle hand stroking the back of her head did wonders as well.

Her state of mind was in such a disarray that she decided to let him.

"This is a disaster," she said into his shirt, which was a

lovely, crisp white button-down that smelled like a heavenly combo of laundry detergent and man.

"For them, yes," he murmured. "Not for you."

"How can you say that?" she wailed. "I literally just talked Sophia into opening the doors in three weeks, only to find out our security is useless, and people are breaking into the wrong trailer. They didn't take anything because the jaguar head wasn't in that trailer. Why are criminals so stupid? Can you hire more guys with guns? We need like ten more—"

"Charli." Heath's voice was so firm and sharp that she glanced up. "Breathe. I'm handling this. This is my job, not yours."

His eyes snapped with an emotion she couldn't name. Maybe because she'd never seen it before on any man in existence. Coupled with the strong arms that were literally holding her together at the moment, it felt an awful lot like he cared about her.

That wasn't right.

It was part of the act.

For some reason that calmed her down. Sucking in a deep breath, she tamped down on her swirling thoughts. This was practice for a real relationship. Sure, it was fun to be Hurricane Charlotte with no worries about scaring off the guy. But taking a step back and handling a crisis like a mature adult counted, too, and she frankly needed a lot more practice at that than anything else.

"Okay." She nodded and heaved another breath. "I'm okay. I trust you."

Instead of clutching his chest in a mock heart attack like she'd expected him to, he did the oddest thing. He leaned into their embrace—somehow, she'd ended up with her arms around him too—and brushed his lips across her temple.

"Good," he murmured. "Remember that."

And then he released her. His heat vanished from her skin, leaving her cold and feeling as if he'd taken a huge chunk of her with him.

"Stay in the house," he ordered as he swung open the door, disappearing through it without a backward glance.

The second the door shut, she locked it. Wrapping her arms around herself, she slammed her eyes closed and let her head thunk back against the wood. How was he so good at reading her? At calming her? At being so thoroughly exactly what she needed when she needed it?

I'm okay, she repeated as instructed. Best way to remember that was to keep it front and center.

But that wasn't the only thing that reverberated through her head.

I trust you.

That's what he'd meant for her to remember.

Chapter 9

The bad feeling in Heath's gut got worse by morning.

The officers from Gun Barrel City personified small-town cops who rarely dealt with anything more serious than burglary, jaywalking and the occasional 911 call from a resident who had seen a shadow outside their window. Despite the connotations, the city's name had come from an early observation that the main road through town lay as straight as a gun barrel.

Heath knew that because Pierce had done a thorough dossier on the town, as well as law enforcement all the way up to the state level. Madden had looped in the Texas Rangers recently—the law enforcement agency, not the baseball team—as a courtesy due to the value of the jaguar head, but thus far, there'd been no need to lean on those resources.

Unfortunately, even this recent break-in hadn't changed that. No one else was impressed with Heath's bad feeling. Or his insistence that something bigger was going on than everyone was crediting.

After all, if Karl Davenport could hire someone to rough up Sophia, he could hire someone to distract everyone on the ranch with a petty crime that amounted to nothing more than misdirection.

These two cops who looked like they'd come from directing traffic near the church weren't going to crack the case of who had broken into the trailer. The patrol car that had rolled up in the yard had the city's motto—We Shoot Straight with You!—for crying out loud, painted on the side. That pretty much said it all.

No problem. Heath didn't need anyone's help to do his job.

Madden took point on giving the locals the rundown while Heath and Pierce stood off to the side of the clearing, running perimeter control. Which mostly looked like keeping the dig nerds out of the way. Easier said than done thanks to the fanfare.

Heath eyed the newest pair of sightseers, both grad students. He'd learned to tell based on how they dressed, which usually consisted of a dirty pair of worn jeans and an even dirtier T-shirt emblazoned with either the name of an indie rock band or a saying that they thought was funny but really, really wasn't.

The scrawny one didn't disappoint. His T-shirt read Pardon My Trench. The other one, Heath didn't like the look of at all. Not only did his shirt have nothing on it—which was its own kind of tell if, say, he didn't want to stand out—but he wasn't skinny. All archeology grad students were skin and bones, apparently, because they had no money and forgot to eat, or at least that's what one of the chattier ones had told him.

Eyes narrowed, Heath watched as the no-logo-shirt guy edged forward, obviously misunderstanding the role of the two former SEALs standing between him and the crime scene.

"Trailer's off-limits," Heath announced and crossed his arms. Usually that gave the dig nerds enough of a warning that they backed off.

Not this guy. He edged forward again, completely breaking free of the small crowd that had gathered to watch the police proceedings.

"Yeah, no, I get it, dude," No-Logo said with nod and took a couple of test steps in the direction of the no-fly zone. "It's just that I left the artifact I'm researching in there and I need to check on it."

"It's off-limits to everyone," Heath repeated as nicely as he could with clenched teeth. "Including you."

No-Logo nodded again. "I'm not going to stay or anything. I just need to check on it and make sure it's still in one piece. It's a bone fragment and—"

"Everything in the trailer is evidence. No exceptions."

"Oh. I see." The guy looked him up and down with an expression on his face that would have earned him some expensive dental work a year ago. "You don't have a degree in anything academic, obviously, or you'd understand the importance of my research."

The frisson at the base of Heath's spine shook loose something black and sharp as he set his heels. "Correct on all counts. My degrees are in black belts. Care to test out which are the most relevant in this situation?"

No-Logo had the gall to laugh and actually take a few more steps toward the trailer. "Is that supposed to scare me? What are you, like a glorified mall cop?"

Must not punch the idiot. Must not punch the idiot. The refrain did not stop Heath from wanting to do exactly that. But unlike earlier, when he'd clocked the dig nerd who had gotten handsy with Charli, he didn't have an excuse this time.

Pierce strolled over at that opportune moment looking an awful lot like Heath's savior. "Problem?"

"Yeah, this guy is not taking the hint," he growled as he

shoved a thumb in the direction of the interloper, who had actually edged closer to the trailer, clearly working out in his head how to duck under the yellow police tape.

"You want me to talk to him?"

"No, I want you to rearrange his face," Heath spat.

If there was a way for Pierce to push up his metaphorical glasses, he would have. "I'm the brains. I don't hit people."

This from the guy Heath had watched dispatch three unlucky insurgents who had stumbled over him in what should have been a hard-to-find location in the top of a bell tower, where Pierce had hidden to operate a drone over hostile territory. If Heath hadn't been so far away, he'd have been there in a heartbeat to help, but it turned out Pierce hadn't needed it.

"But you could. You act like you sit in front of a computer for eighteen hours a day and have the complexion of bread dough."

"You're acting like you couldn't put him in traction with one hand tied behind your back." Pierce eyed him. "You feeling okay?"

"Fine," he snapped as No-Logo edged closer to the trailer. "I'm just...working on a new approach to how I handle situations like this. I'm not in the Teams any longer. Maybe it's time to hang up the Enforcer."

Pierce laughed and then broke it off abruptly when he caught sight of Heath's glower. "Oh, you were serious? What are you even talking about? That's who you are, man. You take care of things. I've never once thought that was a problem you should fix."

"Well, it is."

And he left it at that, even as Pierce shook his head. "Happy to have you in my corner no matter what. Meanwhile, your rabbit is itching to cross the finish line."

Heath glanced at the trailer and swore as No-Logo dropped to his knees and crawled right under the yellow police tape, then stood, heading straight for the door of the trailer. With no time to waste and a trailer full of CSI who would not be thrilled with an interruption they'd specifically asked Madden's team to help prevent, he stalked across the clearing in two seconds flat.

His temper boiled over faster than that.

He ducked under the police tape easily thanks to a rigorous morning routine that included squats, and halted No-Logo's forward progress like a record scratch when he snatched the back of his jeans. "Not so fast."

The grad student glared at Heath over his shoulder. "Let me go. You can't stop me."

"I can. I am," Heath countered, forcibly keeping his fist by his side as he dragged No-Logo in the opposite direction, which to the guy's credit wasn't as easy as it sounded.

He fought the entire way, digging in his heels and babbling threats, all of which Heath ignored. Instead he focused on breathing in hopes it would do something to reel back the black edges riding shotgun through his bloodstream.

With a loud rip, No-Logo's jeans came apart in his hand. Great.

Instead of squawking about it, the guy actually reversed course again, heading back toward the trailer without the force of Heath pulling him away. Why? Why did it always come down to this?

Rolling his eyes, Heath took off after the idiot and didn't bother to check his strength when he gave him a hard shove to the ground, then dug his knee into the back of the dig nerd's neck. The black edges softened and immediately stopped trying to hack through his veins.

But they didn't vanish completely. Heath tried to make his peace with that.

"I said the trailer was off-limits. Which supervisor am I speaking with about banning you from the premises?"

No-Logo sputtered and spat out a mouthful of dirt. "I'll have you fired for this."

Yeah, good luck with that, kid. "Since you're not being forthcoming with the details, I'll drop you with Dr. Low and she can sort out your transfer paperwork."

This threat did the trick. No-Logo stopped struggling and blanched. Bingo. Dr. Low probably wasn't his academic advisor since she was at the top of the food chain, but she wouldn't take kindly to a grad student who couldn't follow the rules.

A few minutes later, No-Logo sat with his head in his hands outside of Dr. Low's personal trailer, which she used as an office. His duty done, Heath slapped the dirt from his jeans and stalked back to the clearing to ensure no one else thought they were above the law.

Apparently, his little show of force had convinced everyone else to scatter. Only Pierce remained, his expression unreadable. "Guess you figured it out."

"Save it," Heath suggested, his mood veering back toward black.

It wasn't that he was mad at Pierce for pointing out the obvious flaw in Heath's plan to hang up the Enforcer while on a job that required him to be exactly that. What else would he contribute to the team if it wasn't the muscle? But why did his resolve constantly have to be tested? Couldn't the universe find a way to allow him to just stand around and *look* threatening?

When he got back to the house, Charli was in the kitchen looking for all intents and purposes as if she might be waiting for him. Good night, the woman shouldn't be such a sight for sore eyes, but he couldn't stop himself from drinking her in, letting his eyes feast on the way her leggings clung to her thighs and the enormous T-shirt she wore sat kicked off to one side, exposing a healthy slice of shoulder that he imagined would smell divine.

She was just as sexy in casual clothes as she had been last night wearing couture and stilettos.

That put him a worse mood. Because he shouldn't be thinking about her as much as he was.

"What do you want?" he snapped, crowding into her space in hopes of picking a fight, which did not improve things as the light scent of woman curled through his senses.

She stopped him with a well-placed palm on his chest but the way her fingers curved to nip in told him that she enjoyed touching him as much as he enjoyed letting her.

"Food," she advised him, her brown eyes missing nothing. "I thought you might be interested in taking me out to make up for our cancelled date from last night. So I haven't eaten yet."

Oh, yeah, he was interested all right. But that didn't magically transform his life into something more manageable. Why everything seemed to be conspiring against him lately, he had no clue.

"I can't." He slapped a hand over hers, searing her palm into his chest before she got the idea that she should step back. Because he really liked her where she was. "The place is crawling with cops who may need extra security help at any moment. The best I can offer you is leftovers while watching a movie upstairs."

One of the bad things about being so far from Gun Barrel City—you couldn't order food for delivery way out here.

Which made date night far less spontaneous. But he'd work with what he could.

"Guess I put on the right outfit for that," she said sunnily.

That she had. Almost as if she'd read the room ahead of time and realized he couldn't actually leave the premises. Which begged the question of why she'd opened with the invitation to go into town for to dinner.

Warily, he swept her with a once-over that revealed exactly nothing of her motives. She had one, though. "What gives? You're being far too conciliatory."

"Now, that is a word I don't hear often in conversation with a hot cowboy." Her gaze burned with a thousand other things that she'd elected not to voice. "Would you like me to argue with you a little bit? Sock you on the arm to make a point?"

"It would make me a lot less suspicious, yeah."

She laughed and smoothed her thumb along the ridge of one rib as if she didn't mind that he'd captured her hand there the slightest bit. "I heard from Sophia that you've had a tough day. I figured you didn't need my crap heaped on top of it."

Really. "So you're fine with having a date night here at the house?"

"Oh, no, sport. Do not get ahead of yourself." She gave him the slip and waltzed out of reach to check out the contents of the refrigerator, presumably for the aforementioned leftovers. "This is not a date. You promised me something spectacular for our first date, so this doesn't count."

She was giving him a pass. That's what this was. Slightly dumbfounded, he scrubbed at his beard. "Then why would you take me up on the offer of warmed-up leftovers and a movie? You should go back to your room and do something you want to do."

"I am doing something I want to do."

The grin she shot him was full of mischief that he couldn't quite wrap his head around Charli's angle here. "Sure. You're volunteering to hang out with me but not insisting on counting it as one of the three dates you agreed to. And you're not giving me grief. What's your game, Charlotte?"

"You've cracked the code. I was totally trying to get you to full-name me," she said with a smirk that was so animated it almost came with its own soundtrack. "Don't bust a gut trying to figure it out. You're not the only one who can practice being in a relationship at a time when it's not strictly required."

That pronouncement whacked him upside the head so hard that it rendered him speechless. Heath didn't have a lot of relationship experience himself, but Margo had never once given him the impression she'd be fine with it if he suggested a movie at home. And as far as he knew, she didn't own a single T-shirt, nor would she be caught dead in leggings. Stilettos she had dozens of, but they were more arsenal than accessory. Most of what Margo owned could be considered as such.

Honestly, he'd describe Margo as high maintenance on a good day. Usually he hadn't minded that, but today it sounded…exhausting.

Practice sounded a whole lot less demanding. It loosened his spine a notch. None of this counted. Not even toward their bet. He didn't have to do anything except eat and pretend to like whatever lame chick flick Charli threw on the TV.

There was zero pressure—from any direction—for the first time in ages. Heath rolled his neck and realized all the tension in his shoulders had eased off. He might even be able to describe himself as relaxed if this kept up.

Instead of standing there like a bump on a log, he helped Charli heat up the leftover tacos she'd found in the refrigerator, but she didn't put them on a plate. In a stroke of genius, she broke up the shells and dumped all the filling in a bowl with some shredded lettuce for an instant taco salad.

"I'm a fan of the way you practice being in a relationship," he mumbled around the first bite as they settled into the ancient couch on the second floor of the house.

This room had been deemed off-limits to future guests and would be for family use only once the ranch began operating as a hotel. That meant it had stayed comfortable instead of getting a makeover like the rest of the place.

"You haven't seen nothing yet," she advised him with an eyebrow wiggle. "Tell me about your terrible day. There was a guy giving you problems?"

Heath scowled at the mention of No-Logo. "Yeah, let's just leave it at that."

"I hope you broke his nose," she said so matter-of-factly that he blinked.

"I, uh…didn't. Not every problem should be solved with fists," he quoted without meaning to drag Margo into this conversation, but since her aversion to violence was to blame for his current sabbatical, it wasn't inappropriate.

Besides, he *should* be thinking about Margo. And how nice it was going to be when she smiled as he told her— showed her—that he'd changed.

"And sometimes it just feels good to watch cartilage crunch," she countered darkly. "Like when you hit that guy who was bothering me. That was hot."

Since none of those words belonged in a sentence together, his immediate response was to stare at her. "Come again?"

She sighed dramatically. "You're going to make me say it, aren't you? It was one of the sexiest things a guy has ever done in my presence. And I mean that exactly the way it sounds. I'm not proud of it. But there you go. You're my hero and you can't make me stop thinking that way."

What way? As if it was perfectly fine in Charli's world if he flexed the muscles in his arms instead of just the ones in his head? As if she found him *more* attractive when he took care of things according to his natural inclination?

If that wasn't enough of a revelation, he spent the rest of the night wondering if this was Charli practicing a relationship, what did the real thing look like?

Chapter 10

If Heath on the ground got Charli's motor humming, Heath on a horse should come with a surgeon general's warning—Caution: may cause heart palpitations, sudden swooning and temporary loss of feeling in your legs.

He also should have mentioned that he wasn't a slouch in the saddle, or she'd have totally brushed up on her equestrian skills. As it stood, they'd barely cantered out of the yard, and she'd already had to resituate herself twice. Though that might have more to do with the fact that she'd been watching him handle the reins and letting her mind connect a few dots about how well he'd grip other things in a wholly different scenario.

Which she should not be thinking about.

She and Heath were barely friends, let alone in a place where any *scenarios* would happen. There had been that almost-kiss, though…

"Thanks for coming with me on this practice trail ride," she said when they slowed their mounts to a walk once they cleared the split-rail fence enclosing the pasture the dig nerds had claimed for their campground. She was riding Ricky, a sorrel male and her favorite horse, while Heath rode the unimaginatively named Hershey, a brown gelding the color of chocolate.

"You say that like I had a choice in the matter," Heath said with a quirked-up mouth that made it seem like he wasn't too unhappy about it. "You're my primary job."

"And this is my job," she reminded him. "Or at least what will be my job in nine million years when we finally open the Cowboy Experience."

Assuming Sophia agreed to open it ever. The three-week delay seemed like a pipe dream at this point after the trailer break-in, but she'd been too heartsick to bother asking her sister for confirmation that the delay might be a lot more permanent now. The police had no leads, but that wasn't a surprise given Heath's professional opinion that Gun Barrel City's finest couldn't find their butt with a map and two hands.

"Honestly, you gave me an excuse to get out of Dodge," he admitted, and she nearly fell off her horse. Again.

"What is this?" she demanded. "You can't be okay with it when I make you follow me some place unpleasant to do your bodyguard duties."

"The sky is blue, the sun is warm. The horses are sprightly, and you needed to practice trail riding. What's not to like?" he asked nonchalantly. "If this is your definition of unpleasant, we need to have a serious conversation."

This was going to be a long ride if he was already this agreeable. Was this how he lulled her into a false sense of security and then pounced? It had been a while since he'd done that, but he still had the capacity to knock her totally off-balance if he wanted to. "Are you trying to get me back for the other night? The non-date?"

He grinned and it was the kind that lit up his whole face, making her sorry he was wearing sunglasses. She liked watching it when his eyes warmed up, turning a pretty color that reminded her of Nordic fjords.

"If by *get you back*, you mean practicing being in a relationship, it's only fair," he informed her. "I can't have you getting better at it than me."

That crossed her eyes a bit. "I didn't know we'd turned it into a contest. Don't we already have a bet going?"

He shrugged without jerking on the reins, and that was hot too. The man knew his way around a horse because of course he did. There was nothing that Heath McKay didn't excel at, including the ability to handle a horse. And Hurricane Charlotte. What was the point of pushing him if he just rose to the occasion and proved he could match her, time and time again? That's why she'd banked the Mach 5 storm surge and just relaxed.

Only it was totally not okay for him to do the same. What would they talk about if they weren't giving each other grief?

"Nothing like raising the stakes, I always say," he commented mildly. "I guess this doesn't count as a date either."

"It absolutely does not."

Though if someone had asked her to list out the qualities of a perfect date, this one had a lot of them: a gorgeous man in a battered Stetson and jeans that fit him so well that they might as well be painted on; an enormous blue sky stretching endlessly to the horizon; nowhere to be and all the time in the world to enjoy being outside with someone who made being with him easy.

Of all things. When had being with Heath become *easy*?

He was right—it was glorious to have an excuse to leave the ranch behind and forget all the mess, the continual cycle of a new crisis every five minutes. There was no one on earth she'd rather do that with than Heath. Practicing had started feeling like the only time she could be herself.

And she'd just keep that information to herself, thank you.

"Just checking," Heath drawled lazily. "At this rate, we'll never get to our first date."

"Nice try," she returned, even as she considered if maybe that might not be a bad thing—wouldn't a real date be sort of anticlimactic by now? "We're not canceling the bet. You'll get your shot at impressing me soon enough."

"I never said anything about canceling the bet."

It was implied, though, as if he'd perhaps caught the slightest hint that she'd started entertaining the idea way in the back of her mind that she might actually lose. Which she'd never admit to, even under threat of death.

So she spent a lot of time not thinking about how different Heath was from any man she'd ever met. And by not thinking about it, she meant obsessively turning it over in her head and then forcing the notion to vanish, only to have it reappear later when her guard was down.

They fell into a companionable silence as they rode abreast toward the back pasture, which stretched almost a mile away from the house, following the trail that skirted the woods. It was a pretty easy ride, which was the intent. This route would be the one she set for guests, assuming that most had never been on a horse before. It wasn't a short ride, though, and guests would feel it by the second hour.

Charli's mount, Ricky, skittered sideways out of nowhere.

"Easy, boy," she murmured and stroked his neck.

Then Hershey did a similar half prance to the side, yanking a few choice words out of Heath as he fought to get control.

Charli exchanged a glance with Heath as their horses continued to shy and spook, snorting loudly with eyes rolled back. He was enough at home in the saddle that he knew something was wrong too. She scanned the trail ahead, braced for literally anything to appear that might explain what had caused their mounts to freak out.

Only the ghastly sight that came into view around a bend eclipsed everything her brain had conjured—several skinned animal carcasses strewn haphazardly across the path. The bloody, flayed bodies of small animals lay in gruesome piles, buzzing with flies and other stuff she didn't want to think about.

She cut her eyes away, but the scene had burned itself into her mind's eyes. So, no sleeping tonight, then.

Ricky spun in frantic circles, fighting the bit. She struggled to calm the agitated animal while Heath dealt with his own panicked Hershey nearby. The stench of death and the visceral carnage was doing a number on her; she could only imagine what the horses were going through.

"I've got to get Ricky calmed down," Charli called over to Heath. "He might throw a shoe if he keeps this up."

"Probably a good idea to check out the scene anyway." His tone had a steel thread running through it that told her he wasn't unaffected. But Heath handled his disquiet a lot better than she did.

They both dismounted with extra care. The animals shifted nervously as Charli and Heath patted their noses. Heath slowly approached the horrific scene. Crouching down, he examined the torn flesh and trailing entrails of the skinned animals.

"What are they?" Charli whispered, not wanted to say out loud that without skins, it was really hard to identify the animal. Refusing to look at them played a factor in that too.

"Foxes and raccoons, mostly. A coyote." Heath's voice got steelier.

Anyone who could kneel down in that kind of horror for the time it must have taken to do this job had more than a couple of screws loose.

A shrill whinny snapped Charli's focus back. She turned

just in time to see both horses rearing up in terror before pivoting and galloping full-tilt back down the trail.

"Ricky! Stop!" Charli cried out in vain.

Stupid horses. Except they were actually a lot smarter than the humans. Of the four, who was still standing around near the crime scene of a disturbed individual? Not the horses.

Now Charli and Heath were stranded deep in a remote part of the ranch. With zero weapons except the ones attached to Heath's shoulders.

"Do you think whoever did that is still around?" she whispered, hand to her mouth and nose to filter the stench.

"Nah." Heath wasn't speaking at a normal volume either, contradicting his denial. "The carcasses are not fresh. Probably closing in on six or eight hours old. Someone staged that scene, probably because they knew ranch personnel use this trail."

His meaning sank in. "Wait, you think someone did this on purpose?"

"No one skins a bunch of animals and accidentally leaves them spread over a trail." To his credit, he didn't add the *duh*, but it was implied.

"This is my first skinned animal crime scene," she shot back defensively. "It's a crime, right? You can't go around doing stuff like this on people's private property."

"Trespassing. At best," he practically spat. "You might could make animal cruelty stick and possibly harassment or some other minor intimidation charges. But this is unfortunately not going to be very high on local law enforcement's radar. Not with the break-in occupying most of their brain cells."

But coupled with the break-in, this was too much to be a coincidence in her mind. "This is sabotage."

Heath lifted his hands. "What? No one even knew you

were going to be out here today. Why would someone sabotage your practice trail ride?"

"I don't know, but they did. Pretty effectively too. You said yourself that someone staged the scene here because they knew people used the trail. I'm people. I own the ranch too. Why not sabotage?"

Oh, goodness. What if she'd been leading an actual group of guests? This sort of horror would stick with a person, and they would definitely put it in their Yelp review. Her stomach squelched for a wholly different reason as she instantly became a fan of the delay in opening that Sophia had forced.

"I can't stand here a second longer," she announced as breakfast threatened to make a reappearance. "I guess we're walking."

Heath nodded. "I'll send some of the rookies out here to clean this up later."

A procedure she wanted to know nothing about. But as the ranch owner, probably she should? Maybe she'd ask him later. At the moment, she was full up on the subject.

As they started back toward the house, Charli pulled out her cell phone. No bars. Not that she was surprised. Reception was spotty at best, especially this far from the house. Sophia had installed a satellite dish for internet service, but the signal didn't extend out here.

They were in for a very long walk. In boots.

"You okay?" Heath asked, his arm bumping hers companionably.

Was she? A quick inventory gave her an answer she wasn't too happy with. "I'm pretty shaky."

"Given the circumstances, that's not too bad." Without a drop of fanfare, he slid his fingers through hers, lacing them tight as they walked. "I won't let anything happen to you."

"I'm aware," she said with a short laugh. "And I wasn't

worried, for the record. It's just…a lot to process with the break-in and now this. It's like the whole universe is conspiring against me."

Not that her lack of success was anything new. If she thought about it too hard, she'd land on the conclusion that *she* was the problem. The Cowboy Experience would be fraught with issues for the whole of its existence solely because she'd touched it. After all, those animals had been carefully placed on the horse trail. The horses were *hers*.

"Don't talk about that, then," he said. "Tell me about what you did before you came to the ranch."

She shot him a sideways glance. "Small talk, McKay? Really?"

"Shh. It's a distraction."

His grin went a long way toward clearing out the squishiness inside, which left a lot of room for her to register complete awareness of the fact that they were holding hands as if they did it all the time, as if this stroll had all been planned from the get-go.

Practice. That's all this was. If she'd been his real girlfriend, he'd do something similar.

And honestly, a distraction sounded heavenly. Especially in the form of an endless conversation with the one person who made her feel like she was standing on solid ground.

"I worked at a pet store. Bird section mostly."

His eyebrows lifted. "A pet store? I expected you to say you came from corporate America. Man-eater division."

"Ha, that was Sophia." One hundred percent, designer clothes and everything. Maybe if Charli had stuck with college, she could have followed in her sister's footsteps, but Charli and school had not gotten along. "Birds paid the bills."

"Did you like it?"

"No," she responded instantly despite not ever having considered the question either way. "The birds were mean to me. They pecked my fingers any chance they got. I think they knew I wasn't really a pet person, deep in my heart. Can we find another distraction? Tell me about being in the service."

"That's not a subject for mixed company." He said it so shortly that she glanced at him. His jaw was clenched the way that usually indicated she'd vexed him in some way.

But this time, she hadn't been trying to. "I'm sorry. I didn't know it was off-limits."

His jaw relaxed a fraction. "It's not. It's just…a lot of stuff along the lines of the scene we left behind. Whatever romantic notions you might have about Special Forces, wipe them from your mind. It's bloody, thankless and soul-draining."

"Well, I'm thanking you," she announced pertly. "For your service. You did something difficult and special, and it means something."

Heath swallowed. And swallowed again. And she realized he was dealing with some emotions she had no idea how to help him through. Or that she'd desperately want to. So she just held his hand the way he'd held hers and they walked in silence.

If he could practice, so could she. And keep her mouth shut about how much she longed to feel like this for real, as if a man like Heath would always be there for her, exactly like this.

After a few minutes, he cleared his throat. "Sorry. That's a bit of a sore subject. I didn't mean to make you feel like you picked up a rock, only to find a rattlesnake under it."

"I didn't feel like that at all," she told him truthfully. "This is a safe space, Heath. No judgment. We won't speak of it again."

"The thing is," he said so carefully that she couldn't help but glance over at him. "Maybe I want to."

Chapter 11

*T*his is a safe space.

The strange thing was that it felt like one. Not just because Charli had articulated it into being. He'd felt like that with her for a while now. As if he could be fully himself, no holds barred.

She certainly wasn't like any woman he'd ever met. He couldn't have come up with the name of one who would have stood in that grisly animal carcass dumping ground and kept their cool the way she had.

Margo would have screamed and thrown a hysterical fit, probably strictly for the attention and to ensure Heath spent a lot of time soothing her emotional distress. Not once would she have clued in on whether he had his own brand of emotional distress.

Charli had, though.

"I know we said no history lesson," he said, and she glanced at him, then back at the trail, which he appreciated. It was a lot harder to talk about some things than others, but she seemed to get that. Almost as if she knew that if she stared at him, he'd never get the words out.

"That was before," she said nonchalantly. "I don't know if you know this about me, but I like to break rules."

For whatever reason, that actually got a laugh out of him.

Which he also appreciated. "I feel like you deserve to understand a few things. And since this isn't a date, I don't have to worry about impressing you."

"Oh, you manage to find ways regardless," she said in a singsong voice. "I don't know any men who excel at identifying skinless animals."

If that impressed her, he really wanted to know more about the ex who had done a number on her. But he wouldn't push—that was hers to share if and when she chose to. At the moment, his most important objective was getting the fifty-ton boulder off his chest. The one that had dropped into place when she'd asked him about being in the service.

"Job hazard, I guess. I learned a lot of things they don't teach you in school while in the navy. I loved being a SEAL," he murmured. "But there's a lot of other stuff wrapped up inside that package that I haven't processed well. It's taken me a while to unpack it, especially because there are complexities."

"That has a woman written all over it," she interjected so matter-of-factly that he did a double take.

"How did you guess that?"

She shrugged, a small smile gracing her face that had a glow from their walk in the sunshine. "No one can introduce complexities like an ex."

Now his need to know about hers had risen to an epic level. He shoved that back in favor of the bigger elephant in the room. "Her name is Margo."

Oddly, voicing the name of the ghost living in his chest lifted some of the weight. As if speaking her name had loosened something inside, something he'd only just become aware of—Margo Malloy had a hold over him that wasn't entirely healthy.

And little by little, he was picking his way through the

obstacles Margo had strewn around him in all directions as far as the eye could see. Only here with Charli in this moment had he paused long enough to see the impediments for what they were—a field of land mines.

"I hate her already," Charli commented and stuck her tongue out. "She sounds exquisitely beautiful and probably speaks three languages. Does she compete in marathons too?"

Heath chuckled. "I think she speaks more like fourteen languages, but if she's ever run a day in her life, I'll keel over in shock. I don't even think she owns a pair of shoes that don't have four-inch heels."

"Oh, one of those." Nodding wisely, Charli squeezed his hand. "Is she like an interpreter or something?"

"What? Oh, you mean because she speaks so many languages. No, she's JSOC." And then Heath had to roll his eyes at himself because even now, he fell into acronyms to describe things that had been a part of his life for so long but weren't anymore. "Joint Special Operations Command. Margo is an SO intelligence analyst."

The face Charli made had him biting back another grin. Who would have thought she could get him to laugh in the midst of unloading all the crap Margo had piled up inside of him?

"Smart and beautiful. I definitely hate her."

"Jealousy might be my favorite look on you," he mused, earning a sock on the arm courtesy of Charli's non-hand-holding fist. "Y'all are completely different women, and trust me, that's a good thing."

She got quiet for a long minute. "Can I ask what happened with Margo?"

"Why wouldn't you be allowed to ask? I wouldn't have brought it up if I was just going to shut it all down."

They'd been walking long enough that the sun had shifted, throwing the shadows of tree branches across her face. "Because that gives you the right to ask me similar questions."

She didn't want him to. That much was clear. So he wouldn't, no matter what. "Safe space, Charli."

That's when she let her gaze slide toward his, locking in place. A wealth of things passed between them, and he found himself stroking her thumb in some kind of half-comfort, half-caress combo that felt so completely right that he couldn't fathom how he and Charli hadn't always been like this with each other. How he hadn't known instantly what *wrong* felt like—the same wrong he'd felt for so much of his life.

"Duh," she returned loftily. "Do you think I walk through scary woods possibly hiding serial animal killers with just anyone?"

Holding hands, to boot. But he didn't point that out in case she had a mind to change that part of the equation and he was not done touching her. Not by a long shot.

"Margo coordinated missions," he said, figuring it was better to get this part over with before he forgot the whole reason he'd brought up Margo. "Mine, a lot of times. We worked together. Pierce was her go-to guy since he did intelligence for our team, but we were often in the same meetings. One thing led to another and before long, I was dreaming up perfect proposal scenarios in my head. Spoiler alert. She wasn't rehearsing how to say yes."

"Ouch," was her only contribution to the conversation, a rarity. Usually, she had plenty of commentary or a smart-aleck comment. Or both.

Apparently, she was taking the safe space rules to heart. Despite the fact that they were wholly unspoken, they both seemed to know what they were. No grief. No giving each other a hard time. Not out here.

This wasn't *practice*. It was something else entirely.

"Margo hated my job," he said bluntly. "She's not a fan of violence."

Charli blinked. "Maybe she should have picked a different career. And a different boyfriend."

Yeah, the irony wasn't lost on him, but if his Trident had been her only problem, they'd still be together. "You have to understand that Spec Ops is nuanced. Sure, I did my share of cleaning out terrorist hidey-holes in godforsaken places, but a lot of warfare is strategy. That's what JSOC does. They're analyzing intercepted data. Making decisions about strike zones and drone range. Margo and her team fight our enemies from a war room. They're somewhat removed from the actual logistics."

"So?" Charli's scowl plucked at a string inside him that he didn't know was pulled so taut. "What's that got to do with the price of rice in China?"

"She didn't like that my fondness for getting physical is pretty much my default," he admitted, scrubbing at the back of his neck, which had grown hot enough to get itchy. From the sun. Probably. "Even when it's not strictly warranted."

Throwing up a hand, she waved it in a broad circle as if shooing away flies. "What in the Sam Hill is that supposed to mean? Last time I checked, you have a body that won't quit and a very good command of it. That's sexy, no two ways about it. Which part of getting physical did she have a problem with and are you sure she's smart? She doesn't sound smart."

Oh, yeah, the back of his neck was hot all right. Along with the rest of him. Charli hadn't meant all of that as a compliment—at least he didn't think so—but he *felt* complimented. And a little objectified. Which worked for him in *so* many ways.

"Not that kind of physical," he growled. Though now that the subject had been broached, he had to stop himself from the instant denial that had sprung to his lips. Because honestly, Margo hadn't appreciated his tendency to be touchy-feely. And he'd never thought about the correlation. "Okay, yeah, maybe that kind too. She mostly didn't like that I get into fights occasionally."

She'd called him a brawler at heart often enough and he knew *she* hadn't meant it as a compliment.

"Sounds like Margo needs to date one of her robot drones," Charli informed him with an animated fierceness that dug into his skin. "She picked a guy with one of the most physically demanding jobs on the planet. One who likes being in the moment, who gets a sense of satisfaction from protecting those who can't do it themselves and then tells you she doesn't like the thing that makes you who you are at your core. If I ever meet her, I'm going to punch her for you."

Heath stopped in the dead center of the trail, accidentally swinging Charli around to face him since their hands were still connected. But that was fine. He wanted to see her the way she saw him. Unlikely. Her skill at peeling back his layers was unparalleled.

"I do like being in the moment," he said, a sense of wonder coating the realization. "Do you really think about me like that? As someone who uses his fists to defend people?"

"Duh," she murmured. "Instead of stopping you, Margo the Idiot should have sat back and watched occasionally. You're like a poem in motion sometimes and it's so beautiful it hurts my chest."

She was looking at him again, the way she did sometimes, the way that made him think she had things on her mind that were best taken behind closed doors. He liked that look on her. Liked the way she made him feel.

Except the whole point of *practicing* with Charli had been to win Margo back. That's what he should've been focusing on, not the fact that Charli had called him beautiful with that catch in her throat.

"I'm sorry Margo did that to you," she murmured. "She made you think you needed to do something different."

"Yeah," he admitted readily, grasping at the threads of the conversation. At all his reasons for why Margo's opinion counted. "I need to become someone she could see herself marrying. Because she couldn't. Said I handled myself like a hormone-hopped-up teenager who wasn't husband material, whatever that means."

"I wondered why you'd make that bet with me," she said, her expression lightening with dawning certainty. "It didn't seem like there was anything in it for you. But I get it now. That's what you wanted to practice. Being husband material for Margo."

The reminder was a bucket of cold water.

With that, Charli stepped back and pulled her hand loose. His felt strange and empty without hers in it, which shouldn't be a thing. The moment was over, if there had ever even been a moment in the first place.

She dusted off her hands and smiled, clearly of the same mind. But her smile had an edge he didn't like.

"You should have said so from the beginning," she told him brightly, almost too much so. It felt a little forced. "I had no idea we were whipping you into shape so you could strut your husband-material stuff in Margo's face. That is a challenge I can get behind in a hurry. When we're done, she'll be asking you to marry *her*."

And then Charli set off toward the house again, the intimacy between them completely broken. What was he supposed to do, tell her she was wrong? She wasn't.

This whole bet had been strictly to get Margo back. That's all he'd wanted for ages. Charli was on board with helping him get there—and she'd provided the much-needed reminder that Margo was the goal, not cozying up to Charli. What wasn't to like about this plan?

Everything. And he had no idea when that had changed.

Chapter 12

Charli's relationship with Heath was *practice*. It always had been. No matter how real it had started to feel.

Thankfully, he'd reminded her before she'd done something totally stupid, like kiss him.

Heath was still in love with Margo. That much had been obvious from the way he talked about her. Good. *Great.* This was perfect. One more step toward winning the bet—after all, if he spent a lot of time pining after another woman while on a date with Charli, that totally violated the whole point of the bet. It was basically over before it started if he couldn't focus on Charli for more than five minutes.

Granted, they'd have to go on a date for that to be a factor. During which, she'd be totally aware the entire time that he was thinking about Margo as he practiced being the perfect mate on Charli.

She'd give him points for the excellent distraction. Not once on the walk home had she thought about the skinned animals.

When they got back to the ranch, she had to think about them, though. Heath called a meeting that he conducted at the kitchen table and for once, she wished she could bow out. Not only was the subject terrible, Ace sat next to Sophia and Paxton took the very far end of the table, leaving Charli to sit next to Heath.

Her knee brushed his thigh as she slid onto the long bench seat that she'd never minded before, but not having her own chair meant that it was completely obvious that she'd opted to sit as far away from him as possible. He spared her a glance laden with meaning, but what was she supposed to do, sidle up to him and coo all over his manly muscles while he treated her to that megawatt smile that she'd started thinking he only gave to her?

Firming her mouth in a straight line, she stared at the table as Heath outlined what had happened, leaving out the grisly details, which she appreciated for both her sake and Sophia's. Her sister didn't need the image of all those animals in her head, the way they were in Charli's, and neither did she want to relive them.

"They were planted?" Ace asked, his tone razor-sharp.

Heath nodded once. "Very clearly. The carcasses were stacked in pyramids."

She hadn't noticed that detail. Not surprising since she'd studiously avoided looking at the scene with much care. But she had opinions none the less. "Whoever did this knew it was a trail for horseback riding. And was probably aware I was planning to do a practice trail ride today. So that means it's someone on the ranch."

Sophia looked like she'd been punched in the face. "Great. That means we only have a hundred and forty-seven suspects."

"It's okay," Ace said softly and gathered her closer with the arm he slung around her sister's waist. "This is what I'm here for. We'll handle it, Soph."

Soph. The cutesy nicknames and being there for each other with casual intimacy made Charli's eyes sting with jealousy and longing. Sure, she was happy for them, but she wanted a man to look at her the way Ace looked at Sophia. As if he *saw* her. As if he'd cut a swath through hell itself if it stood between him and her.

The way Heath talked about Margo. He was going to enormous lengths to get her back, obviously because he thought Margo was worth it.

And what did Charli have to look forward to? *Practice.*

She glanced over at Heath almost involuntarily. It was her default lately, to seek out his steady gaze, to let him settle her. Except he was already watching her, his expression hooded and stormy. Searching for something. An answer.

What did it mean that she knew exactly what he'd been trying to figure out?

Yeah, she'd been the one to put the distance between them. For a *reason*, one she didn't feel like explaining. Everything was standard operating procedure to him, and why wouldn't it be? Nothing had changed on his side.

He'd talked her into the bet for a very specific reason—to figure out how to be the man Margo wanted him to be—and Charli's job was to help him get there. *While* he treated her with the reverence and respect a man should treat a woman he planned to be in a long-term relationship with. Only Charli wasn't the actual woman he dreamed about at night.

Squaring her shoulders, she tapped on the table to get everyone's attention. "What's the next move, guys? How are you going to handle this?"

Preferably as quickly as possible. But she didn't say that. Honestly, she didn't have a lot of faith that it mattered. They still didn't know who had broken into the lab trailer and even if they caught both guys, it didn't mean nothing else bad would happen.

This ranch might as well be cursed.

And if the Cowboy Experience never got off the ground, she'd have nothing.

"We're going to report it to the police first," Ace said and nodded to Paxton. "Pierce will take point on analyzing all the video footage from the property. Our guy must have left a trail of some sort. We'll find it."

They talked logistics for another thirty minutes, complete with a warning that neither Lang sister should leave the house without an escort. Well, that's what was *said* but they really meant Charli shouldn't. Sophia wasn't the flight risk, apparently.

When the totally useless meeting ended, Charli stalked out of the kitchen, intent on a hot bath and a mindless book. But Heath caught up with her well before she hit the staircase.

"A word with you, Ms. Lang," he drawled, and she rolled her eyes at the firm hand on her elbow that told her it wasn't a request.

Back to that, were they? "I have a date, McKay, and it's not with you."

The volcano in his irises bubbled and frothed. "No dates with anyone other than me. Nonnegotiable."

Well, well, she'd struck a nerve. Looked like her plans for the evening might have changed slightly. He wanted to go a round? She cracked her neck.

This was where they'd find out what he was made of, per his own request. A husband test, so to speak, because she couldn't think of anything more on point than a knock-down drag-out fight that would prove he couldn't hang in there when a woman had righteous indignation on her side.

"Jealousy is *not* my favorite look on you," she lied with a totally straight smile while secretly reveling in the nip of his fingers against her skin. "Careful or I might get the impression you care who I go out with."

"In case it's slipped your mind, my job is to keep you from resembling one of the skinned animals we found in the woods," he shot back with an impressively saccharine tone. "That's my only priority and there is nowhere in my contract that states I have to do it while third-wheeling it with you and another man. Besides, that violates the terms of our bet."

"What in the world are you blathering on about?" she said, shoving her face in the direction of his but he hadn't gotten any shorter, so she only ended up with a nose full of Heath's woodsy-piney-clean-male scent that wafted from the V of his button-down shirt. "I never agreed I wouldn't date other men."

He showed his teeth. "You did. When you agreed to give me a fair shot. Allowing another man to romance you cannot be described in any way, shape or form as a fair shot. Look it up in the dictionary."

A fair shot? Yeah, she'd given him that. Enough of one that she forgot that it wasn't real. Enough of one that she'd fallen for his sorcery and had actually started to think they were being authentic with each other.

"Oh, I see," she sneered, one hand on her hip. "It's totally fine if you're sitting around mooning over Margo while holding hands with me, but the moment I start making eyes at someone else, that's off-limits. What was I thinking? Oh, that's right. That you're a two-timing misogynist who can't spell monogamy with three sets of Scrabble tiles."

Instead, Heath crowded into her space, his frame fairly vibrating with tension that she could feel through her thin shirt. Oh, he was in a mood. She liked it when he was in a mood, especially when it matched her own.

Let's go, McKay.

She slapped two hands on his chest to force distance between them. He was so finely crafted that she forgot for a minute that she wasn't supposed to touch the artwork and let the pads of her fingers slide into the grooves of his ribs.

That's when she made the mistake of meeting his gaze dead-on. The volcano erupted, blue flames engulfing her with heat that rippled across her skin. Oh, my, that was delicious.

"I'm not thinking about anyone but you, Charlotte," he growled, and it rumbled through her fingers. "It's not what I was expecting when I proposed this bet."

That lovely confession melted all over her, softening her ire as she stared up at him. "What were you expecting?"

"A way to make spending every waking second in each other's company tolerable." The brief flash in his gaze spoke volumes. "I may have gotten more than I bargained for."

Two for two. A man who could admit when he was wrong was dead sexy. It was enough to get her to take a step back, even as she recognized that he didn't mean he thought about her the way she thought about him.

"My date is with my bathtub and a book," she murmured but he was still close enough that she could feel the exact moment when his body released its coiled tension. "It wouldn't be entirely inaccurate to say I wasn't expecting to prefer that to going out with another man. As your punishment for assuming that's what I meant, I'll let you think about me in my bath outfit."

It was something she'd say to a boyfriend. Wasn't this practice? Two could play this game.

He made a strangled sound deep in his throat, his expression darkening. "You might have just become the proud owner of a bathing partner. What kind of bodyguard would I be if I didn't ensure your complete and utter safety in all situations?"

Okay, practicing had just gotten a quadrillion times more interesting. And dangerous. But first—interesting. She swept him with a cool, assessing glance. "I don't believe you'd actually fit in my bathtub."

"Wanna bet?"

The laugh that got out of her felt a lot like a palate cleanser. "I'm still in the middle of the last bet you bamboozled me into."

His smile warmed her immensely. "And doing a stellar job at it too, I might add, despite the big mistake I made dragging Margo into this equation. For that, I'm sorry."

The apology was so unexpected and so sincere, it nearly buckled her knees. What was this twist? How dare he change the rules midstream. *This* was the man his ex-girlfriend thought needed a major overhaul before she'd contemplate the idea of marriage?

Nothing inside her skin felt right. When she'd started this fight, she'd expected him to career off the rails, maybe land a few of his own verbal hits. Get back to that place where they barely tolerated each other, and everything made sense. They'd always sparred pretty well with nothing more than their vocal cords and a healthy amount of chemistry. Why would this be any different?

Except it was. Because something *had* changed. What, she couldn't put her finger on, but this was not Heath conducting business as usual. This was Heath being…Heath. Solid. Unyielding, even when she pushed him. Matching her, toe to toe, giving as good as he got, and never, ever dropping the ball.

It was more than sexy. It was…something else she had no vocabulary for.

"I don't know how to have this conversation if you're going to fight dirty with the only thing guaranteed to render me speechless," she grumbled.

"And yet, you're still talking," he pointed out without a drop of irony. "But you still haven't told me what set you off in the woods. That was what I thought we'd be fighting about."

The volcano in his gaze had receded. Slightly. Actually, his eyes still burned pretty bright, but the energy didn't feel like it might lash out and burn her alive at any moment. It just felt…focused. On her. She didn't hate it.

But she did hate the question marks in his comment, and she was woman enough to admit she had played a part in the vibe going south between them.

"It's stupid. I just didn't like the idea of being your testing ground, only to have to give up my spoils to Miss Special Operations. I mean, she already won the interview question and probably the evening gown competition. Thanks to me, she's getting the husband of her dreams and all I get is the satisfaction of watching your shame sign video."

His lips quirked. "If you wanted to poke the bull, you picked the right way. That sounds a lot like you think you're winning our bet. Nothing could be further from the truth."

"Except the bet is that you'll change my mind about men," she reminded him, though why she had to was beyond her. "And here we are with another woman in the wings. The exact scenario I was expecting. Which means you lose."

Instead of immediately flaying her with his argument to the contrary, his gaze softened, drawing her in, settling around her like a soft blanket. Swallowing her whole before she could blink, wrapping her in something that felt a lot like gentleness.

That, she had no defense against.

"The difference here is that I'm being up-front with you," he murmured. "Isn't that the whole point? You're mad at men who keep secrets. Jerkoffs who tell you one thing and do another. Make you believe something that isn't true. I'm not hiding anything from you. Margo is the reason I made the bet and I've never given you one reason to think this is anything other than practice."

Oh geez. He wasn't wrong. That mean *Charli* was the other woman in this scenario.

And she had it totally backward. The more he practiced with Charli, the closer he'd come to winning. Because it wasn't real. Because the more he didn't put the moves on Charli, the more apparent it would become that he could, in fact, spend a great deal of time with another woman and not cheat on Margo.

Completely off-balance, she scowled. "You have a long way to go before you convince me you're different."

"How long? Tell me what I'm up against," he suggested with the gentleness that might be her undoing, but the point still stuck in her gut like a word spear that shouldn't hurt as much as a real one.

He'd been nothing but honest with her and she'd thus far refused to return the favor. How could she say she'd won the bet if she didn't tell him what was on the mind that he'd volunteered to change?

"His name is Toby."

"I hate him already," Heath ground out with gritted teeth in a parody of her comment about Margo, which oddly relaxed her spine. Unexpectedly.

"Not so much fun being on the other side, is it?" she commented with a tiny smile. "I'll make it worse by telling you *her* name is Mandy. Which I know because she came on to him right in front of me. Then I had the pleasure of realizing he'd taken her up on the blatant invitation later when I walked in on them."

Heath's hands had curled into fists by his side, the white knuckles giving her an unparalleled amount of joy. This was what someone having your back looked like.

"I hope you punched her."

"I didn't, no." Though now she was thinking she should have. It might have been a form of closure that she'd thus far been denied. "I turned around and walked out. It was easier. At least until I tried to get my stuff back and he refused to open the door. He was in there too. I could hear his phone buzzing when I called it."

"Please tell me he then gathered everything up and placed it carefully in a box for you to retrieve later."

She shook her head. "I've made my peace with the fact that I'll never get my stuff. He's probably dumped it in the trash by now."

Heath's glower could have singed the paint off an iron fence and she should probably be ashamed at how giddy his rage made her, but come on. No one in her life had ever been even slightly ticked off on her behalf. Heath didn't even know Toby and she had a feeling if they happened to be in the same place at the same time, Cheater McCheaterpants would not come out the better for it.

"Get your purse," he growled. "We're going to pay Toby a visit."

Chapter 13

"You know you can't actually break any of Toby's bones, right?" Charli commented from the passenger seat of Heath's truck where she was sitting way too far away from him.

"Says who?" he snarled, aware that he'd done very little actual talking since she'd confessed the details of the raw deal her ex had treated her to.

Pieces of work like Toby needed a few broken bones. It wasn't quite the same as crushing his spirit the way he'd done to Charli, but it was a close second, and it was the only pain Heath had the capacity to inflict.

"Margo, apparently," she informed him with a smirk that did not improve his mood. "And since you've appointed me as the judge, jury and executioner of your Win Back campaign, I guess me too."

The face she made distracted him from his grim determination as his flatbed ate up the miles between Gun Barrel City and Dallas, where they were headed for the reckoning she'd been denied. He would fix that for her. Possibly with a few less fists than he'd set out to use.

But not because his temper had abated even one tiny iota. Because she wasn't wrong and that pissed him off even more. "Your job is to keep an open mind about relationships and my role in one. Not tell me what to do."

Now he was snapping at her. Mostly because she was still too far away, and his fingertips ached to feel her skin against them. Just one little hit of Charli would soothe him, he was sure, but he refused to reach out. If he could power through without that fix, it meant he wasn't addicted, right?

Everything was fine. Just because he'd started craving Charli's brand of humor and her tendency to be 100 percent on his side no matter what didn't mean anything. They were spending a lot of time together. It stood to reason they'd start to appreciate things about each other.

"Beg to differ," she said mildly, not even the slightest bit cowed by his mood. "When you're on a mission to right a wrong on my behalf, the least I can do is make sure you're staying on the straight and narrow. It's what you asked for, McKay. If this was up to me, I'd pay extra to see Toby in traction."

"You're not paying me in the first place." But the sudden image of her jackhole ex in a full-body cast did cheer him up a bit. Instead of sitting here stewing in his own righteous fury, maybe he could lean into this unexpected fantasy she'd introduced. "What else would you like me to do to him? If it was up to you."

The look she shot him said she knew exactly why he'd asked. When she smiled, it was purely diabolical, and he had a very hard time tearing his gaze away from her in favor of focusing on the road to Dallas.

"Oh, I like this game," she announced with undisguised glee and clapped her hands. "You could break all his fingers. You threatened to do that to Trevor, and I have to admit it was a nice touch."

Heath lifted a brow, amused all at once. His knuckles

gained some color as he eased off his grip on the steering wheel. "Trevor? That was the dig nerd's name? Precious."

"He introduced himself to me," she explained, distaste coating her tone. "Like we were at a club, and he was gracing me with his presence."

Now he wished he *had* broken all of Trevor's fingers, even though the university had kicked him off the project. Couldn't dig up many treasures if you couldn't hold a shovel, and surely he'd dialed up Daddy as quickly as he could to get a new assignment.

"What else?" Heath demanded. "And let's stick with Toby since he's the one who hasn't suffered yet."

"Well, let me think. It's not often I'm asked to get creative about how to torture someone who hurt me."

Charli shifted in her seat, angling toward him and lifting one knee onto the bench seat so that it grazed his thigh. She didn't pull away. It was a subtle move, but it was clearly not accidental, and it tore through him with unexpected fire.

Margo, Margo, Margo. It shouldn't be this hard to remember why he'd cared so much about her.

"Let your imagination run free," he insisted magnanimously, since this was all hypothetical anyway, and his mood had just mysteriously improved.

Toby might not even be home, which would be a shame. Heath wouldn't hesitate to break down the door to ensure Charli had a chance to search the entire apartment for any item she wished to retrieve—whether it originally belonged to her or not—but scaring the bejesus out of her ex would be the likely extent of his satisfaction given the warning he'd just received.

No, he couldn't punch Toby in the solar plexus like the jerk deserved. And wasn't that a kick to know that Charli had appointed herself his keeper?

"You know what would really set him off?" she mused thoughtfully. "If you kissed me in front of him."

The sudden image of doing exactly that flooded him and he had a hard time shutting off the accompanying heat for more reasons than one. But he did have enough brain cells left over to be impressed with her brutal brand of retribution, which so neatly fit the crime.

That didn't make it a good idea. "I'm not kissing you for the first time in front of Toby."

"Eliminate that as a factor, then. Pull over and kiss me now."

Heath nearly swerved off the road and it was only the steady drum of the rumble strips that jolted him into correcting course. Her smile held way too much satisfaction for his taste. Oh, she didn't even have the first clue how much he wanted to do exactly as instructed.

And how conflicted the whole thing made him.

"Let's keep thinking," he suggested darkly as she laughed.

"I'm only kidding, of course. I know your heart belongs to Margo." She waved a hand at him abracadabra style. "But it's not my fault that you have all of that going on along with a healthy side of Neanderthal. It's apparently working for me."

And it worked for him that she appreciated the full package. What was he supposed to do with all of this?

A road sign for Dallas flashed by, indicating they had another twenty minutes until the city limit, which wasn't nearly enough time to sort out the mixed messages his body was giving him. Guilt at the mention of Margo wasn't pairing well with the sizzle in his blood. Hyperawareness of Charli's knee against his thigh wasn't slowing down the sizzle any. And knowing that she'd be totally fine with it if he did rearrange Toby's face might be the best adrenaline high he'd ever had.

Scratch that. *Worst*.

It was the *worst* high. Adrenaline wasn't his friend. If he ever hoped to reel back the part of his personality that would always be the Enforcer, he had to stop enjoying it when Charli encouraged him to be himself. She wasn't the one he needed to be thinking about impressing.

But he couldn't stop himself from imagining how Charli would react if he did pull over and kiss her. That occupied him until she told him to take the next exit and soon, they'd pulled up to a nondescript beige apartment building in Richardson that refused to distinguish itself from the ninety others they'd passed on the way here.

"Far cry from a six-hundred-acre ranch and a three-story Victorian house," Charli commented, her voice flat enough for Heath to figure out that she had some emotions about this trip that she hadn't shared.

He didn't hesitate to lace their fingers together—strictly for her comfort, not because the contact skimmed through his blood quicker than lightning. "You're better off. Let's get your stuff back."

Logistically, it made sense for Charli to lead since he had no idea where they were going, but it chafed not to be the one in front. It hardly mattered. There wasn't a single thing in a hundred-mile radius that could get the drop on him, even if it had been months since he'd depended on his reflexes to keep himself and his team alive.

Some things would never change, though. As they mounted the stairs to the second-floor apartment near the parking lot, his senses cleared and the slight uptick in his pulse flooded him with crackling energy.

The fact that Charli had opted to keep their fingers laced

had something to do with it too. And he didn't even mind that it had probably been for show. This arrangement benefited him as well for reasons he didn't want to spend a lot of time analyzing.

He did steal the task of announcing their presence from her, though. When Heath beat on the door, the sound reverberated through the wood with some oomph that gave Loverboy plenty of warning that answering it wasn't optional.

Unfortunately, Jackhole Toby was slightly smarter than he sounded and swung open the door, ruining Heath's plan to kick it in. He shuffled Charli behind him, just in case, but honestly, she could probably take Toby in a fair fight.

"You Toby?" he growled at the scrawny weakling who either used a ridiculous amount of sunscreen or never went outside. Plus, he had *gel* in his hair that sculpted it into a fan over his forehead. It was literally the most nauseating hairstyle Heath had ever seen.

"Yeah. Who are you?" Toby gaze shifted to Heath's hat and then swept him with an assessing glance all the way down to his boots. Which took a minute since the guy was a head shorter than him.

Then he caught sight of Charli peeking out from behind Heath's arm.

"What are you doing here?" he said with a scowl.

"No. You don't talk to her." Heath snapped his fingers in Toby's face and reversed his index finger to point at himself. "You talk to me if you decide you have something to say. Meanwhile, you're going to stand aside while Charli spends as long as she likes gathering whatever from this residence she wishes to take. Got it?"

"What is with this guy?" Toby asked Charli, completely ignoring Heath and his very patient explanation of what was about to go down. "If you want to talk, I have a few min—"

Heath pushed open the door, effectively shoving Toby out of the way. "You listen about as well as you do relationships. Move aside and keep your filthy mouth away from Charli."

Then he crossed his arms and crowded Toby until he backed up defensively, trapping him against the wall of the entryway, which allowed Charli plenty of room to navigate behind him into the apartment. In another subtle move, she pressed her hand to Heath's back as she passed.

"It's okay. This won't take me very long," she said.

Her tone was off. The Charli he knew spit fire when she got riled and if there was ever a right time to be riled, this was it. But he hadn't imagined the warble in the last couple of syllables. Whatever it was about this situation that had made her feel vulnerable wasn't okay, and he had his guess about where to place the blame.

Heath eyed Toby, who was frowning at him as if he had a right to be annoyed or put out by this surprise visit.

"Problem?" Heath growled.

"Yeah. But it's between me and Charli. I don't know who you are—"

"The person who is going to break your face if you so much as look at her again," he informed Toby succinctly. "She doesn't owe you one second of her time. And you don't deserve a millisecond."

"Look, man, I don't know what she told you, but—"

"She didn't tell me anything. I just don't like the look of your face." Heath's fist ached to plow right into the jawline of Loverboy, to inflict more pain than this loser would have the ability to deal with. But he kept his arms crossed.

Because as his newly appointed Win Back campaign manager, Charli expected him to. And he didn't want to disappoint her.

He'd finally gotten his chance to stand around and look threatening instead of being forced into using his strength to make a point. Was he really going to waste it?

Toby scratched his neck, finally looking a little uneasy. "I didn't think she'd move on so fast."

Heath didn't bother to respond to that statement when the reason for that should be perfectly obvious—that's what a woman did when she found a real man. Except she hadn't moved on, not the way Jackhole thought she had. This was all for show. And wasn't that a shame?

Charli deserved to have a man treat her well, especially after the way this one had treated her. Yet, she'd have a pretty difficult time meeting one when Heath was the only man she was spending time with.

The thought should have him stepping aside. He shouldn't care who she went out with. But when she'd told him she had a date, a red haze had filled his vision. Kind of like what was happening now.

Imagine if he actually had to watch her go on a real date. And he would have to watch. His job would still be his job, even if Charli elected to give him a taste of his own medicine and find some other guy to take her to dinner since Heath couldn't seem to find the time to do it.

More to the point, a date with Charli still wouldn't be anything other than practice. It shouldn't bother him so much.

"Where did you meet Charli?" Toby asked, as if they were having a chat in his foyer and he had every right to ask questions. "She's never been into country music. I can't believe she went to a honky-tonk."

The sneer was implied. Amusing.

"She's my boss," Heath told him just for fun.

Technically it was true, though he doubted Charli had

ever thought about it that way. Neither had he, honestly, and now he had a lovely fantasy about her sitting on a desk with her legs crossed primly as she bossed him around with that smart mouth of hers.

Charli reappeared from the back of the apartment, lugging a box filled haphazardly with stuff, including a hoodie slung across the top that hid the majority of the other contents.

"Hey, that's mine," Toby protested and actually took a step toward Charli like he planned to wrestle the hoodie from her fingertips.

"You gave it to me," she insisted.

She paused near the door, releasing the box, but grabbing the hoodie protectively in a way that made Heath's stomach clench. Maybe he'd misread some of her cryptic emotions from earlier. Did she miss this guy? Seriously? Was that why she hadn't found a replacement yet?

"To wear, not to keep," Toby informed her and reached out, as if he intended to grab the hoodie in a forcible takeback.

Heath stepped between them. "She gets the hoodie. You get the waitress. Everyone wins."

Toby glared at him. "I didn't think she told you about that. You don't understand, it was a one-time thing. A mistake." Then, he actually tried to step around Heath to speak to Charli. "She meant nothing to me, I swear. I tried to call you, but—"

Heath stepped between them again, and this time, it was easier to keep his fists from clenching. This guy wasn't worth it. "Charli, go to the truck. I'll carry the box down. We're done here."

Thankfully, she did as ordered. Heath hefted the box into his arms and walked out of Loverboy's apartment, leaving him sputtering about the hoodie. The fact that he was more concerned about the sweatshirt than Charli pretty much summed up the entire altercation.

After stowing the box in the bed of the truck, Heath slid into the driver's seat. Charli was already in the passenger seat, buckled in, and uncharacteristically quiet as she sat there clutching the hoodie.

"I'm sorry," he offered since it was clear she still had big emotions seething around inside. He got it.

She glanced up at him, her gaze snapping. "For what? You're the only person in this equation who did the right thing. I should have been the one to smash a fist into his nose after he had the audacity to try to explain away his cheating."

Heath grinned. "I would have paid extra to see that."

The joke seemed to break the dam and Charli rewarded him with a watery laugh as she tossed the hoodie to the floorboard and stomped on it. "I cannot wait to get home and burn that thing."

"Oh, is that what you wanted it for?" he commented with far less glee than what was happening on the inside. What was wrong with him that he felt such a blinding sense of satisfaction that she wasn't pining over Loverboy?

"It certainly wasn't to wear," she shot back and then her eyes widened. "That's not what you thought, right?"

She smacked him in the arm, and he caught her hand, pulling her close with it until he could see the slight smattering of freckles over her nose. "Your decisions are your own. Wear it if you want to. But I would have a very hard time not ripping it off you."

Charli shuddered but he didn't mistake it for a temperature-related reaction when heat climbed through her expression simultaneously. "Well, that just sounds like a challenge."

They stared at each other as the atmosphere sizzled between them. "You're not supposed to be challenging me to get physical. It's the other way around."

"That's the thing, though, Heath," she murmured. "Everything you do makes me feel safe and protected. No one has ever stood up for me like that before. You're amazing and you did it without grinding Toby into the carpet. If you'd needed to, you would have. I trust your judgment because you know the difference between when to stand down and when you can't."

The clearest sense of awe flooded Heath's chest as Charli's lips tipped up in a small smile.

"Now I need you to trust yourself," she said.

Chapter 14

Heath was waiting for Charli outside the door of her bedroom by the time she rolled out of the shower the next morning. Despite the door being closed, she knew he was there. She could feel his energy seeping through the walls. That was the problem with a man who had as much going on inside him as Heath McKay—he couldn't contain himself even if he tried.

Most of the time, she didn't mind just soaking him up. It was a guilty pleasure that she'd deny if asked. Thankfully, there was no enforcement agency questioning her motives when she allowed herself to bask in the way he made her feel. *Feminine. Heard. Understood.*

They might even be friends at this point.

Except she'd never had a friend who treated her like Heath did. Nor had she ever had a friend who set her blood on snap, crackle, pop mode with nothing more than a look.

That's why she couldn't face him today. Not after the way he'd handled Toby. Yeah, she'd heard every word of their exchange yesterday. The whole scene had settled into her bones—along with Heath. She didn't think she could dislodge him if she tried.

So that was a problem. This thing she'd developed for him, it had to go.

They called it a crush for a reason. It perfectly described what was going to happen to her sooner rather than later. Like the moment Heath realized he was already husband material times infinity.

And then he'd go back to Margo.

Miss Special Forces would take him back because of course she would. The woman had probably already cried herself dry over her idiocy at letting him go in the first place.

The broken heart in Charli's future was exactly what she'd been trying to avoid by not going out with him the first time around. The bet should have provided enough of a cushion to fall back on. But no. He had to be wonderful and strong and perfect at pretty much everything. Handling her ex had been the straw that squished the camel's heart.

How was she supposed to avoid Heath when she'd agreed to be joined at his hip? How was she supposed to stay away when all she wanted to do was throw open the door, drag him inside and start something he would never finish?

Or would he?

That was the other thing that was burning her up. If this was all practice, why did it seem like he wanted to kiss her for real sometimes? Why hadn't he taken the bait in the truck yesterday? Sure, she'd used her flirty I'm-not-really-serious voice when she'd dared him to pull over. No, she hadn't missed the way he'd said he didn't want to kiss her the *first* time in front of Toby. Like there'd be a second and third and fourth time.

There weren't going to be *any* times. She had zero desire to find out how principled he was. Because if he did kiss her, then he was even more of a dog than she'd pegged him to be. But if he didn't, she'd lose the bet. And know forever that he'd found a better woman, one he couldn't get over ever. Charli wasn't even a blip of temptation on his journey back to happily-ever-after with Margo.

It was killing her. That's why she'd slept a measly two hours last night. Why she was pacing in front of the door, glancing at the knob every forty seconds as she contemplated opening it and acting like everything was fine. Or not opening it and leaving Heath to cool his heels for a few hours while he guarded the pathway to her door, a grumbly bear who would gladly bite the head off anyone who tried to get to her.

That part might be the worst of all. It was becoming way too easy to believe he'd started to care about her the longer he defended her against all manner of evil in the world.

Before she drove herself to the brink, she grabbed her phone and pulled up a calendar. They still had two more weeks before the arbitrary deadline she and Sophia had agreed to. Two weeks to find the other jaguar head before word got out that it existed.

The university people had agreed to keep it a secret as much as they could, given that everyone involved had cell phones and social media accounts. Charli knew they'd focused almost all their dig nerds' efforts toward locating the hiding place of the other head—assuming it was also hidden somewhere on the ranch.

It was highly likely that the jaguar head was here somewhere. Charli's luck didn't work any other way.

And if she had a prayer of getting her life going, the stupid thing needed to be in that safe on its way to Fort Knox, or wherever university people kept ancient statues worth millions of dollars.

"I can hear you pacing, you know," Heath called through the door with barely concealed amusement.

"So?" she shot back. "This is my room. I'm allowed to pace if I feel like it."

"Fair. It just feels like restless pacing. Something on your mind?"

Trust Heath to correctly interpret the way she paced. She rolled her eyes. The man paid far too much attention to her, and she liked it far too much. "I have so many things on my mind I couldn't possibly describe them all to you."

"Do any of them have something to do with breakfast? I'm starving."

"I'm not hungry," she lied. "You can go on without me. I'm working on ranch plans."

That much was true. But if she didn't send him away, the temptation would still be out there in the hall, wearing jeans so worn they were practically a butter-soft second skin.

And the fact that she knew the texture of his jeans might be at least half the reason she'd had trouble sleeping. The other half could be the fact that she also knew the density of the powerful thighs encased in those jeans. The things you could catalog by firmly wedging your knee against a man's leg in a truck could not be overstated.

Heath wasn't leaving. His presence hadn't budged from the hall. "The day you're not hungry hasn't arrived. What's going on?"

This was the one time she wished he wasn't so dialed into her. Other times, it felt...nice to know that he'd started to figure out some of her tells. That was part of the problem. She enjoyed the way he paid attention to her. It was going to her head.

"Nothing," she responded brightly. "I'm just rearranging some of the stuff I got back."

Honestly, she hadn't bothered. The box of her belongings had been meager at best. The retrieval had been largely symbolic, and instrumental in bringing about her current mood.

Because it had solidified something for her. She'd never felt like her life had really started back in Dallas. Walking back into that apartment she'd shared with Toby had rung some of her bells the wrong way.

It had never felt like her place.

This ranch? *Home*. Just not *her* home. Not yet. Making her mark with the Cowboy Experience would go a long way toward fixing that. That's why she needed to focus on figuring out how to move forward. Sophia had all of her own tasks laid out in her millions of planners. Charli had never been one for making lists, but she had a running agenda in her head. That counted.

And the first item on her mental to-do was finding that jaguar head. It could lead to clearing out the entire place of dig nerds because why would they stay after that? Even the single jaguar head was the find of the century. Once they had the other one, it was all over. They couldn't possibly justify hanging out in hopes of hitting a third jackpot. Right?

So that meant Charli had a vested interest in being the one to locate the head.

"You're still pacing," Heath called.

"You're still not eating," she pointed out. "I'm fine. Go eat."

Just to throw him off, she scampered to the box and pulled out the handful of paperbacks she'd never gotten around to reading but liked the look of on her bookshelf. It made her feel like she could be the kind of person who read for fun. Eventually. If things settled down enough and she found some downtime, she could totally be a reader.

Carefully, she placed the books on the dresser since

this bedroom she'd chosen didn't have actual bookshelves. Which was fine since she didn't have an actual library. The four slim volumes of classics fell over immediately.

"What was that?"

"A noise," she informed Heath grumpily. "One you wouldn't have heard if you'd gone to the kitchen like I told you to. My books fell over."

"You have books?"

"I can have books," she returned defensively, hoping he didn't ask her the titles because obviously he was the type who did actually read, and he'd probably read all of these multiple times. She'd fail the quiz and then he'd ask her why she didn't have bookends.

And the answer was that she'd never had bookends because she'd leaned the books up against the end of the bookcase, but she didn't have a bookcase anymore so that was a logistical issue she hadn't solved yet. The whole thing was giving her a headache and all she wanted was for Heath to leave her alone so she didn't have to spend 24/7 trying to figure out how he'd gotten under her skin.

"Do you want some help putting your stuff away?"

Oh, he'd like that, wouldn't he? An invitation into Charli's room where his Heathness would spill over into all the empty spaces, including the ones inside her, and warm up everything, reminding her how bleak and horrible it felt to be in here alone.

She hugged her abdomen with both arms, wondering if it was actually possible for a person's guts to spill out strictly from longing.

"That's okay. Thanks," she called as an afterthought.

"Now I know something is wrong," he said with an edge to his voice. "You never say thank-you."

"That's not true, I say it all the time." Didn't she?

"Not to me," he commented. "I'm starting to get a complex about it."

She rolled her eyes again. "Thank you, Heath. You're the best, Heath. I don't know what I would do without you, Heath."

"Never mind," he muttered. "I definitely didn't have a lack of your sarcasm in my life."

Now he sounded vaguely...something. She frowned. That was one thing she couldn't do with the door closed—read what was going on in his eyes. So maybe she *was* a reader. Huh.

When she flung open the door, against her better judgment, mind you, he was leaning against the wall with that loose, lazy pose that screamed exactly how comfortable in his body he was, one booted foot crossed over the other. That hat pulled down low over his face that he hadn't bothered to shave. Again. Even the scar near his collarbone screamed *too hot to handle*.

He was so delicious that her skin actually reacted, a swath of goose bumps racing across it, chasing the flush of heat that accompanied her first visual smorgasbord of the day.

Then she met his gaze and what she saw there set her back a step.

"Did I hurt your feelings?" she whispered as something flickered in his depths.

She had. She'd stumbled somehow while wallowing in her own crap.

"Men don't have feelings." His voice was oddly flat. "We have urges. Mine is usually to break something."

She suspected he hadn't meant to answer the question, but he actually had. "I'm sorry. I'm not in my right head yet. Thank you for taking me to get my stuff yesterday. It was implied, but that's not good enough for the effort. It was really amazing."

Heath's arms were still crossed but they relaxed a fraction as he tipped his head in acknowledgement.

"I'm fine," she told him. "I also appreciate that you're concerned. No one else pays enough attention to me to figure out if I'm anything, let alone not okay. Thank you for that too."

He eyed her suspiciously. "That sounds like a lead-in if I've ever heard one."

What was wrong with her that the one person who spent the most time in her company accused her of never saying thank-you and of having an ulterior motive when she did?

No wonder he preferred Margo. Charli was a hot mess who destroyed stuff simply by breathing on it. She had to do better. That's what this bet was about, after all. Practice. On both sides. If she'd never had an adult relationship before, one where each of them treated the other with respect, how could she expect to get it right unless she started figuring it out right now?

Despite knowing it would set off a chain reaction of butterflies in her stomach, she reached out and placed a hand on his arm. "No agenda. Just...thank you."

Without a lot of fanfare, he covered her hand with his. "You're welcome."

Something passed between them, and it was so light and bright that it filled her chest so fully that she couldn't breathe.

She yanked her hand free. "I'm really not hungry. Go. I'm going to finish putting my stuff away."

Thankfully, he nodded, his gaze searching hers, but he didn't seem to find whatever he was looking for. "I'll be back later to catch up with you on your plans for the day."

Since she didn't have any, other than making doubly sure she avoided Heath the rest of the day, that wouldn't take long. "Have a good breakfast."

The moment his bootsteps faded from the stairs, she bolted back into her room and slathered on some sunscreen, then changed into old clothes, shoving a baseball cap over her hair. Giant sunglasses hid her face and with any luck, she'd pass for a dig nerd if none of them looked at her too hard.

Hiking boots in hand—no reason to alert anyone to the fact that she was creeping down the stairs—she made it to the front porch without anyone seeing her. Sophia would have ratted her out in a heartbeat and Ace probably would have too, but thankfully they were nowhere to be found.

She had to get out of this house. Out of the sphere of Heath's influence before she lost her mind. She needed fresh air, stat.

Taking a horse would be too obvious, so she laced up her boots and put her legs to good use, vanishing into the trees as quickly as possible, her back on fire as she braced to be stopped with a solid hand attached to Heath's body.

Nothing happened. Somehow, she'd legit managed to give her bodyguard the slip.

Now she could breathe again. And find that jaguar head.

Chapter 15

Clear air. Yes, that definitely should have topped Charli's list a lot sooner. This was her ranch, and she should be spending a lot more time on it—all of it. She'd headed in the opposite direction of the university people's camp, not that it mattered. They'd spread like ants over the entire property.

No problem. She could avoid the dig nerds if she tried hard enough.

The ranch property opened up into a number of pastures just down the hill from the new barn. Sophia had filled her in on how the old barn had collapsed, which had happened before Charli had gotten her head wrapped around the concept of being named as one of the new owners.

Inheritance. It was one of those words that you heard applied to other people. Not to yourself. It hadn't meant much to Charli at the time, for sure. Some money maybe. But Sophia hadn't wanted to sell. Veronica, their younger sister, emphatically insisted they shouldn't keep the ranch.

Charli had been caught in the middle, totally unsure which side she should pick. Story of her life. The money from the sale would have been nice, but she knew herself. It would have slipped through her fingers with little to show for it other than a new car and some expensive shoes. The rest would have gone unaccounted for.

Veronica would have used the money to do something smart like start her own business or invest it. Sophia would have stuck it in a savings account and kept on being Super Sophia at whatever corporation she'd elected to tame next. The only one who would have kept drifting was Charli.

Because she was the most like their father.

It was an ugly truth she'd always known in the part of her heart way in the back. That's why it had been so important for her to put a stake in the ground at the ranch. To make it a home. Her home.

Being out here in the midst of it—*alone*—did wonders for her state of mind. This was hers. All of it. Sure, technically she owned one third of it, but there wasn't a way to divide it up like a pie chart. She liked to think of it as all three of them owning the entire ranch. As if their shares sat on top of each other instead of side by side.

This was what she'd expected to feel during the horseback ride. A sense of pride. Ownership. *That's my tree. This stretch of grass? Mine. That fence post belongs to me.*

Instead, she'd spent the entire day engrossed in her riding companion, even after they'd found the animals. That's what Heath did to her—took her brain hostage—and if she was being honest, he commanded the attention of most of the rest of her too.

That's why this break from him had been so sorely needed. She could think about important ranch things and forget about Heath. He certainly didn't think about her when he wasn't in her presence. All his mental energy went toward Margo.

This part of the ranch contained remarkably few people. Most of the nerds had focused their dig sites in the woods, which stretched along the east side of the property. That's where the creek ran, but you had to know where to look for it. She remembered that from the few times she'd visited her grandparents. It was a bit of an inside joke for Sophia to have named the place Hidden Creek Ranch, but Charli appreciated it.

Since she'd wanted to avoid the university people, she'd veered toward the pastureland. Plus, if the dig nerds spent all their time in the woods, odds were high they'd find the jaguar head...or they wouldn't because it wasn't hidden there. No reason for Charli to duplicate their efforts.

No one was in this far-south pasture. Jonas, the ranch manager, kept the horses closer to the house in deference to all the treasure hunt activity. It was more work to feed them, but it eliminated a lot of hassle and prevented the university people spooking them. Which just proved the urgency of finding the female head—the sooner they got these extra people out of here, the sooner the ranch could return to normal. And the sooner they could get the Cowboy Experience up and running.

And finally, Charli would have a place to belong.

No more Tobys. No more pet stores with the pecky birds. No more running from real life, her default. *That* was the inheritance she'd gotten from David Lang. That was what she was up against—the DNA her father had infused into her blood. She could consciously put that behind her and *belong*.

Charli's boots crunched through the tall grass as she trudged across the neglected pastureland. A slight breeze blew against the long grasses, rifling through the split ends for acres upon acres. It would take forever to search every square inch, especially without tools, which she'd forgotten about in her haste to give Heath the slip.

Well, this wasn't wasted effort. She could still enjoy the breeze and feeling her own earth beneath her feet.

The breeze picked up, flattening the grass and then releasing it to gently bob. There was one place where the grass seemed shorter, as if it had been trampled or mowed recently. Except that would be really weird, considering the horses hadn't been in this area for weeks.

Curiosity piqued, Charli set off for the cleared-out area because, why not investigate? As she got closer, she could see the outline of a circular something, overgrown with weeds and vines.

She pulled one of the vines away and saw that it clung to stone covered in moss. What was this, some kind of grave marker? She knelt down, wishing she'd worn gloves, and yanked another vine free, a long one that curled over the top of the circle. A lizard darted away from her hand, and she yelped, jumping a solid four inches.

Oh, thank god. One of the little green ones. Those she didn't mind but there were probably other ones—and maybe snakes too—that she did not want to come across.

She shuddered. Well, too late to worry about that now. If she cared about snakes, traipsing around in a big field full of things they liked to eat was not the way to avoid them.

Another yank and she had partially uncovered the circle. It was a hole in the ground ringed by stones, so deep that she couldn't see the bottom. A well. Right? What else would be out here in a pasture meant to hold animals who would need to drink a lot of water?

More to the point, it was a deep hole in the ground that would be a great hiding place for stuff. Like a gold jaguar head worth a lot of money. Best of all, probably no one else had found it yet since it was out here in the middle of a field the university teams cared nothing about.

Enthused by her find, Charli leaned closer to inspect the well. The ancient stones creaked beneath her weight.

Wow, this thing might be older than she'd first assumed. She shone her phone's flashlight down into the darkness, cursing her lack of foresight in bringing a real flashlight.

There were still a few stupid vines stretching over the opening, casting too many shadows. She pulled at a couple with her left hand. The earth shifted and she lost her balance. And her grip on her phone, which tumbled into the hole.

That had *not* just happened. Charli cursed.

Her phone's flashlight was still shining, and she hadn't heard a splash. That was a good sign, right? But geez, it was so far down the hole. She could barely see it, even if she angled herself right over the opening.

The stones of the well's edge crumbled under her weight. With a *crack*, the whole edge collapsed. Flailing, she grasped at thin air as she fell into darkness.

The fall was quick and brutal. Her wrist absorbed most of the impact, sending a searing pain through her arm. Her hip glanced against something hard. Maybe her phone. Or the well floor.

Her lungs on fire, she struggled to catch her breath, heaving great gasps of air. The opening above her let in a bit of light but not nearly enough. Given her luck, she'd landed on her phone and killed it, which had also effectively eliminated her one light source.

It was dark. She was in a hole. No one knew where she was. She was *so* screwed.

Panic edged in faster than she could check it. A scream clawed its way out of her throat, which did zero good and got the rest of her body in on the panic. She started to shake as pain forked up her arm, sharp and agonizing.

Okay, this was probably the worst thing that had ever happened to her, but just like anything else, there was no one to rescue her. She had to figure this out on her own. What would Black Widow Hurricane do?

Climb.

Sucking back the panic, she crawled to her hands and knees, whimpering as she accidentally put some weight on her wrist.

So that was a problem. Broken probably.

Well, she'd just have to use it anyway. This well wasn't going to lift her out via a magic carpet. She felt around for some crevices in the well wall. It seemed to be made of the same stone as the part above ground. If her arm didn't hurt so badly, she might have a second to appreciate the construction quality of this well. How had they gotten the stones all the way down here?

And where was all the water? Had this well dried up at some point—or was it not a well at all?

Honestly, she didn't care enough to spend a second more of her precious brain power wondering about the creation and maintenance of whatever this hole in the ground was. Tentatively, she reached up to search for a niche or a ledge to hoist herself up, the fingers of her good hand scrabbling for purchase. Finally she got a solid enough grip to try to pull.

Okay, good. This was working. She levered herself up, slamming her feet into tiny cracks between stones, gasping as one boot slipped off the weatherworn stone. Barely managing to avoid sliding back to the floor, she froze, locking her fingers in place.

Somehow, she kept her position. But she had to *move*.

Now came the hard part. She stretched her left hand high, wincing as pain radiated from her wrist, but she didn't have the luxury of being a baby about this. Her fingertips found the next ledge about a foot higher than the stone she clung to with her right hand.

The second she put her weight on her injured wrist, a lightning bolt sailed down her arm and lit up her entire body with agony. It was so bad that she lost her grip and fell back to the floor in a heap, a torrent of angry tears cascading into the dirt beneath her cheek.

She felt sorry for herself for exactly thirty seconds, during which she cursed Heath for not realizing she'd given him the slip and then following her on this ill-advised adventure, Sophia for telling the university people they could look for more Maya crap, and David Lang for giving her not only a tendency to drift but a healthy amount of curiosity and zero fear.

Except for right this minute. She had a lot of fear. It was suffocating her.

But she couldn't give up. Something was poking her hip and that needed to stop. She felt around and her fingers slid over a smooth flat object. Her phone. She nipped her fingertips around the edges and when she tilted it, the screen lit up. Glory be. She'd been sure she'd smashed it in the fall. Somehow, she'd managed to switch off the flashlight with her hip. Bet she'd never be able to do that twice.

No bars. Not that she'd thought for a second cell service would pop up on the screen. She'd had to check, though. At least she had light for as long as the battery lasted. This was a positive. *Focus on that.*

Rolling—carefully—she sat up and fumbled with her phone, shining it around the bottom of the well. Or whatever it was. Because it didn't really seem like it had ever held water. Wouldn't it have mold or something along the edges? And it was kind of wider at the bottom, like a…cave.

Sort of similar to the ones closer to Austin in the Hill Country, where the water table had carved out the limestone.

She ran the light along the edges until she couldn't swivel any further, then scooched around until she could sweep behind her. Oh, man. There was a wide passageway from the main area, which would have been super handy if it had still been another exit point, but it looked like it had caved in on itself several feet back.

And there was something over there. A few piles of what looked like old fabric.

Charli blinked and held the phone up higher. Had someone used this area for storage at one point? That seemed so unlikely. Wouldn't it have flooded when it rained?

But if there used to be a different entrance, anything might be possible.

She climbed to her feet, wincing as her abused body let her know that she'd fallen twice in the last few minutes, and limped toward the piles. She nudged the one closest to her with her foot, expecting the fabric to disintegrate, but whatever was under it was pretty solid.

Kneeling gingerly, she used her good hand to pull on the fabric, but it was wrapped tight. One good push up allowed her to free the dusty covering, which reminded her of the stuff that covered patio chairs with the rough texture, and then the wrapping came loose.

She yanked it free and gasped. Never, never again could she claim she had anything but pure, blind dumb luck because holy ancient Maya gods, she held the other jaguar head.

The statue gleamed in the light from her phone, unmistakable even though she hadn't studied the other one at length. This one had the same burnish to it, as if it needed to be polished, the black markings of the jaguar's spots fading into the gold along the edges. The flat, black eyes stared at her.

This one, which surely was the female, had a similar round, collar-type thing ringing the base of the head, like the other one. That's what the statue stood on and the collar was covered in what looked almost like cartoons, but she was pretty sure it was the Mayan language, which kind of resembled Egyptian hieroglyphs but not really.

Oh, man. She definitely couldn't climb out of here with *that* tucked under her arm, even if she felt stronger in an hour or so. Which wasn't likely with no food and water.

Okay, think. Could she dig out where the tunnel had collapsed? She stumbled over to the giant pile of dirt, rock and a few tree branches, but she couldn't budge even the very top layer.

Frustrated, she stepped back and kicked one of the other piles of fabric, the ones she had forgotten about instantly. Boy, she was some kind of adventurer. What if she'd hit the mother lode of Maya treasure and all she could think about was escape? Wasn't there some saying about one jaguar head in the hand meant there were two more in the bush?

She poked at the pile of fabric, but this one wasn't solid like the other one. Plus, it was a lot longer and thinner. Running her light up the length, she got a funny squiggle in her gut that the pile of fabric looked like...pants. That led to a shirt. And a face. Or what was left of it.

Not a Maya treasure. But a body. A dead one. And she was trapped with it.

Chapter 16

Heath shoved his hat back further on his head and jammed his finger in the direction of the pastures.

"Spread out," he barked. They'd been messing around in the woods too long and had almost lost the light. "Do not miss a single inch of ground. You shoot a flare if you find so much as a piece of thread that might be from Charli's clothes. Got it?"

The group of dig nerds nodded solemnly, and the leader held up his flare gun, the one Heath had painstakingly showed him how to use. Meanwhile, he was counting down the seconds with his thundering pulse because it was yet another delay in getting to Charli.

The woman was going to kill him. Only fair. He was pretty sure he was going to return the favor. As soon as they found her. *Assuming* they found her, which given their lack of success over the last eight hours wasn't a given.

"Move," he instructed the dig nerd team, who'd volunteered to take the front section of pastureland. They meekly complied, trotting off like a herd of lazy buffalo.

Heath, Pierce and Madden were leading a second team including Sophia and a few of the ranch hands. Their objective: combing the back section of pasture along with the dogs, where they obviously should have started instead of wasting time in the woods. The dogs strained on their leashes, and Jonas spoke to them in the same soothing voice he would use with a spooked horse. They were itching to get going and so was Heath.

Pierce settled a hand on Heath's shoulder, his expression calm. "We're going to find her."

If only faith worked in these situations. Heath bit back a testy reply because they'd all been at this for eons already. He wasn't the only one who was hot, tired and terrified. Sophia hadn't stopped pacing on the porch, even though she'd personally walked the entire front half of the fence line with Madden earlier this morning. This was after she'd called every single person she could think of who knew Charli or had spoken to her recently.

Nada. Just like everything else they'd tried. Charli was missing. Like, full tilt, dropped off the face of the earth, no note, car in the half-circle driveway, purse and wallet still in her room, missing. Just…gone.

He'd do a repeat call to everyone in the county if he could do that and ride a horse at the same time, but so far, he'd been wildly unsuccessful dialing while at a full gallop.

Madden crossed the yard and shoved a sandwich into Heath's hand, obviously sensing it was the opportune moment since this was the first time in over eight hours that he'd been in the same spot for more than five minutes.

"Passing out from lack of protein isn't going to help anyone, McKay, least of all you," Madden murmured and jerked his head. "Sophia called her mom. She's on the way."

Oh, God. If Sophia had finally given in and called Mrs. Lang, that meant she didn't have a lot of hope for a positive outcome. Well, he wasn't giving up. Period. Guess he hadn't lost his blind faith after all.

After all, Heath had extracted a high-profile Taliban

prisoner from a compound hidden in the extensive cave system of the Spin Ghar Mountains. In the dark. He could find Charli.

He'd been standing here immobile during their regroup session for too long, that was the problem. It made his mind spiral, worrying that she'd been kidnapped by one of the unsavory characters lurking in the shadows of this long-drawn-out assignment.

And that was the rub, right? He had no clue who he was up against, if so.

What if they'd taken her somewhere off the ranch? He'd never find her. And he was way past the point where he'd deny caring if asked. This went beyond an assignment, and it wouldn't surprise him if everyone had guessed that already. Madden and Pierce had wisely kept their cracks about it to themselves, which he appreciated, because he did not want to break his vow of nonviolence by knocking out the teeth of one of his friends.

But that didn't mean he planned to spend a lot of time examining the curl of panic in his gut or why it was making his throat hurt. Why everything inside screamed at him to move, to find her. What if she was hurt? What if she was lost? She needed him and he was failing her.

Plus, this whole situation had smacked him in the face with the fact that he needed her too.

Sophia paused midwhirl and buried her head in her hands, scrubbing at her eyes. "If she just took off for a spa day and didn't bother telling anyone, I'm going to dis-own her."

"She didn't just take off," Heath said for the millionth time. The worst part was that he almost wished she had. That would be better than the alternative. "If she had, she'd be back by now. Or she'd have called."

Anyone with a cell phone had been tasked with trying to call her but she never picked up. So that eliminated any possibility that she was ducking Heath or Sophia's calls. They'd even tried getting Veronica to call her. She had nothing to do with the ranch, so even if Charli had descended into some sort of temper tantrum over Heath's method of personal security, she wouldn't have suspected her younger sister of wanting to locate her.

And honestly, Charli had stopped causing him problems a while back. They'd been on the same page lately. She wouldn't do this to him deliberately.

This was a bad situation. He could feel it in his gut. And it was getting worse. Statistically speaking, the odds of finding Charli went down exponentially with each hour that ticked by.

They'd crisscrossed the woods twice already, working in teams since he couldn't physically search an entire six-hundred-acre ranch himself, not in a few hours. If something didn't break soon, he had a feeling he would be personally going over every inch with a flashlight before too long.

Shoving the last of his sandwich into his mouth, he chewed and swallowed, wordlessly taking the bottled water Pierce had pressed into his hand. He checked his walkie-talkie—again—as the others did the same.

"Let's go," Madden said and led the charge, but only because Heath's knees had gone a little weak. From lack of food combined with physical exertion. Probably.

Was it worse to admit he was out of practice at executing an operation with stone-cold reflexes or that the mission itself had personal undertones that were messing him up?

Stalking ahead, he ignored everything but the terrain beneath his feet.

They were walking this time, at Heath's insistence. He'd been so sure they'd find Charli in the woods and in his arrogance, he'd also made the wrong call of being on horseback. Better to cover a lot of ground, in his mind. Wrong. They'd do this section on foot and that's what was going to make a difference. It had to.

"Cut the dogs loose," he instructed Jonas, who had maneuvered the hounds to the search party's twelve o'clock position.

Another necessary shift in strategy that he'd felt in his gut. Jonas unsnapped the leashes, still stone-faced as always.

Madden glanced at Heath as Pierce caught up to them both, but it was a testament to their partnership that neither of them questioned his directive. These guys had his back no matter what. It was nice.

Shrugging, Heath kept his gaze on the ground, scanning for visual clues as he explained anyway. "We tried following the dogs in the woods, hoping they would lead us to her. That didn't work. We don't have time for that now."

The sun had started to set. Charli had been missing since nine twenty this morning, when he'd realized she wasn't refusing to answer the door for some mysterious reason, but because she wasn't actually in her room. After an hour of assuming she'd reappear, he'd known in his soul that she was in trouble.

The dogs seemed to sense that they were the stars of the show, eagerly pushing their noses along the ground despite not being trained bloodhounds. Putting his faith in them might be another problem, but Heath had few options.

If this had been Afghanistan, he'd have military-grade equipment at his disposal, complete with infrared scanners, drones and night vision goggles. In East Texas, he had his eyes, his brain and some dogs Charli petted occasionally.

The breeze from the north fluttered the split-seeded tips of the overgrowth in this pasture. Another problem. Under normal ranch operations, Jonas would be rotating the horses through these pastures, which would have naturally mowed down the grasses as they grazed.

Instead, the search party got to contend with acres and acres of tall foliage that would easily hide a small woman who might be passed out cold from who knew what.

Heath bit back an order to hurry. The dogs needed to be thorough, not rushed.

As he scanned the field to the left, the breeze ruffled the grass differently in one particular section. He shaded his eyes against the glow of the setting sun. It definitely looked like the grass was flattened in that area in comparison to the rest.

It might be Charli.

Without a word, he shifted his trajectory to head in that direction. Pierce automatically split off from the group and followed him. Madden stayed on the group's course with Sophia, but he'd redirect everyone in a heartbeat if Heath called him on his walkie-talkie.

The flat grass area was a hole in the ground. An old well by the looks of it, but the stones around the edges were crumbled in on the edges closest to the center. It looked fresh.

"Charli?" he called, and his heart stumbled as he heard scrabbling inside.

"I'm here."

The sound of her voice emanating from the hole unleashed a slew of sensations that swept through Heath's body and not one of them he could name. Except mad. That he knew he was plenty of.

"Why don't you climb out now," he instructed as calmly as he could, given the adrenaline levels currently flooding his veins. "I'll grab you when you get close to the top."

"As fine an idea as that is, McKay, don't you think I would have already done that if I could?" she shot back with far less sarcasm than he would have expected.

She sounded so weak. It was alarming. "Is the shaft blocked or something?"

After a long pause, he heard her response drift up to him. "I broke my wrist when I fell. I can't put any weight on it."

"Call the others," he instructed Pierce over his shoulder. "Have them bring a rope."

Then he wasted no more time, slinging a leg over the edge of the hole. He couldn't wait for proper gear, not if Charli was hurt. If he'd known he would be descending into the pits of hell with nothing more than his best ninja skills, he'd have worn something other than cowboy boots, but he'd done worse in far more desperate circumstances.

Never with someone he cared about deep in a hole in the ground, though.

Calf muscles screaming, he braced both legs against the outer walls, pushing out to keep from sliding. Gymnast he was not, but he could brute-force his way down in a controlled descent with the best of them. As he shimmied down the stones one agonizing inch at a time, the flashlight and walkie-talkie clipped to his belt loops slapped his hips with each jerky movement.

That was going to leave a mark.

"Are you practicing to be Spider-Man for Halloween?" Charli called up the shaft wryly. "Because you're nailing it."

His chest heaved from the exertion. Man, he was out of

shape. Something like this wouldn't have even winded him a year ago. "If you want to be rescued, save the small talk."

Finally, he hit the dirt floor and shook out his aching biceps, then resituated his hat, which he hadn't lost in the descent, so he'd count that as a plus. It was pretty dark down in the depths, but he could sense Charli just off to the right. His fingers yearned to reach out, just to assure himself she was safe. The rest of him just wanted to fold her into his embrace and never let go.

He crossed his arms. "Not the locale I would have picked for a date."

"Good thing this isn't a date. How did you find me?"

Heath switched on the flashlight. The glow lit up her face, highlighting the smears of dirt across her cheeks. She had a twig in her hair, and she cradled her right wrist against her body. The sight of Charli injured put him in a dangerous mood.

"Well, it was simple really. I read the note you left and decided to let you suffer for your sins, then went to a bar to live it up since you so magnanimously gave me the day off." The edge in his voice echoed off the worn, dingy stone surrounding them. "How do you think I found you? I kept looking until I did. Eight hours we've been at this, Charli. Everyone. The entire ranch. Your mom says hi, by the way."

Charli's mouth tightened. "I didn't ask you to come after me. I didn't leave a note for specifically that reason."

His laugh sounded as forced as it felt. "You're so welcome, Charli. I'm glad you appreciate the effort. No, no, I refuse to leave you here despite your very compelling arguments to the contrary."

"Don't be a jerk," she returned and shifted her arm, wincing.

"Let me look at that."

The mulish look she shot him didn't do his mood any favors, but he wasn't here to make friends. Setting the flashlight down, he pulled her closer by the shoulders and took her hand, gently turning the wrist over. When she cried out, his stomach clenched.

"Yeah, it's broken," he said gruffly.

"Thanks, Sherlock, I am thrilled to hear expert medical opinion comes along with your manly muscles. Whatever would I have done without you?"

Her exhausted expression pulled at some other parts of his chest that he'd rather remain unaffected, but that ship had sailed a long time ago. He sighed.

"Let's not do this, okay?"

"Do what? Practice being a couple?" she practically sneered. "Guess what? The bet was your idea, and this is what people in a relationship do. Fight. Especially when one of them is being horrible to the other one."

Heath checked his eye roll because yeah. She wasn't wrong. "I'm tired. It's been a long day."

"Back atcha," she said with one hip jutted out like a supermodel on the catwalk with plenty of lip and attitude that convicted him for that crappy non-apology. "You didn't ask, so I have zero motivation to tell you, but we're not alone down here."

Instantly, his spine stiffened, and he hustled her behind him, his feet spread and arms poised to take apart any threat that tried to get to her. They'd have to come through him and hope he let whoever had threatened her keep their limbs attached.

"Relax, Rambo," she huffed on a half laugh, half snort. "It's of the not-currently-alive variety. And I don't mind telling you that being stuck down here with a corpse has scarred me for life."

"A...did you say a corpse?" Heath swept the well area beyond where he stood with Charli and saw the body in question that was decaying enough to have him cover his mouth with his shirt.

"You get used to it," Charli commented with a wrinkled nose. "But that pales in comparison to what else I found."

She pulled something shiny out from under a tarp and he blinked. "Is that the other jaguar head?"

Dumb question. It matched the first almost exactly and what else would anyone expect to find in the hiding place of a five-million-dollar statue but a dead body—which he'd lay odds had not ended up that way accidentally. But why kill whoever the unfortunate soul was, only to leave the ancient statue behind?

"The one and only." Her grin came out as a half grimace. "I quit feeling lucky about three hours ago when I started accepting the fact that there would be two corpses in here before too long. I...well, I had a lot of time to reflect on how dumb it was to ditch you. I shouldn't have. If you promise not to look at me while I do it, I'm going to admit I was wrong and say I'm sorry."

The catch in her voice undid him. Flat unwound everything that held his heart, his lungs—his soul—together, all of it uncoiling in the depths of his stomach. He muttered a curse and yanked her into his arms, tucking her deep into the place that she'd just emptied out.

Charli snuffled against his shirt, her bad arm hanging at her side, but the other one clung to his waist and she felt like heaven against his body.

"I'm sorry too," he murmured into her hair as she filled him up again to the brim, with heat and light and pure bliss. Whatever he'd been furious about blew away in an instant and he forgot everything but this woman, here, now. "You scared me."

"I'm sorry," she whispered again against his shirt and repeated it mournfully. "All I could think about was you. That I'd never see you again and how mad you must be. I thought I was going to die and the last memory you'd have of me is how crappy a practice girlfriend I am."

"This is not practice, Charlotte," he growled. "Safe space. Take a time-out for a minute."

Just as she drew back, her gaze searching his, a rope hit the ground behind him. He looked up to see a dark head leaning over the edge of the well.

"You guys ready to get out of there?" Pierce called.

Chapter 17

Charli's brand-new cast sucked. All she wanted to do was sleep when they finally got home from the emergency clinic in Gun Barrel City, but the skin under the plaster itched and everything hurt. Especially her throat. From holding back the screams, most likely.

Predictably, Heath followed her up the stairs to her room, his hand at the small of her back like he was afraid she might pitch backward down the stairs if he wasn't there to catch her.

Well, that made two of them afraid of that, dang it. She had plenty of other things to worry about too, like blubbering gratitude for his heroic efforts to make sure she didn't die. And maybe some other stupid feelings churning around in the mix that felt an awful lot like fodder for losing the bet.

He *was* different. He'd proven that over and over again. What he was not? *Hers*. The time-out at the bottom of the well notwithstanding.

Whatever that had been about. A time-out from what? The bet? Practicing? That wasn't a thing, not in her world.

Heath paused at her door, dropping his hand. "Want me to help you get ready for bed?"

"You'd like that, wouldn't you?" she said with a smirk,

desperate to get back to a place where she understood the dynamic between them. Understood why her chest hurt when she looked at him.

"Yeah, a woman with a broken arm is my kind of hot date," he muttered, his eyes on the ceiling in what looked like a not-so-veiled attempt to keep his temper in check. "But sure, try to take your clothes off with one arm. I'll wait."

"I can call Sophia."

"The same sister who walked all over half this ranch today and is currently about to slide into a bubble bath drawn by her equally exhausted boyfriend?" Heath crossed his arms and leaned on the doorjamb. "That sister?"

Yeah, she hadn't thought that through. She sighed.

The man would not stop showing up for her and she was sick and tired of pushing back the tendrils he'd snaked around her heart. Especially when he said confusing things like *this is not practice*.

Was he saying it didn't feel like practice because she'd messed it up or because he'd truly been worried about her? As a friend. Right? And why didn't she know? Because she didn't want to ask. Didn't want to have it clarified so she knew for sure it had been a friendly hug that had felt anything but.

As soon as his partners had lifted them out of the hole via the sturdy rope they'd thrown down, Heath had driven her into town to have her wrist checked out with Sophia and Ace in tow. Sophia because she'd refused to let Charli out of her sight and Ace because he'd refused to let Sophia out of his. Heath had stayed glued to her side because he was Heath.

Paxton had stayed behind to call in the body they'd found, then planned to assist the local police with securing the scene. No one knew about the jaguar head except the five of them, per Sophia's directive. Which Charli appreciated. Tomorrow morning, they'd figure out how to manage what would surely become a forty-seven-ring circus combined with a petting zoo and a rave once word got out that they'd located the second head.

There better not be any jaguar babies or extended family statues out there somewhere or she'd punch something.

"I'm running on fumes, McKay," she said as it all hit her like a ton of bricks. "I can't do this now. Please just let me be for tonight and I promise, tomorrow you can go back to being your domineering, confounding, hotter than asphalt self and I'll be in a much better place to take you down a few pegs. Deal?"

Heath nodded once, though his expression could give a mule a run for its money. He didn't argue thankfully, and it felt like a small win as she shut the door in his face. Until she tried to wrench her shirt off with her good hand and wound up smacking herself in the face.

Cursing, she eased off her hiking boots and jeans, which went easier, then padded into the en suite bathroom. Dear God, was that her face? It was practically unrecognizable under a layer of dust and some black streaks of who knew what. Bat poop probably.

It took four million years to scrub her face clean with one hand, only to find some of the black was bruising—nice—and another four to get a brush through the bird's nest on top of her head. An actual twig fell out, so that was lovely.

Exhausted all over again, she opted to get into bed with her shirt still on. She could surely wash sheets with one hand after she'd slept for twelve hours. But her brain would not shut off long enough to sleep. For one, she was still filthy, and she had a hard time not thinking about what kind of ick she might be spreading around in her bed.

She eased off the mattress and trudged back into the bathroom to wet a washcloth, then ran it all over her body, only to realize as she collapsed back into bed that she'd just splatted right in the middle of the dirt she'd transferred there earlier.

Another futile struggle with her shirt later, she sank to the floor and slumped against the wooded rail of her bed frame, cradling her cast. Angry tears pricked at her eyelids. For what? Because she was in pain, emotionally overwhelmed, and weak from not eating but not hungry enough to actually put something in her stomach.

And her throat still hurt.

Maybe a glass of water would help. She stumbled to the door and flung it open, nearly tripping over the cowboy spread out on the wooden floor of the hall with his back to the doorframe, which had to be uncomfortable.

"What are you doing out here?" she grumbled, annoyed that her McKay-dar seemed to be busted. How had she not realized he'd made himself at home outside her door?

He rolled and climbed to his feet with a grace that shouldn't seem so effortless on a body with so much bulk. Even bootless, Heath towered over her, his hair adorably rumpled and untamed without his hat. Good gravy. This version of him might be even more delicious than the put-together one.

"Dancing the cha-cha, obviously." His voice sounded like he'd gargled gravel and the lines of exhaustion around his eyes aged him instantly.

Nope, no feeling sorry for him. She clamped down on the wash of emotions, especially the tender ones. Coupled with the precarious vibe between them, she had no choice but to go on the defensive until she knew how to manage the things zinging around in her heart. Preferably without giving him an advantage that would crush her, at least until she understood what he meant by *this isn't practice*.

"I wasn't going to ditch you again," she told him. "At least not tonight."

Heath's gaze flickered. "That wasn't my concern."

It took her a second to figure out what he meant. Because they'd found a body. And a jaguar head. He'd been worried about someone trying to get to her in the middle of the night, and instead of scaring her, he'd elected to forgo his own comfortable bed.

Her heart stopped zinging and started tumbling.

"I didn't ask you to do this. I can take care of myself," she returned hotly.

"Yeah, I can see that," he said without a drop of irony as he eyed her dirt-streaked shirt. "Meanwhile, I'll sleep better knowing that you're inside your room, safe and sound."

Sleep better on the floor? Sure. The warmth of his stupid self-righteous hero complex would definitely lull him into a peaceful slumber. "This is not one of those times I'm going to say thank-you."

"I wasn't confused."

Her eyelids fluttered shut. Could he be any more unflappable at midnight? Or anytime? They were standing in a semi-dark hallway, the house hushed for the night, and all she could think about was this man spider-crawling his way down a well shaft to get to her. There was no reason for him to have done that. He could have told her to hang on while he went to fetch the rope or waited for the others to get it, then lowered himself down.

But he hadn't.

She ached to ask why. She wanted to hear him confess that hearing her voice after spending a very long stretch of time convinced he never would again had opened up a place inside him that he'd had no clue existed. That's what had happened to her. She'd basically given up hope and then her name had floated down from heaven on the lips of Heath McKay and everything had shifted.

And she'd thought her feelings for him had been jumbled *before* she'd fallen into the well. Add the ghost of Margo into the mix and she had no clue how to be in her own skin.

The angry tears resurfaced. One splashed down on her cheek and she swiped it away, but not before Heath noticed. His expression caved and he muttered an expletive, drawing her into his arms without explanation. Since that was exactly where she wanted to be, why would she argue?

"Don't cry, slugger," he murmured into her hair, which quite frankly might be her favorite way for him to speak to her. "Let's reel it all back for a while and just…"

"Stop practicing?" she suggested as he walked her into her bedroom, leaving it open.

"I was going to say sleep."

Apparently, only he could call a time-out. She clamped her mouth shut as Heath gently spun her around and peeled her shirt from her sore body. It wasn't the slightest bit sexual. It was worse. Tender and intimate, as if they'd done this so many times that the ritual had become as familiar as her own skin.

With only two false starts, Heath found the drawer in her dresser with the oversize T-shirts she slept in and expertly drew one over her head, settling it on her shoulders as he threaded her arms through the holes. Who knew a man *dressing* you could be so…actually she had no idea what this feeling was.

Wordlessly, Heath led her to the bed, settling her into the correct side of the mattress without asking because of course he would be observant like that, then nodded once.

"I'll be in the hall if you need anything."

She needed *him*. How pathetic was that, to yearn for a

man she couldn't have? "You can't sleep on the floor. It's ridiculously uncomfortable."

Hands shoved in his back pockets, he shrugged. "I've done worse."

"Not after spending all day searching for me without stopping," she correctly him crossly. "Get in the bed and don't argue with me. It's big enough for two adults who have a tenuous friendship and one of them is in love with someone else besides."

He hesitated long enough that she almost called his name, worried that bringing Margo into the mix had been a mistake. But she'd wanted him to know that she got it. He'd never pick Charli. It was fine.

"I won't maul you in your sleep," she said, the scowl on face hurting the bruised places. "And think how much better you'll be able to take out an intruder if you're well rested."

That seemed to be the deciding factor since he shed his clothes without a word and slid beneath the covers.

Oh, my. When she'd offered, she'd sort of expected him to stay dressed. Every drop of moisture fled her mouth. She lay there, senses on such full alert, so painfully aware of Heath that her teeth hurt.

She'd promised not to maul him in his sleep, but she'd never said a word about what she might do while he was awake. All that Heath-ness was right there in touching distance, and she wanted to reach out more than she wanted to breathe. But she wanted to be shut down far less.

Plus, she wasn't that woman. His heart belonged to someone else. She could not in good conscience go after a man who was committed. Even as a part of her knew deep down that she didn't have a prayer of dislodging Margo in the first place.

"The sound of you not sleeping is so loud, I can hear it

way over here, you know," he murmured, flipping to face her and that was so much worse.

She rolled away, facing the wall. "I'm overtired. It's not a big deal."

"Yeah, same," he admitted, sounding as weary as advertised.

Her fault. She'd led him on an exhausting search and rescue mission that shouldn't have happened. Finding the other head via her pure, dumb luck remained the only good thing that had come out of it.

She owed him. She rolled back. "Turn over."

"What? Why?"

"Just do it, McKay." She didn't even have the strength to snap at him but he did it anyway. Probably too tired to argue.

When she threaded her hand through his hair and started massaging his head, he let out a husky moan that nearly undid her.

If he kept that up, she'd forget all her principles in under point-zero seconds. Because now all she could think about was getting a repeat of that sound, but in wholly different circumstances.

"How did you know that's exactly what I needed?" he murmured.

Her eyelids slammed shut. His rich, decadent voice in the dark did sinful things to her body, things that she hurt too much to enjoy. And she really, really wanted to savor all the sensations Heath caused, even if he didn't mean to do it. Even if all of this wasn't real.

"Oh, you know me. Always practicing," she said lightly, reveling in the feel of his hair against her fingertips since this was the perfect excuse to touch it. "Since there's no time-outs tonight."

He fell silent for a beat. "Is that what we're doing? Practicing?"

"Sure. You're exhausted thanks to me. This is what I would do for you if we were together for real. Take care of you. Isn't that what an adult relationship is all about? Seeing that the person you love needs something and doing it."

"Your arm is in a cast," he pointed out needlessly since it currently lay wedged against her leg, probably adding to her bruise count.

But she wouldn't move for a million dollars. His masculine, clean scent had drifted over her, winnowing down into her blood. "So? My other arm is fine."

"I should be taking care of you," he grumbled and suddenly rolled to face her so unexpectedly that she didn't have time to fully prepare.

Who was the genius who had decided to switch off the lights? She was missing out on a whole experience here of seeing his beautiful cheekbones up close and personal, plus the chance to memorize what he looked like in her bed so she could conjure up the image later.

"My turn," he told her. "Roll over."

Oh, that was an unexpected twist. She couldn't comply fast enough.

But he didn't rub her head or even stroke her hair, which would have felt nice. Instead, he gathered her in his arms and spooned her against his delicious heat.

Instantly, she relaxed despite her previous conviction that having a hot cowboy in her bed would produce the exact opposite reaction. But this was something else. Something she'd craved without knowing it would be the glue that fixed broken places inside.

She'd never been this warm and this content in the whole of her life.

"Just to be clear," she murmured against his well-defined arm muscle that shouldn't be such an excellent pillow. "I do not sleep with men on a first date."

She could feel his lips turn up against her cheek. "This is not a date, Charlotte."

"Why don't I hate it when you call me that?" The claws came out when anyone else full-named her.

He was silent for a beat. "Because you know I only use it when we're being genuine with each other."

How could she be anything but genuine? She'd never succeed at being anything else with him. "I generally only think of myself that way when I'm at my worst. Hurricane Charlotte, at your service."

His thumb brushed against hers. "But that's when you are your truest self."

The certainty of that settled inside of her, not feeling as foreign as she would have expected. Neither was the hard press of his legs against the backs of hers. All of it overwhelmed her, beating against her rib cage to escape. "What are we doing, Heath?"

His thumb stilled. "Practicing?"

With a question mark and an implied *duh*. Because what else would it be? That's what he meant by being genuine— he genuinely didn't feel anything for her. Fine. That was perfect. It allowed her to stuff everything back in the box, where it should be.

"Yep," she agreed brightly. Too brightly for the middle of the night. "I've never slept like this with anyone, so we'll have to see how it goes. I might be terrible at it. It's a good thing—"

"Shh," he said into her hair and his breath floated over her. "You're still not sleeping. That was the point of this. So we can both rest."

And he needed to. He'd more than earned the right to rest, to have a respite from her. She could read between the lines. What she could not do was sleep, not with all the stuff churning through her head and her heart.

She was falling for him.

She could feel it happening, powerless to stop it. This man could break her. Shatter her into a billion unrecoverable shards.

It was exactly what she deserved for putting herself in this position, for pining after another woman's man. For letting him scoop her up into this wholly improper, wholly delicious embrace under the guise of *practicing*.

None of this felt like practicing. Worse, whatever she learned here would go to waste because she couldn't imagine being like this with any other man.

Apparently, Heath could also market himself as a sleeping pill because the next thing she knew, it was morning, and she woke draped over him. He slept flat on his back, and she'd wiggled her way into the crook of his arm, one leg thrown over his.

Shameful.

But when she tried to work herself free without waking him, his arm tightened, clamping her in place. And then Heath opened his eyes, still heavy with sleep, and the bottomless abyss of blue scored her on the inside where a man should never have been able to touch.

Which scared her more than anything else that had happened to her in the last twenty-four hours and that was saying something.

"Hi, good morning," she said with fake cheer. "I need food and ibuprofen stat."

Prying herself loose only worked because he let her and then she fled.

Chapter 18

When Heath came back to the house after taking a shower in the ranch hand's quarters where he normally slept, Charli was right where he'd left her, sitting at the breakfast table sipping coffee like he'd asked her to.

He paused before announcing his presence to just…take a minute. Man, she was so much stronger than any woman he'd ever met. Not only had she survived a fall into a well, she'd found the jaguar head and a human body, and somehow resisted curling up in a ball in the corner after finding herself trapped with a corpse.

She was something else. Someone he'd never have said he'd be attracted to, but here they were. His skin still tingled from the feel of her against his fingertips.

Nothing in his head or his chest lined up quite right when he looked at Charli. She'd destroyed him and then knit him back together with nothing more than her fingers in his hair. Tending to him. Because that's what a woman did for someone she cared about in Charli's world.

Not in his. He'd never even dreamed that someone could pay that kind of attention to him. Or would. Especially after a day that included her being trapped in a well and breaking an arm.

What was he supposed to do with her?

Charli wasn't alone in the kitchen. An older woman who must be her mother sat with her, both of them glancing up when he made a noise to let them know he was here before his silent reckoning got creepy. Yep. They had the same eyes.

Mrs. Lang insisted that Heath call her Patricia, taking his hand and warmly thanking him for saving her daughter. Which was a totally legit thing to be grateful for, but geez. What was it about mothers that made him want to duck his head and get a haircut?

Maybe it was because he and Charli had crossed some kind of line last night. What line, he didn't know, but everything had changed and yet nothing had. It had always felt like they were entangled in ways that were difficult to explain.

Nor was anyone asking him to, least of all Charli. She couldn't leave the bed they'd slept in together last night fast enough. He got it. Everything had turned upside down and it was big and strange. He should probably check in with her.

But the security company that bore his name had multiple things going on today and he owed it to his partners to show up. Despite the fact that all of them needed some downtime after the long darkness of the day before, no one was going to get it.

Before the craziness started, he planned to dump copious amounts of caffeine down his throat. As he pulled a mug out of the cupboard above the coffee maker, Charli joined him, sliding right into his space as if they'd always stood here together in a scene straight out of the domestic bliss playbook. She even smelled perfect, like vanilla and woman.

"Let me," she murmured and took the mug from his hand. "I owe you this, plus about a million other things."

Speechless, he watched as she grabbed the carafe and poured the coffee, then dumped two spoonfuls of sugar into it, stirred, then added the exact right amount of creamer. She'd even done it in the same order as he always did, which he'd honestly never even thought about as a routine, but she'd somehow learned his coffee preferences expertly as if she'd memorized the steps.

"What is all of this?" he asked suspiciously.

"Do I need a reason?" When she glanced over her shoulder, she must have realized the answer to that was *duh*. She rolled her eyes. "I like being able to take care of something for you. You run around being all capable and stuff. Makes it hard for me to reciprocate. Deal with it."

She handed him the mug and he sipped, biting back a moan as the first rich taste hit his system. "How did you know how to make this for me?"

She flashed him a guilty grin. "I can't tell you on the grounds that it might incriminate me."

"You have a spy camera set up in here?" he guessed and glanced around for show despite being 100 percent aware there was no such thing thanks to Pierce's careful sweeps for any foreign equipment.

"Which part of *I can't tell you* wasn't clear?" She hip-checked him and winced, instantly sobering the vibe between them. "I guess I fell on that one."

That hip and a lot of other places that he'd personally cataloged while helping her change into her T-shirt last night. She'd heal but the rage that had built in his chest as he'd noted the marks on her skin roared right back. There wasn't anything he could break that would fix it for her. That was the problem. She hurt and he couldn't do anything about that or his urge to plow a fist through something.

"I'm sorry," he murmured. "Want me to kiss it and make it better?"

She glanced at her mother, still seated at the table on the other side of the kitchen and turned her back to the table deliberately, leaning in to whisper. "Heath McKay, are you flirting with me?"

That teased a smile out of him, because of course Charli would have the power to amuse him even in the midst of his physical response to her pain. "Yes. Strictly for practice, of course."

Her expression instantly flattened as she nodded. "Of course. I knew that. The coffee is practice too."

That was the same voice she'd used last night, after she'd asked what they were doing and he'd answered the question with a question because he had no idea. He loved Margo or at least that's what he'd been trying to tell himself for quite some time. But at this point, he didn't have a lot of confidence he'd be able to pick love out of a lineup.

Margo had never done anything like rub his head or make his coffee. What did that mean? He was driving himself nuts with questions that shouldn't be so hard to answer.

Heath tipped up Charli's chin with his thumb so she could see his sincerity. "The coffee was a nice touch. I'd like to stand here and flirt some more, but I'm afraid today is going to be a nightmare. For both of us."

Which started almost immediately when Madden, Sophia and Pierce rolled into the kitchen, business faces on. Everyone took a spot at the table.

Beneath it, Charli slipped her hand into his, warming him in places he hadn't realized were cold. He suspected she'd needed the connection to settle something inside.

At least he could do that for her. And would, as much as she wanted. It worked out that it settled something inside him too. Who knew secret hand-holding would be so affecting?

"Logistics meeting," Madden announced.

Sophia touched her mother's shoulder. "Mom, this is going to be so boring. You're welcome to stay if you would like but Ace is going to be talking about some of the security changes that have to happen now that we've located another jaguar head."

And a dead body. But Heath kept that to himself. Everyone was enough on edge without the added fear that there might be a killer on the loose. Though it had to be on Madden's mind.

"*Another* head?" Charli stressed. "You mean *the other* head. Right? The only one. Say that's what you meant."

Sophia glanced over at Charli, her expression grim. "I talked to Dr. Low about that. She's pulling in some other experts from the museum in Mexico who might be able to verify if there are more."

Charli groaned and tried to rub her forehead with the arm encased in the cast and nearly hit herself in the eye. "No more heads. We need these people to leave, not bring more experts to the ranch. We might as well move the opening date of the Cowboy Experience to next year at this rate."

"Actually," Madden interjected. "That's not a bad idea."

If Heath hadn't been holding her hand, he might have missed how agitated that statement made Charli. He stroked a thumb down hers, but her spine didn't loosen, and he needed it to.

"Can we table that conversation for the moment?" Heath wasn't asking, though, and plowed ahead. "We need double the number of armed guards pronto."

That did the trick. She relaxed, letting her shoulder graze his arm in a way that set off sparks in places that needed to stop sparking ASAP. This game required his head in it with no distractions, and all he wanted to do was wrap himself and Charli back up in the cocoon of darkness where they could keep pretending the real world didn't exist, that they hadn't made the stupid bet, and he'd never let Margo get her hooks into him in the first place.

"Already on it," Madden confirmed with a nod. "They'll be here by noon."

"No one leaves the house without one of the three of us," Heath continued, wagging a finger between himself, Madden and Pierce. "I'm thinking it wouldn't be out of place for us all to renew our acquaintance with our friends Smith & Wesson."

Sophia glanced at Madden and the look they exchanged carried a lot of unspoken language meant to leave everyone else out of the conversation. Normally Heath would be the one Madden shared his concerns with, but things had subtly shifted with the introduction of his friend's relationship with Sophia. It should bother him more, but given the vibe between him and Charli, and the ways they'd been learning to read each other, he got it all at once.

This was what a relationship looked like. It was mind-blowing how wrong he'd gotten it with Margo. How right it felt with Charli. Did she feel it too?

"Everyone should make that decision for themselves," Madden said quietly.

"Can I have a gun then?" Charli wanted to know.

"No," Sophia and Heath answered at the same time. Charli looked so crestfallen he rushed to amend that with, "At least not until I teach you how to use one."

That got him a smile and a head bop on the arm, which seemed to raise her spirits. Until there was a knock at the front door and Sophia left to answer it, then returned in seconds with the sheriff in tow. His badge gleamed against his sedate brown uniform, both ominous this early in the morning.

"I'm glad you're all here," the sheriff announced gravely, his hat in his hand. "Thought I would come by personally to tell you some difficult news. We've positively identified the deceased as David Lang."

Forget a pin—you could have heard a feather drop in the room.

Heath immediately removed his hat in kind, wishing he hadn't seen that bombshell coming a mile away. Charli sucked in a breath, her grip on his hand tightening, but otherwise, she accepted the news stoically.

Sophia, not so much. She started crying and Madden folded her into his embrace, murmuring to her while he stroked her back. Which Heath totally would have done for Charli if she'd seemed like she needed it, but in her typical fashion, she met this challenge head-on.

"Are you sure?" she demanded of the sheriff. "No question?"

The sheriff nodded. "We used two corroboration methods to verify."

Because of the level of decomposition, no doubt. The sheriff was being discreet by leaving out the details, but most likely the police had access to Lang's dental records and possibly existing DNA samples since he'd grown up here at the ranch, likely utilizing still-existing medical services in town.

Mrs. Lang, who had returned to the room with the arrival of the sheriff, stepped forward, her face frozen. "Do you know how long he's been dead?"

The sheriff met her halfway and extended his hand to shake hers. "You must be Mrs. Lang. I am very sorry for your loss and to be meeting you under these circumstances. I'm afraid I can't give you specifics yet. We've ordered an autopsy, which will help us determine cause of death as well as the date. Rest assured we'll open an investigation immediately if foul play was involved."

Mrs. Lang murmured her thanks and put a comforting hand on each of her daughters' shoulders. Heath's skin got tight and started feeling like it was on backward, so he bowed out, catching Madden's eye and jerking his head toward the door.

Figuring it was better to let the Lang women grieve without an audience, he hightailed it to Charli's bedroom to wait it out. Man, that was a rough scene. He didn't do grief well in the first place. It was one of the few things that couldn't be pounded out of his system, and it hurt to watch other people hurting.

Especially Charli. And wasn't that a kicker to find out that he could bleed just as easily when someone else took the hit.

Some forty-five minutes later, Charli wandered through the door, not seeming overly shocked to find him lounging on her bed, boots kicked off and hat on the floor next to them. Which he'd done strictly to show her that he was here and present for as long as she wanted him there.

"Heath," she croaked, looking as if she might faint at any second. Before he could spring out of the bed to catch her, she held up a finger. "Time-out. No questions."

He nodded. As if he'd have denied her anything.

Without a word, she crawled onto the bed and right on top of him, collapsing against his chest. Automatically, his arms came around her, cradling her close. She was shaking.

"Hey," he murmured, inhaling her scent, which inexplicably calmed him. "I've got you. Breathe with me."

She did, falling into the rhythm that he set. He stroked her hair, pausing occasionally to circle her temples soothingly. After an eternity of his heart feeling like she'd seared it with a hot knife, the trembling eased off, finally stopping entirely.

"Good girl," he whispered and lifted her face with his thumbs. Then wished he hadn't.

Charli's expression was ravaged. Coupled with everything else, it put his body on simmer, the edges of his vision going black. Not a good thing, especially when there wasn't a target for him to punch. But this was where he would temper his tendencies, pull it all back. For her. Because she needed him to.

"What can I do?" he almost bit out and course-corrected quickly, leveling his voice on the last syllables.

"You're already doing it."

Her accompanying sigh reverberated through his chest, the sentiment likewise spreading through him like warm honey, soothing him in the same vein as he'd tried to do for her. Who knew that they'd be so good like this? That they could pull each other off the roller coaster at a time when they both so desperately needed it?

She sat back on the bedspread, her legs under her, taking all her heat and light and vanilla-y scent with her. But she threaded her fingers through his and it was enough. They clung to each other as they each processed their own very different emotions.

"It doesn't feel like enough," he muttered. "I hate seeing you so upset."

Charli shook her head. "The terrible part is that I'm not upset that he's dead. It's fine, he's basically been the equivalent of dead for a long time anyway. But now it's like…

final. We can't ever have a conversation where I tell him what a lousy piece of filth he is for leaving us."

"And what if you find out he's been dead for years?" he added because he got it. It was a lot to take in.

"Exactly. It changes things. It changes how I think about myself." She eyed him. "Why are you here? You left the kitchen and I thought I'd find out you'd galloped off on a horse or something."

He scowled. What kind of man did she take him for? "And leave you to deal with all of this by yourself?"

To be fair, he had actually left her in the kitchen, but he had good reasons for that. She'd needed to be with her family, not a bunch of onlookers.

She stared at him, and he had the distinct impression she wasn't at all sure what to make of what she saw. That made two of them. "I don't get any of this, Heath. Why the bet? Why frame all of this as practice? Because it doesn't feel like you need much."

Oh, he definitely did. Whatever had just happened between them, whatever you called it, he could do that a hundred more times and still not feel like he'd mastered it—but more to the point, no other woman had ever made him want to try. Or afforded him the opportunity to.

This bet with Charli was 100 percent practice, but not for the reasons he'd originally laid out. Not anymore.

He forced a chuckle. "If it makes you feel any better, this is not the kind of thing I've ever done before."

Disbelief climbed its way up Charli's expression. "What? Show up for me? That's what you do, Heath. It's like you can read my mind and know exactly what I need from you."

"Took me way too long to find you yesterday," he muttered as everything inside revolted against what she was telling him. That he was good at this relationship business when in reality, he was stumbling around blindfolded, depending on his senses to guide him. "I meant I've never done *this* before. Whatever *this* is."

He waved his hand in a circle to encompass the two of them, punctuating the point.

"It's practice. Isn't it?" She stared at him, her eyes huge and damp and full of something he couldn't look away from. "That's what we agreed to. The bet is almost an afterthought now. Because somewhere along the way, I realized how much I want to get it right."

He let himself fall into the possibilities that she meant she felt the way he did, that it had stopped feeling like rehearsal a long time ago. That this might be the realest real deal there was.

"I want to get it right too," he murmured.

"Of course you do," she said and squeezed her eyes shut. "For Margo. It's a lot easier for you because you have her in mind when we're practicing. I'm turning myself inside out for some nameless, faceless dude I haven't met yet. He's going to be different. What if getting it right with you is wrong with him?"

White-hot rage stole his vision as he processed the idea that for one, he and Charli were not in fact on the same page with what was happening between them and two, at some point she'd move on. Into someone else's arms. Who was not Heath.

He wanted to destroy that nameless, faceless dude.

Just as the black edges bled into the field of white, she squeezed his hand. It centered him. Brought him back from the edge in a blink.

"Thank you for introducing the concept of a time-out," she told him. "Our friendship means a lot to me. In a lot of ways, that's practice for a relationship too. Because this matters to me in a way a romantic relationship wouldn't. I can tell you things I would never say to someone I was dating for real."

So...that's what all of this was to her? Them becoming *friends*?

The tiny sound he heard inside could quite possibly be his heart breaking a little. But honestly, it was the best scenario. He did love Margo. Probably. And did want to impress her with his new personality, the one that could come back from the brink of hulk-smashing drywall with nothing more than a squeeze of someone's hand.

"That's what I'm here for," he said weakly but meant it.

This was how it should be. If he got back together with Margo, she'd become better too, simply by virtue of seeing what lengths Heath had gone to in order to win her back. That's how it worked with Charli. They both tried, they both gave, they both course-corrected when needed.

Like he needed to do now. Charli expected him to act like a friend—that's what he'd be.

Feeling as if he still wasn't quite on the track he'd expected to be, he ran his thumb over Charli's, gratified she'd never released his hand. "We're both learning how to have an adult relationship without the risk of screwing it up."

Her expression grew thoughtful. "I'm realizing I've never had one. An adult relationship. You see what my model for relationships is. My dad ending up at the bottom of a well, leaving all of us to believe he abandoned us. My ability to take things at face value is broken. It scares me. Maybe I'll do all this practicing and screw it up when it comes to the real thing. Maybe I'm broken."

The utter bravery it took for her to admit that she was scared crushed him.

"I want you to hear that you're getting it right," he said

fiercely. "Safe space, Charli. I wouldn't lie to you. You're not broken."

If there was ever a moment in their history when he wished he could call a time-out, it was this one. No one else existed in the world except her. A time-out would allow him to do exactly as he wished, and if he had that latitude, it would be to kiss her. To explore the way she made him feel, as if they were embarking on something new and wonderful together.

That wasn't what they were doing here, though. The romance part of their relationship didn't exist. But naming it and claiming it did nothing to lessen the tide of Charli in his blood.

Neither did the look on her face, as if she'd found something precious and could hardly believe her luck. He wanted it to mean something other than what it did.

"You heard me, didn't you?" he said, his voice huskier than it should be given the circumstances. "All this practice is not for nothing. You're this close to winning the bet."

He held up his finger and thumb with zero space between them and a smile curving his lips that he almost didn't have to fake.

Tipping her face up, she caught his gaze. "Does this mean you're finally going to take me on a date?"

Chapter 19

Straightening things out with Charli should have worked to clear Heath's head. He shouldn't be so distracted. But the fact of the matter was that he couldn't concentrate on the security issues that should be his sole focus. Instead, the entire breadth of his mental capacity was going toward planning a perfect first date.

She deserved that. After learning to make his coffee and giving him a fair shot and a dozen other things that signified her commitment to their practice relationship, he needed to step up his game.

"Would it be totally cliché to just make reservations at a nice restaurant in Dallas?" he asked Pierce as they walked across the yard to debrief the new security guards their third-party company had sent.

Pierce rolled his eyes. "Yes, McKay. It would. Try again."

"A picnic?"

"Let's keep thinking," Pierce suggested, as if he could claim the title of Most Romantic Man Alive without breaking a sweat and Heath was merely a bothersome novice.

"If you're so smart, what would you do?" he shot back.

"I don't know Charli very well, so I can't tell you. That's for you to figure out. It's supposed to show her that she's worth the effort to take five minutes and plan something that is meaningful to *her*," he stressed. "What does she like?"

"To antagonize me," he muttered with a double take at Pierce's eyebrow lift. "What? It's her favorite hobby."

To be fair, he poked at her in kind pretty frequently. Maybe he even started it on occasion. But when she faced him down with that snap in her gaze—she was the most beautiful woman in the world.

The times they reeled it back...those were the best and came far too infrequently. Was it at all in the realm of possibility to call a time-out for an entire date?

Except that pretty much negated the experiment. Plus, he liked sparring with her as much as she seemed to. That's why this was such a strange, wonderful relationship—and yes, they had one. A friendship. Officially. It was new, and difficult to quantify, but real to him.

And so different in a good way than any relationship he'd ever had before. They were *friends*. It wasn't as terrible as it sounded. Plus, it was what he had to work with.

Pierce was right, but Heath had no plans to admit it out loud. Charli warranted whatever it took for him to find the perfect first date and he'd think on it until the idea unfolded naturally. It wasn't like he could spring for the time off tonight, not with all the additional security logistics.

The gun tucked into the holster at his hip was a part of that, a necessary one. That was the beauty of a place like Texas with open carry laws, and Heath had wasted no time getting the additional license to complement his concealed carry license the moment he'd arrived.

He just hadn't expected to use it in quite such an obvious way. Anyone in a half-mile radius—or further, pending their surveillance equipment—hopefully had zero question about his willingness to use his weapon to keep the peace.

Or destroy it if someone came after Charli. With or without his firearm.

He and Pierce got the new guys organized, showed them the extra beds in the bunkhouse where they would sleep during their off hours. They were running armed guards around the clock, three on the trailer where the jaguar heads lived in the safe bolted to the floor and two making rounds between the house and the woods, with unscheduled loops around both.

The hope was that this would be temporary, just until the university people rolled out with their treasure and took the chaos with them.

"If we're set here, I'm going to spend a few hours on my drone code," Pierce announced once they were able to leave the guards to their jobs. "The quality of the thermals is not where I'd like it to be given the circumstances. I got some new sensors that should solve the issue with the denser brush near the creek too."

Since all of that sounded like as much fun as learning Swahili, Heath waved him off to go do his geek things in solitude. That's why God made people like Paxton Pierce, so the Heaths of the world didn't have to think about the finer points of sensors and whatever nonsense went along with increasing the quality of thermal imaging.

All this tension and attention to the hardware of the surveillance *and* personal protection variety was making him antsy. They'd found the other head. Well, Charli had, by accident, but it still counted. This whole cuckoo environment should be easing up but he felt more on edge today than he ever had before.

But with Charli in the house and everything Madden had asked Heath to do completed, maybe he could spend some time googling date ideas. Nail something down. He wanted to show Charli that he was invested, that he could get this right too. In the name of practice, of course.

Internet reception was better closer to the house, so he headed in that direction, his phone already in his hand as he went with the "on the nose" option and googled "perfect first dates."

That's why he didn't notice the woman standing near the back door until she called out, "Hello, Heath," in that cultured voice that he used to hear in his dreams.

Margo's voice.

It was all wrong in this setting. Margo's voice didn't go with East Texas or the dirt in the yard. Neither did it sit right in his chest.

He glanced up, straight into Margo's stunning hazel eyes that could turn the color of molten silver or iced tea or a moss-covered log pending what she was wearing. Today, the armor of choice was a sleek black jumpsuit with wide legs and a crystal-encrusted belt around her minuscule waist. Barbie pink stilettos, of course, and a pink jacket thrown over her shoulder completed the look that he had no doubt she'd spent a fortune in time and money to pull together.

Her face had a flawless complexion thanks to the trifecta of genetics, expensive skincare routines and a deal with the devil, probably.

Good God, she was still an uncommonly beautiful woman, and he felt absolutely nothing when he looked at her. What was *happening*?

"What are you doing here?" he demanded, so floored that he couldn't have found his manners with a military-grade GPS receiver.

She laughed, the trilling, slightly amused one that used to make him smile, but now only confused his already beleaguered senses.

"No hug for someone who used to pick up your favorite Chinese food?" she asked sweetly, holding up her hands.

Heath's muscles jumped to do exactly as bid in some kind of Pavlovian response before he could check them. Shocking how easily she could *still* evoke a response in him. But then, she'd been doing that for a long time, and he'd always had zero resistance when it came to her.

She folded herself into his embrace, bringing with her a cloud of spicy perfume she regularly restocked from a store in Morocco, which he knew because he'd given her the first bottle for Christmas an eon ago.

Nothing had changed with Margo, apparently, even after she'd given him the boot.

It threw him off-kilter and he'd never quite been on-kilter with her in the first place.

He pulled away and crossed his arms, focusing his attention front and center on facts, not his own stupid hang-ups when it came to this woman. "I can't say a hug is how I thought you'd want to be greeted the first time we saw each other after…what happened."

It's not me, it's you.

That's what she'd said when she dumped him. It still stung, honestly. Not only the smug, sarcastic phrasing, but the whole concept.

What *was* wrong with him, exactly? That he liked being physical? That it made him feel good to protect people and make sure other people knew they couldn't threaten or bully their way through life?

That was Charli's voice in his head. He shouldn't be thinking about her or how much better he liked her narrative.

"Oh, Heath, let's leave the past in the past, shall we?" she murmured, her stilettos inching closer to him as she swept him with an appreciative once-over. "I'm a fan of how you're flourishing in this environment."

His eyebrows shot up so high that they nearly hit the brim of his Stetson. "You hate it when I don't shave, and I've never once heard you say a positive thing about boots."

It was so weird, but he'd sworn he would react differently the next time he came in contact with Margo. He'd planned it all out in his head, how he'd sweep her off her feet with his new, improved, much calmer persona. But here and now, with the real reunion happening, his temper had already started swirling twice in thirty seconds.

Was it possible that Margo *herself* had been the one to constantly provoke him into being such a hothead?

Margo folded her jacket over her arm, contemplating him. "Maybe I've come to appreciate things about you now that I've had time and distance to contemplate our relationship."

That was closer to the conversation he'd hoped to have, but very far from the one he'd expected. "So that's why you're here? You want to apologize to me and start over?"

"As happy as I am to see you again," she said, "I'm actually here on official business."

When Margo's smile gained a strange edge, every nerve in his body blipped into high alert. "JSOC is getting into the Maya treasure business?"

Margo lifted one shoulder delicately. "When the treasure in question is tied to the funding of a sleeper cell out of Iraq, I'm afraid the answer is yes."

His arms were crossed so tightly that his muscles started to ache. "And you naturally requested this assignment when you saw my name come across your desk."

The incredulity dripped from his voice but really, he shouldn't be so shocked. Word had gotten out all right. And brought with it a slew of new challenges that he couldn't have anticipated even with the aid of a crystal ball.

"Life has so few coincidences." She smiled and he didn't miss the glint in her gaze.

This wasn't just a job. Or just a drive-by reunion. It was both. And felt exceptionally mercenary all at once.

His knees actually went weak as he absorbed this blind-side. How like the universe to throw this enormous monkey wrench in his path the second he'd set up a practice run with Charli—which he wasn't done with, not by a long shot. He was supposed to be figuring out how to be in a relationship by spending time with her, not by shepherding Spec Ops representatives around who came with history that suddenly weighed more than an albatross.

The complications, they were legion.

If Margo wanted him back, great. He should *want* to spend time with her. He owed it to himself—and Charli—to try out his new husband material persona on his ex-girlfriend. It was what he'd been practicing for. Why was he being so weird about it?

Heath pinched the bridge of his nose. "How is this going to work, then?"

She smiled and it was the one she used when she wanted something. "I was hoping you'd be my ace in the hole. For old times' sake."

She *would* liken this to a poker match. Heath shook his head. "The jaguar heads are in a biometrically accessed safe and I'm not one of the people with the keys to the kingdom. You'll have to go through the bigwigs at Harvard for that, if they even decide to let you near them. And they don't have to listen to me on that, by the way."

Nor would he advise them to. He wouldn't get near that conversation with a ten-foot pole.

"Well, this is a dilemma," she said smoothly. "What can we do to facilitate my investigation? I don't want to pull in local law enforcement. I thought that by coming to you first, we could avoid all of that."

Yeah, dilemma was the word all right. As not-so-veiled threats went, this one landed a pretty hard punch. If he kept digging in his heels, she'd circumvent him and his partners, then blast onto the property with the blessing of Gun Barrel City's finest. He'd be completely cut out of the picture. That did not sit well, especially not when he still didn't understand what was happening here.

For the first time, he had the luxury of seeing Margo without blinders on. It was quite possible that she'd always used her connection to him in ways he'd never examined fully.

He'd have to play along. At least until he got a clearer picture what in the blazes this was all about. Because he didn't for a second believe JSOC cared about jaguar heads, nor that someone had magically unearthed a connection to terrorists half a world away.

He couldn't discount a sense of edginess since Charli had discovered the body of her father and there were too many other unknown elements in the mix. They didn't have a blessed clue about what kind of buddies David Lang might have picked up along the way. They didn't know how he'd died. The trailer break-in hadn't been resolved, not fully. And there were still too dang many people on this ranch coming and going as they pleased.

Margo was the last straw. How was he supposed to separate his win-back campaign from *his* job, especially when she insisted on combining the two? Funny how that had never been an issue with Charli.

"Fine, I'll be your liaison," he told her, painting a smile on his face that he hoped came across as genuine.

Margo practically purred as she sidled up next to him, heels boosting her into his space in a way that used to feel comfortable. Welcome, even. It was neither all at once.

"We should spend some time debriefing," she suggested silkily. "Maybe over a brandy."

His gag reflex nearly created a soundtrack of his opinion about that plan. Who actually drank brandy on purpose? She never had before. Oddly, that anomaly tripped his radar the hardest. "Sure. Give me an hour to take care of some things. I *am* working."

"Oh, right. Your new job." She said it as if naming a previously unknown virus and hooked her arm through his. "I'm sure I don't have to remind you that the brass at Fort Bragg don't like to be kept waiting. The sooner we can get this pesky terrorist funding issue dismissed, the better."

Was that her goal? To eliminate suspicion cast on this treasure? Somehow, he didn't believe that was her actual assignment. But the only mechanism to figure out what she wasn't telling him lay in playing her game for as long as it took to unwind all the layers of deception going on around here. Neither did he think she was the only one with an agenda.

"Thirty minutes," he amended, silently cursing the satisfied smile she flashed him.

"Great. We can catch up at the same time," she suggested with a heated once-over that had all the subtlety of a warhead.

"Great," he echoed.

Suddenly, he had a very bad feeling he'd been practicing all wrong.

Chapter 20

Charli felt really good about establishing the friendship boundary around her practice relationship with Heath. Sure, it smacked of self-preservation, but he didn't have to know that she'd thrown up as many walls as she could to keep herself on the straight and narrow.

It was far too easy for her to forget that when he took her hand, he was thinking about Margo, not Charli. Then she remembered and it burned through her as if she'd swallowed a quart of battery acid.

He deserved to be happy, to get what he'd been working so hard for without the additional burden of Charli's ridiculous and misplaced feelings.

She hadn't quite figured out what she deserved. To be alone for a while probably. Spend some time working on the Cowboy Experience and then see whether the Heath-shaped place in her heart had shrunk at all.

Ace had taken Sophia and Patricia into Gun Barrel City to talk to the sheriff. They needed to find out how long the autopsy and investigation would take, then drop by a couple of possible venues for a memorial service.

Charli had begged off with the excuse of sticking around the ranch so she could work on the guest menu for meals they'd serve once they were able to open. Sophia intended to hire a full-time chef who would probably have some ideas as well, but given their lack of income thus far, the pay range wouldn't attract top-tier talent at first, so Charli had volunteered to do some research.

That lasted all of fifteen minutes, the longest she'd ever sat in Sophia's desk chair, and it felt like fourteen minutes too long. How did her sister sit in this thing for hours on end?

Fresh air needed, stat. Charli pushed back from the desk and wandered outside. Maybe she could quiz some of the hands about their favorite dishes and call the menu Rustic Ranch Fare.

The moment she stepped outside, the entire ranch panorama fell off the face of the map. All Charli could see was a svelte blonde viper wrapped around Heath, a solid dose of possessiveness dripping from her fingers. There was practically a pop-up bubble above her head with *mine* in capital letters and flashing lights.

Heath's chin swiveled and he locked gazes with Charli. His expression flattened as if he'd snapped a cable supplying all his emotional energy. She barely recognized him, as if she'd stumbled over a doppelganger who definitely looked like Heath McKay but had actually been born in Argentina and didn't even speak English.

"Ms. Lang," he called, his voice a match for his expression.

Since she was the only Ms. Lang around thanks to her ill-timed bailout from the memorial service, she crossed her arms so neither he nor the viper could see how her hands shook to hear Heath address her so formally.

"What's up, McKay?" she said.

Heath walked toward her. Viper on the other hand, no. The woman strode across the yard as if she owned it and everything around her, including the town and possibly the whole state. If this woman had ever suffered from lack of confidence, Charli would eat Heath's hat.

"We were just coming to the door," Heath said flatly. "So I could introduce you."

"You must be Charlotte Lang," Viper said and even her voice had been specially crafted to be mesmerizing.

There was no reason to hate her. But Charli did. Instantly.

"It's Charli," she corrected. "No one calls me Charlotte."

Except Heath. But if he recalled their conversation about what it meant when he Charlotte-ed her, his expression sure didn't show it. His current one resembled granite.

Charli stuck out her hand, figuring it was her job to be civil to someone who was a guest on the property. Surely the practice would come in handy for when real guests came, because odds were high she wouldn't like everyone who paid to enjoy the Cowboy Experience.

"This is Margo," Heath added almost as an afterthought.

Charli's hand turned to lead and dropped to her side.

The name rocketed through Charli's soul like a throwing star ricocheting inside her, its cutting points drawing blood with each tender surface it hit. The viper was *Margo*. She had every right to wrap herself around Heath, and he had every right to enjoy it as much as he could.

"Oh," she croaked. "That's, um, nice. It's nice to meet you, I mean. Margo. Hello."

Margo ignored the fact that Charli stood there like a wax statue and extended her hand with enough grace to convince anyone that if her mother was a viper, her father had been a gazelle. "Margo Malloy. Intelligence analyst with JSOC. I'm happy to meet you. I'm here to investigate the recent discoveries on the ranch."

Woodenly, Charli clasped the viper—Margo's—hand and released it immediately.

"Investigate?" Apparently, Charli's ability to use her brain had been sucked out of her by the force of Margo's presence. "I don't understand. You're here to investigate something?"

Like, whether Heath still belonged to her? That was a quick one, requiring no intelligence whatsoever. There hadn't been a whole lot of pushing her away on Heath's part, after all, and the woman had practically been climbing him like a tree.

"Yes, the recent discoveries," Margo repeated without a drop of frustration, as if she had no clue she was speaking to an idiot who hadn't gotten her wits about her yet. "The Maya jaguar heads. JSOC has an interest in delving further into this situation."

Oh. *Those* recent discoveries. Charli blinked. Margo was here because of the stupid gold heads? If she didn't have an audience, Charli would scream. Actually, she might anyway. It wasn't like she could pale in comparison to Margo any further.

"Investigate away, then," she muttered. "Don't let me stop you."

Margo glanced between Charli and Heath, who'd turned into a mute bump on a log. Probably because he wished he could be done with his bodyguard duties so he could have a proper reunion with Vip—Margo.

"I'm told you're the best person to assist?" Margo said with a lilt on the end as if not sure her intel was correct.

Assist? Was that military speak for getting Margo coffee? "I own the ranch. Is that the skill set you're looking for?"

The joke fell flat. But it wasn't much of a joke.

Not only did Margo not laugh, she cocked her head, studying Charli curiously. "I just need someone in charge. If that's you, great. I hope we can work together so I can get out of your hair as soon possible. My goal is to make this investigation fast and painless, especially for you since I've descended on you with no warning. The more you co-operate, the quicker I can leave."

Well, that sounded fantastic. Anything that would get the viper off the ranch and hopefully take Heath with her worked for Charli and then some.

The idea didn't relax her an iota. "Happy to help. What are you investigating exactly?"

Margo brightened, a feat since she'd walked into this conversation with a great deal of animation, as if she didn't have an off switch. "I'm so glad you asked. Most of the details are classified but the basics I can share. We intercepted some intelligence that suggests the jaguar heads you found might be linked to an organization we have eyes on. We think the treasure was intended to help fund their activities."

An organization? Like the government of a foreign country or the Boy Scouts? Charli had a feeling if she asked, Margo would say that information was classified, which was a handy way of never having to admit to anything. "What will you do if you can prove it?"

Margo smiled. "Shut them down. They can't operate without money."

But the treasure wasn't in their possession. It was in the hands of the Harvard people and heavily guarded besides. If Charli hadn't come into this conversation already intimidated, she might have a better handle on how to ask the right questions, but as it stood, she didn't want to stand here jabbering with Special Ops Barbie any longer than she had to, so she bit back her questions.

Probably she just didn't understand how any of this worked.

Heath picked that moment to join the conversation. "Margo will be here for a couple of days. She'll be combing through the sites where the two heads were found. I'll run point on security, to ensure she can come and go at will."

That made even less sense. After all this time, what possible clues did Margo expect to find?

"Great," Charli forced a smile. "Let me know what I can do to help."

"You can speak to the head of the dig," Margo suggested immediately as if she'd been waiting for that exact offer. "I'll need full access to the treasure so I can catalog it as evidence. Also, if this isn't too delicate of a request, I would really appreciate some assistance navigating your father's finances. We'd like to look for transactions that may tie him to the organization under investigation."

Follow the money. That part Charli got. But that didn't make it any easier to comply. "Sorry, I have no idea who could help with that. My father didn't live here or, like, communicate with us too much."

Or at all. Though it wouldn't shock Charli to find out her father had gotten killed by some nefarious "organization" out of the Middle East that he'd tried to sell his treasure to.

Margo nodded. "Okay, that's completely fine. We'll work with what we have."

That was not the first time she'd made reference to a *we*. "Do you have a team arriving?"

"Just me." The woman's smile hadn't slipped once, which was starting to grate on Charli. "Though I do plan to borrow Heath as frequently as I can."

"Heath?" His name on Margo's lips dumped a bucket of ice water on Charli's head. And she'd been off-balance in the first place.

Every scrap of Charli's spare energy funneled into pretending she hadn't just realized Margo's presence meant the end of practicing with Heath. Which didn't leave a lot left over to keep her on her feet. She might even be weaving.

This morning, Heath would have caught her. Not now. She was on her own.

Margo leaned in, tilting her head as if imparting a secret. "I'm sure I don't have to tell you how handy he is in the field. We used to work together. He was the kind of operative you could count on to get the job done."

The thread running through the other woman's voice carried more than a hint of longing. And familiarity. Neither did Charli think the phrasing was accidental—she'd totally meant it as a double entendre.

It put Charli's back up. "Yeah, he told me. Along with the rest of your history."

That got a rise out of the ice princess, who had thus far maintained a completely even keel. Challenge flittered through her hazel eyes as she evaluated Charli. "Then you know we were more than colleagues."

"That's not relevant, Margo," Heath interjected, his voice still oddly flat.

"I'm fairly certain that it is." Her gaze narrowed a flick. "I hope we can all be professional about working together, Ms. Lang. I've been looking forward to renewing my acquaintance with Heath."

Yeah, and Charli looked forward to acquainting Margo with a pile of horse dung, but she painted a smile on her face anyway, one that carried its own challenge. Whatever

Margo thought she'd picked up on, it didn't exist. But Charli knew what a threatened woman looked like, and this was it.

Margo thought Charli represented some type of *competition*, here. Which was hilarious. But inexplicably put Charli in a much better mood.

She showed her teeth. "I can take you out to the site where I found the second head. Hope you brought horse-back riding clothes."

"Horseback?" Margo blinked. "Can we use the ATV I saw around the corner?"

"That belongs to the university people." Charli crossed her arms, leaving out the part where they let anyone use it who asked. She shot Heath a glance, but he didn't correct her.

"Oh, all right," Margo conceded with a faint voice. "Let me see what I have with me."

And like that, Charli was dismissed. "We'll be here when you're ready," she called after the rapidly disappearing Margo.

Charli double-timed it to the house so she could beat the viper back to the yard. And not be near Heath.

"Charli, stop walking away," Heath called and followed her up the stairs.

She liked it better when he called her Charlotte. At least then she knew nothing had changed. "I'm not walking. I'm stomping. There's a very clear difference."

She hit the last stair extra hard to prove her point.

The svelte viper was *Margo*. Of course she was. A living, breathing Barbie doll, with the perfect accessories and a sexy job, plus the preemptive claim on Heath's heart. No mystery any longer why Heath had framed the bet as practice. The real thing was leagues better than his practice field.

"Then stop stomping," he ground out as she strode into her room. "And talk to me."

"I have to change clothes to take your girlfriend out to the well."

She slammed the door in Heath's face, which helped her mood a little. It slid right back into a black place when he slung the door open, crashing it into the back wall, then stormed into her room as if he had every right to be there.

"Acting childish is not going to work," he said.

"Back at you. Go away."

This was her sanctuary and he'd invaded it. Of course, he'd done a thorough job of that the night they'd slept together. She could still smell him on her sheets, which she should have washed and hadn't, like a big Loser McLoserpants who could only score the faint scent of a man. The real Heath belonged to the viper.

She made a big show of vanishing into her closet in search of riding jeans and her boots, so she didn't have to look at his stupid face, which was not disappearing into the hall as she'd instructed him.

"Stop pushing me away," he told her, and the door opened wider.

He crowded into the space that a real estate agent would have called a walk-in closet with plenty of room for clothes and two people, but really, really wasn't big enough for all of the stuff in her chest plus Heath.

"I'm not," she countered sweetly, clamping down the keening sound desperate to get out as every cell in her body sucked in Heath's essence, so close, but so far away. "Why would I do that? We're done practicing. The bet is over. Now we can move on. What's not to like?"

Heath stood there, his eyes the color of thunderclouds, hat in hand as he ran stiff fingers through his hair. "What is going on with you? I want to talk to you and you're being…"

"Hurricane Charlotte?" she supplied and shoved at his chest.

Big mistake. Huge. She'd only meant to get him out of her closet so she could switch her pants for jeans, but the wall of Heath didn't budge an inch. Her fingertips had amnesia and forgot that they weren't supposed to be enjoying the rock-hard feel of him.

"Yeah," he growled, smacking a hand over hers and lacing their fingers together. "I thought we were friends."

The tic at the corner of her eye picked that moment to flare up as she stared at him, all her ire leaking out of her pores, leaving her feeling deflated and like a crappy, jealous witch who couldn't get out of her own head long enough to see that Heath needed her to get this right.

"We are," she said with completely fake cheer. "So that's Margo."

"Yeah. That's her." His voice had lost none of its edge. "I didn't invite her here if that's what you're thinking."

No, that hadn't been what she'd thought at all. "Why didn't you? It's totally fine if you did. It's Margo. The pot of gold at the end of the rainbow. The prize in your Cracker Jack box. A—"

"I get it," Heath snarled. "What I don't get is why everything went sideways between us."

"Really? You don't?" Charli squeezed her eyes shut. "You were the one being weird. You could barely look at me out there. I felt like—"

My soul had been crushed.

She couldn't say that out loud. He hadn't done anything

wrong. Just like he'd told her a long time ago, Heath had been nothing but honest with her.

Charli was the one who had fallen headfirst into their practice relationship and done the one thing she shouldn't have.

"Charli." She could hear him scrubbing at his beard in frustration. "Look at me. Please."

Ha, he'd like that, wouldn't he? Because then she'd start crying and she never cried. Except for the six or eight times he'd been so supportive and strong and beautiful that he wrenched that vulnerability right out of her, and she was not in the mood for a repeat, not under these circumstances.

She had to reel it back. Be the friend he expected.

She opened her eyes. The storm had passed in Heath's gaze, leaving behind a few choppy waves and darkness in the distance, but mostly calm. And a thread running through it all that she couldn't help but cling to.

This was the Heath she'd fallen in love with.

"This is so not what I planned," Heath murmured. "I was looking for perfect first date ideas when she showed up."

Well, this situation was not much better than when they were sniping at each other. "Good thing she did. It was time. You don't need any more practice."

Charli didn't either. She was done. There was no way she could step back into her role as his proving ground, knowing that's all she'd ever be. Knowing she was the other woman and Margo would be the one hurt by it. If she knew.

Charli wondered all at once if Heath would tell Margo that he'd practiced his skills with another woman. That it was Charli he'd spider-crawled down a well to rescue and cuddled later that night when she couldn't sleep. That he'd held Charli's hand while she navigated skinned animals and her father's death.

"Charli." He sucked in a breath and exhaled it on a broken note. "This is not—I'm having a hard time figuring out what to say."

She threw up a hand, stopping the flow of words that she already knew had the power to eviscerate her. "There's nothing to say. Margo is a lovely woman. Clearly gracious, and well, she's obviously not ever going to need rescuing. She probably spends her Saturdays volunteering at the animal shelter and befriending every person she's ever met."

"Yeah, no," Heath drawled with his eyes rolling heavenward. "If that's the impression you got from her, you need your eyes checked. She spends Saturdays eating navy SEALs for breakfast when they don't perform operations to her exacting standards."

"Then on Sunday, she'll spend it with you, marveling over how much you've changed." Forcing the words out of her mouth was getting a little easier the longer she did it. Practicing paid off. Who would have thought?

"That makes one of us who is sure."

Oh, man. He was adorably scared that his practicing *hadn't* paid off. That Margo wouldn't recognize the lengths he'd gone to in order to win her back. Her heart cracked.

"You've been working hard on yourself, Heath," she told him earnestly and squeezed his hands. "Safe space. I wouldn't lie to you. She'd going to be so wowed by you. You deserve to be happy. With Margo. Nothing else matters but that."

His expression flattened and he nodded. "You're right, of course. Nothing else matters."

Except the fact that Charli might possibly be in love with him herself. If Margo hadn't shown up, there'd been a lovely scenario running through her head where she told him and he smiled, his own heart in his eyes as he kissed her senseless and told her he'd been working up to a similar confession.

Obviously that wasn't happening.

"This is your chance," she said and bopped him on the arm. "You're one hundred percent grade A husband material now. Through and through. Margo showing up here now is the universe's way of rewarding you. The timing is too good to be a coincidence. Go get her and show her how much she means to you. She'll honor all the effort you went to."

I would.

Her chest caved in, and she struggled to breathe. Impossible when these tight bands had constricted so hard that it hurt to try to get a deep enough breath.

Heath's eyelids dropped as his mouth firmed into a line and he nodded once. "Yeah, okay. We've already jumped out of the helicopter. It would be ridiculous not to pull the parachute's rip cord now."

She gave him a watery smile. "I'm sure Margo would love to hear you compare her to a parachute. You should tell her that one."

Heath rolled his eyes. "She would love four dozen Dendrobium orchids in an heirloom vase."

"Then you should get her some," she insisted, refusing to think about how *she'd* have been thrilled to be presented a wildflower he'd picked in the fallow horse pasture.

"This is not how I thought this conversation was going to go," he muttered. "I thought you were mad about Margo."

Mad? No. Heartbroken might be closer to the truth, but she'd choke on it before she let even an inkling show. He didn't need her emotional crap piled on top of his reunion with Margo. It would make her seem pathetic and petty, especially since he'd always been very clear with Charli about the bet. And that this was practice.

"Oh, well." She ducked her head and warbled out a laugh that nearly made her wince. "I mean, she's beautiful and could give Blake Lively lessons on accessorizing. Who wouldn't be jealous, right?"

"She has nothing on you," he murmured, his eyes burning with intensity all at once.

She has you. "You don't have to say stuff like that to make me feel better. I have my own brand of awesomeness."

"That you do," Heath conceded and stepped back. "If you're sure there's not more to talk about?"

Like what? How it felt as if her insides had been scooped out with a shovel? Smiling brightly, she shooed him away so she could change. "We're totally good. I'm over my hissy fit about how unfair it is that she can prance around a horse ranch in heels and not trip. Do you think she'd tell me where she got those shoes?"

Chapter 21

"I hate her," Charli muttered as Sophia slid into the chair behind her desk, coffee in hand.

"Who, Margo Malloy?" her sister asked with an eye roll. "She is something all right."

Something Heath preferred. And as much as Charli would like to deny it, she could totally see how any red-blooded man would find himself slavering after her. The woman was gorgeous and cultured and orchestrated a lot of secret military stuff, particularly with Heath, once upon a time. Whom she clearly wasn't over.

His campaign to win her back was a cinch.

"Yeah." Charli sipped her own coffee glumly, her second cup on what was already a very long morning. "I thought I had her with the offer to take her out to the old well on horseback, but it turns out she can stay on a horse. And that she packed six-hundred-dollar jeans that she didn't mind getting dirty."

Plus a pair of riding boots of the English variety meant for fashion, not form, but Margo made it work with a laugh, telling Charli that she'd never expected to actually be on a horse in those boots. Joke was on Charli, then.

Plus, she'd had to watch Heath ride next to Margo, his stoic face back in place, uncharacteristically quiet.

No, that's how he'd been back at the beginning. All the time. They rarely spoke to each other after their one botched date, the only real one they'd ever been on. And then something had happened. Changed. They'd talked all the time after that.

She missed it. She missed *him*.

Heath had left early this morning to take Margo out to the site where they'd found the male head. They'd been gone for over an hour already. Not that she was watching the clock, but with each minute that ticked by, the jumpier she got.

Why, she didn't know.

It was the perfect opportunity for Heath to make a move. They were going to be alone in the woods. Why wouldn't he take advantage of it, spring a well-timed kiss on the woman he dreamed of getting back into his arms?

Good thing Charli hadn't eaten any breakfast, or it would be threatening to make a repeat appearance.

The doorbell chimed and Charli held up a hand to stop Sophia from standing. "I'll get it. I need the distraction."

She started to swing open the door and heard Heath's voice in her head warning her to be cautious, especially when he wasn't around. Good grief, the man had infiltrated even her conscience. But it wasn't bad advice, so she peeked through the peephole to spy her younger sister standing on the porch.

Veronica.

Oh, man. Not who she'd been expecting. Despite Sophia informing her that Veronica was coming down from Dallas for their father's memorial service, Charli hadn't realized she'd be here today. Or sporting a new haircut that put the *sever* in *severe*.

Charli flung the door open to admit her sister to the

house, meeting her at the threshold for an enthusiastic hug. It had been way too long since they'd seen each other.

"Hey, what's all this?" Charli called and riffled her fingers through the extremely short razor-cut ends of her sister's hair. "This is rocking."

Veronica touched her dark brown hair almost self-consciously. "Time for a change."

Oh, geez. Every woman on the planet knew that a man had to be at the root of that sentiment. "Did you and Jeremy break up?"

"Yeah, but right after Christmas," Veronica said vaguely and waved that off. "It's not a big deal."

Charli bit back the slew of questions that her sister clearly didn't want her to ask, meanwhile calculating how she was just now hearing about this. Hadn't she texted Veronica a couple of months ago to check in? Maybe it had been closer to three months. With everything that had been going on in her own life, she and her younger sister hadn't talked in far too long.

That was on Charli.

"Want some coffee?" Charli offered. "Sophia and I were just going over some business stuff. You can hang out with us if you want."

"Sure, that would be great."

Okay, now Veronica was scaring her. "I was expecting you to say no," she countered with a laugh. "You don't care about the ranch business. You were the one who was heavily in favor of selling, remember?"

"I remember."

Something was really off with her sister, and it wasn't just the breakup with her boyfriend of four years. There were fine stress lines around her brown eyes that aged her. Also, Veronica had never met a situation she didn't want to talk to death, usually with well-researched bullet points and a multimedia presentation.

"Everything okay at work?" Charli asked as her sister followed her into the kitchen.

Veronica laughed, a short brittle sound that didn't sound the slightest bit amused. "I have no idea. I quit."

Charli practically dropped the carafe in her left hand, which she'd been forced to use more often thanks to the cast on her other arm. "Oh. Are congrats in order? Did you get a better offer from a bigger law firm?"

There was a strange shadow in her sister's gaze, and it definitely didn't have a lot of better-job-more-pay type vibes. "No, I quit-quit. As in I'm not employed. It's still new and I'm still processing."

Carefully, Charli slid the carafe back into the coffee maker, wishing not for the first time that she had the money to spring for a Keurig. But all of the ranch's cash flow was tied up in renovations, and of course no guests meant no income.

No guests also meant Charli would have plenty of down-time to be there for Veronica. Something was clearly going on, but the fact that her sister hadn't immediately spilled all her secrets told her that it was more than a run-of-the-mill adulting dilemma.

She handed Veronica the coffee mug and tilted her head at the silver canisters full of creamer and sugar. "Help yourself. By the way, I know a little something about quitting your job and showing up at the ranch because you have no place else to go. So does Sophia. If you wanted to talk about it."

"I'm fine," Veronica said shortly and ran fingers through her hair with a jerky motion that maybe meant she still wasn't used to the new length. "I mean, I'm not here because I quit my job. I'm just here for the memorial service. Then I'm going to figure out the rest of my life."

She and Sophia knew a thing or two about that as well, but Charli kept that to herself since Veronica didn't seem to be in too much of a chatty mood. "Okay. I'm glad you came. It's going to be a little weird to have a memorial for someone who's been dead to us for years already."

Their mother had been the one to request that her daughters attend and insisted that everyone treat the service like a normal one, even though the forensic pathologist hadn't determined the cause of death yet, so the body hadn't been released to the family. Neither did Charli think she should point out that none of them had many fond memories of their father.

Veronica nodded, looking relieved at the subject change, and she followed Charli out of the kitchen, trailing her to Sophia's office. Sophia wasn't behind her desk, though. She was standing at the window, watching something out in the yard as she drank her coffee.

Curious, Charli joined her. Veronica took a second to give Sophia a hug and then did a double take as she caught sight of what had so thoroughly captured Sophia's attention. Not shockingly, her sister's boyfriend stood on the slope between the house and the barn, a small semicircle of ranch hands intently listening to whatever Ace was saying. Paxton stood directly to his right, listening with crossed arms.

"Who is *that*?" Veronica asked.

"That's Ace," Sophia said with a small smile. "Isn't he gorgeous?"

"Yes, I've seen nine hundred and forty-seven pictures of him on your Instagram," Veronica said dryly. "I meant the other one. The only one not wearing a hat."

"Paxton," Charli supplied helpfully. "He's cute, no?"

The three of them shifted their attention to the third partner in Heath's security firm, the one Charli had once thought might break her bad luck in the man department. Paxton was objectively handsome, but he couldn't hold a candle to Heath's sheer, rugged male beauty. Plus, it was entirely possible that she might be a little too much for someone with Paxton's mild demeanor. He kept to himself and caused zero waves, choosing to fade into the background when possible.

Heath was totally it for her. He'd ruined her for other men, and she couldn't even be mad at him over it.

Veronica on the other hand clearly appreciated the view. "He's definitely easy on the eyes. How do you get any work done around here if that's what's going on right outside your window?"

"Oh, it's easy," Charli replied with an eye roll. "We don't do any work. We sit around and wait for one of the *ologists* to show up with more bad news."

As if giving voice to that thought conjured the woman herself, Dr. Low exited the trailer perched at the edge of the wide space near the barn, closing the door behind her and locking it. One of the armed guards let her clear the short staircase and then took up a new position in front of the door, his semiautomatic rifle crossed over his chest. The scene was straight out of a movie full of special effects and actors with chiseled jaws, but this was Charli's real life and it kind of sucked.

Veronica watched with unveiled interest, the shadows Charli had seen in her eyes earlier completely banked. Maybe she'd imagined her sister's disquiet. But she didn't think so.

"Are we safe here?" Veronica asked, sounding more like her lawyer self than she had since she'd walked into the house. "When you said there were armed guards on the property, I guess I pictured it a little differently, like maybe they were doing rounds at the fence line and staying out of sight. But this is quite a bit more in your face than I was expecting."

Sophia sipped her coffee and nodded. "I'd trust Ace with my life and have, more than once. Heath is keeping up with Charli, no small feat, but I think he's the right man for that job."

"Hey," Charli protested without a lot of heat. But only because that wasn't wrong. "I have to do my share of keeping up with him too."

Ugh, she hadn't thought too much about what *that* would look like. On purpose. The bet had been designed to keep Heath entertained while he protected Charli, but at the end of the day, he still had a job—as Charli's bodyguard. Could her life get any worse?

The university people needed to clear out *soon*.

Veronica glanced at her with an eyebrow quirked, her gaze sharp as she took in Charli's expression, apparently seeing something there. "Sounds like a story there. Spill all the tea, Char."

A tight band snapped tight around her lungs all at once.

"There's no tea," she mumbled and drew in a breath. It didn't help.

Sophia bumped her with an elbow. "Oh, there's tea. It was a little hard to miss that he slept in your room the other night instead of the bunkhouse."

"Oooh," Veronica trilled and settled, her posture expectant, into the love seat Sophia had pushed against the far wall. "Tell, tell. This is a big development, yes?"

"Not even a little bit." It hit her all at once. Margo. The

bet. How far she'd taken *practicing*. "It's not like that, not like you think. We're just friends."

Veronica and Sophia glanced at each other, but it was Sophia who spoke. "I've seen you two together. You could light firewood from ten paces. I know you said it wasn't working out after that one date you went on, but I thought… well, I mean, couples fight and make up all the time. I kind of assumed you were figuring it out."

"Yeah, we were," she responded glumly, slumping to the floor to lean against the wall under the window so her eyes would quit flicking to the horizon to see if Heath had come back from his jaunt with Margo yet. "Figuring out how to get him back together with Margo."

Sophia visibly flinched. "What? What is that supposed to mean?"

She told her sisters about the bet and how Heath had flipped it on its head by introducing the idea of practicing. It sounded ridiculous out loud. Even to her, and she'd been the one to blow it way out of proportion.

"That's…" Veronica blinked a bunch. "Fascinating. I didn't think people did stuff like that in real life."

Yeah, well, she didn't need her sister's hypercritical tone to feel stupid. And now she wished she'd kept her mouth shut.

"Judgmental much?" Charli shot back and set aside the coffee that had turned to mud in her mouth. "I just wanted to win. I wasn't expecting to fall—"

Abort, her brain screamed, and she clamped her mouth shut. Too late.

Sophia brightened and clapped like she'd just descended the stairs on Christmas morning to find Santa had dropped half of a Tiffany's store under the tree. "I knew it! I knew you guys were falling for each other. Ace owes me ten bucks."

Ace had bet against Heath falling in love with Charli? The bands around her lungs became knives instantly. "That was a sucker's bet, Soph. He knows Heath is still in love with Margo. And it's fine. There's nothing between us."

Rubbing her forehead, Sophia sank into her desk chair, fiddling with her coffee mug, contemplating Charli with an unreadable expression. "If that's what you want to believe, okay. But I don't think that's even a little true. I've seen you together. There's a mirror on the wall behind the kitchen table, or did you forget? Every time y'all sit together, he's holding your hand on the down-low. You're constantly on his mind, whether it's to make sure you're being taken care of when he can't be around or talking about you to Ace."

This was news she hadn't heard. "He talks about me?"

Sophia rolled her eyes. "If I'd known any of this was in question, I'd have clued you in a long time ago, but yeah. Ace thinks it's entertaining, so of course he mentions it to me."

"Then why did Ace bet against me?" she couldn't help but ask. "Because he knows Heath is still in love with Margo. Like I said. They've been friends a long time."

The question was rhetorical, but Sophia treated the answer like she'd wagered everything on final Jeopardy. "I don't know why he took the bet. Ace never said anything of the sort, plus how would he know that? Men never talk about important stuff, just sports and firearms."

That didn't mean Ace hadn't figured it out. Her sister's boyfriend was sharp and intuitive, which made him good at his job, plus he'd worked with Margo too.

"I think the most important question is whether you've

told Heath you're in love with him," Veronica said in her opposing counsel voice.

"What?" Charli croaked. "Why would I tell him that? It's not true. I would—"

"You're lying," Veronica interjected simply. "I have a very expensive degree in psychology and another one that says I can practice law, plus a dozen cases in my rearview mirror that every partner at my law firm said were unwinnable. I win because I pay attention to what people don't say. You're in love with him. It wasn't practice for you. Does he know?"

"No," she said flatly, figuring it was better to come clean instead of throwing even more kindling on the fire of her sister's argument. "And no one in this room is going to say a word. He's in love with Margo and that's that."

Honestly, his commitment to his ex-girlfriend spoke volumes about his character. Ironic that his most attractive feature meant that he'd never be hers. And that she'd lost the bet.

"Oh, honey." Sophia clucked. "Did he tell you that? He's a moron."

"He didn't have to say it," she insisted, letting her head thunk against the wall. "I saw them together. Plus, he's been really clear since always that he wanted to get back together with her."

"Sometimes people's feelings change," Veronica muttered, sounding as if she might have a lot more to say about that, but opted not to.

"And sometimes they don't," she countered.

"Sometimes they don't," Sophia agreed and pointed at herself. "And that's a good thing. I had to tell Ace how I really felt, or I might have lost him. Now we're talking about the kind of forever I didn't think was possible."

"Yeah, exactly," Charli said with her brows raised. "We don't have a lot of positive relationships to look at for inspiration. What if I do tell him and we ride off into the sunset? There's always a sunrise and those don't always bring good things. His feelings might change about *me* at some point. That's a running theme here."

Men *never* picked her. Not the way Sophia was talking about. It was too big a risk to lay it all out there, only to be left once again, either by cheating or abandonment. Same end. It was so much better to step back than to invest her entire soul in someone who would ultimately wind up shedding their relationship one way or another.

"Besides, it doesn't matter," she said and pushed away from the wall, done with this subject. Past done. "We have a lot of other things to worry about with everything going on around the ranch."

That's where her attention should be, with the treasure still on site, plus the unanswered questions about the trailer break-in and their father's cause of death.

Veronica seemed to realize it was time for a subject change and smiled slyly. "Does that mean I get my own personal bodyguard? Because I can do math and there's one left who doesn't seem to be otherwise occupied."

"Yeah," Sophia said, her mouth flattening out as she considered the point. "I wasn't thinking that would be necessary since you're only here temporarily. But it wouldn't be a bad idea to ask Paxton to keep an eye out for you and Mom while you're in town."

Veronica cleared her throat, her expression decidedly wry. "I was thinking more about the *personal* part of the equation, not the danger."

When Sophia gave her sister a strange look, Charli translated for her. "She and Jeremy broke up. I think we are witnessing a rebirth of her interest in jumping back into the dating pool. Perhaps we could ask one of the auxiliary guys to watch after Mom and arrange for Paxton to be directly assigned to Veronica."

"Oh." Sophia flashed a broad smile. "I will see what I can do as the employer of Madden, McKay and Pierce's services. No promises. Keep in mind that the danger is real, though. You can't treat him like his protection is optional, which some people seem to forget occasionally."

Charli shot Sophia a withering look. "Most of the bad stuff happened around the house or in the woods. Nothing exciting has ever happened in the horse pastures."

"Except for you falling in a well and breaking your arm," Sophia pointed out with a nod toward the cast on Charli's arm. "Fortunately, Heath has stellar tracking abilities, or you might still be down there."

"Wait, what bad stuff happened in the woods?" Veronica wanted to know.

"Charli and Heath ran across some dead animals that appeared to have been planted," Sophia supplied.

"Rather not relive that," Charli said with a shudder. "Let's just say I've never more strongly considered being a vegetarian than I did in that moment."

"So one of the trailers was broken into, someone planted dead animals, and Dad was found dead under mysterious circumstances." Veronica ticked off the points on her fingers. "Did I miss anything?"

Charli and Sophia glanced at each other and shook their heads, Sophia speaking for them both. "I don't think so. I mean, there was the incident when I was kidnapped and I guess before that, the same guy broke into the house. But Cortez is in jail. Why?"

Veronica stood and paced, looking every bit like a high-powered criminal defense attorney addressing the jury. "The animals and the trailer break-in are recent, and Dad's death is likely several years old, which means they're probably not related. It would be highly unusual for a murderer to return to the scene of the crime so much later and terrorize the victim's family."

"The statues alone are worth ten million dollars," Charli reminded her. "That means all bets are off. It's too much money to assume anyone is doing anything rationally. Plus, we already know that Karl Davenport is an associate of the guy who kidnapped Sophia."

And they knew that Karl was their father's treasure hunting partner. Anything their father may have been involved with, Karl would know about. The mystery of their father's death might be years old, but they'd just found his body recently. It didn't feel like a coincidence. Or unrelated.

"That's true," Veronica said and turned to pace in the other direction. "But why murder Dad and then leave the extremely valuable statue you killed him for with the body?"

No one had a response to that, least of all Charli, who had actually asked herself that same question during the hours she'd been alone with both her father's body and the statue. But if the recent threats weren't related to their father's murder, that meant they were dealing with two different people, not one.

And the danger quotient might be even higher than they'd assumed. That was the important thing to focus on right now, not all her confusing feelings for Heath.

Chapter 22

The jaguar heads were gone. *Stolen.*

Heath stared at the open—empty—safe, his heart doing a tango and his stomach threatening to squeeze out through his throat. Outside the trailer, people shouted and milled about, crossing in front of the large picture window above the desk like panicked ants as their mound collapsed in around them.

"How are the statues gone?" he repeated for the fourth time as Dr. Low wrung her hands uselessly, the same thing she'd been doing since she'd reported that the safe had been broken into. One of the guards had grabbed him as he'd crossed the yard on his way to the house.

"I don't know," she mumbled, which was the petite academic's equivalent to a wail. She'd remained largely composed in the scant few minutes since chaos had erupted. "I came back from a meeting with Dr. McDaniel in her trailer and found this."

She gestured to the empty safe, her face etched with disbelief. The thief had carefully dismantled the silent alarm in a feat worthy of someone with Pierce's level of skill. They were dealing with a professional, obviously.

His eyes darted around the small, dimly lit space, taking in Dr. Low's undisturbed laptop, several labeled artifacts standing intact on a shelf near her desk, and her personal items, including a phone and an expensive-looking hand-bag. Nothing else had been so much as touched.

Just the safe.

Heath cursed as blue and red lights flashed against the far wall announcing the arrival of the local law enforcement. At this rate, they should get a room in the house and stick around. Save time on their commute out to the ranch.

Of course, there wasn't much left to protect.

The three guards who had been on duty at the time of the theft stood behind him, silently accepting their complete failure. They weren't the type to wear their emotions on their sleeves, but he could feel their nerves as they exchanged glances.

"Outside," he snapped to the guards, who immediately did as bid, likely aware that their employment contract with Madden, McKay and Pierce was not going to end with a favorable review.

He followed them so the police would have room to start cataloging the disaster, and then stopped where the three guards stood in a defensive clump. Nothing would save them from his wrath, but before he destroyed them, he needed answers. "What happened? How did the thief get past you?"

One of the guards, a burly man named Murray who had twenty years at the St. Louis PD in his rearview, shook his head. "You know as much as we do. Dr. Low went to her meeting. I saw her lock the door. Wilson took up position in front of the door like he usually does when she leaves, and Jones and I took perimeter. She came back and rushed out to announce the safe was open. I grabbed you. End of story."

Not end of story. This was not happening. Not on his watch. "There has to be something you can remember.

Some detail. Thieves do not wave wands and magically appear inside a locked trailer."

The trailer was in view of the house and the barn, deliberately. The clearing had fifty feet of visibility from all sides. Only a ghost could have accomplished this feat.

Then there was the interesting timing, given that they'd only recently discovered the second head—and David Lang's body. Someone could have broken in and stolen the single head, especially since there was a period of time when the security hadn't been as strong, well before they'd found the second one.

Had someone been lurking in the wings, waiting for them to find the second head? Someone who knew there were two? Like Karl Davenport, David Lang's former partner, who topped the list as the likely suspect. And fit the profile of a ghost quite well since no one had actually seen him in the flesh.

Had he been one of the two people who had met at the fence line near the cigarette pile Heath had found?

Heath pinched the bridge of his nose as Murray, Jones and Wilson shifted restlessly. Finally, Jones offered, "That intelligence lady was asking questions yesterday. About the safe."

Of course. That was her job. "I'm sure she asked a lot of questions about everything."

Murray nodded. "That she did. For about an hour. I think she spent at least two with Dr. Low."

And two with Heath this morning. Margo was nothing if not thorough. He'd walked her to her car and as far as he knew, she'd left to fly home, since she'd finished the on-site investigation. She'd mentioned that she would be subpoenaing David Lang's financial records, but that would take weeks to be granted.

The rest of her investigation could take place at Fort Bragg. Such as it was. She'd invited him to stay at her place for an extended visit when he finished his assignment here, heavily alluding to an enthusiastic kiss-and-make-up session in the future. Until the theft had been reported, he'd thought of nothing else except why the idea of taking her up on it made his skin crawl.

Eventually, he'd have to let Margo know the statues had been stolen. But the trail was fresh at the moment and daylight would only last another four and a half hours. Madden was occupied with the local police, acting as their liaison while they did their initial pass on the crime scene, while Pierce had holed up with his surveillance footage looking for a shot of the thief.

That left Heath to do the legwork.

"You three," he said to the guards and pointed at the knot of locals who looked to be a mix of badges and possibly CSI, probably borrowed from a bigger city's department. "Give your statements to whoever is handling that, then park somewhere. Don't leave. You'll be dismissed when I say you are."

Satisfied that they would do as ordered, Heath set himself the task of looking for clues. With everyone else occupied, including the police who were good at taking statements and not much else, someone had to get the jaguar heads back.

The thief had entered the trailer some way and he wanted to know how. Pierce might turn up something in the recorded footage, but that would take hours, and Heath needed to be doing something now.

Preferably something that would burn off the adrenaline pumping through his blood and ease the black edges crowding his vision.

Except he'd taken no more than a half a step toward the trailer when Charli burst from the woods behind him. Alarm flared in her eyes, widening them, and her hair fell around her face in a disarray that sent his pulse into the stratosphere.

"What's wrong?" he demanded.

She bent at the waist, breathless, but finally wheezed out, "Heath, someone's breaking into your truck! I saw him from the house and had to go out the front door, then double back—"

"Get behind me," he ordered, his brain already connecting dots. "Stay close."

It was the thief. Trying to escape with everyone's attention stuck on the crime scene. Clever.

But the filth hadn't counted on Charli still being in the house, likely with her gaze glued to the window since he'd explicitly told her to stay inside with her mother and sisters. He'd yell at her later for disobeying him.

Or maybe not, if her quick action helped him catch the thief.

He dashed toward the truck, his boots pounding on the ground. There was no time to ensure Charli could keep up, but he couldn't protect her if he opened a gap between them. Instinctively, he matched her pace, and automatically took her hand to pull her along.

The thief would not get away. Not from Heath.

But when he rounded the corner and his truck came into view, the figure crouched near the truck's wheel well was not stealing Heath's truck. He was vandalizing it.

And his name wasn't Karl.

"Harvard," Heath snarled as the kid jerked his head, dropping the can of spray paint in his hand.

It rolled under Heath's truck, right beneath the expletive marching across the door in three-foot letters.

The guy who had manhandled Charli leaped to his feet but didn't run like Heath had expected him to do. Instead, Harvard stood his ground in some misguided show of bravado. As if Heath wouldn't tear him apart in seconds with zero provocation.

Blackness edged through his vision, tempting him to act, pushing him to destroy.

"What do you think you're doing?" Heath barked and the kid had the audacity to sneer.

"Payback," he said with a cocky grin.

He'd gotten his nose fixed. It would look much better broken again and Heath's fist ached to repeat their first encounter. But there was so much more at stake here.

"Is that why you stole the jaguar heads?" It would explain a lot. Who else would have enough knowledge of the university's equipment and procedures to bypass security but an insider?

"Jaguar heads?" A glint of confusion flitted through Harvard's gaze as he glanced at Charli, who hovered at Heath's elbow, thankfully staying out of the line of fire. "Is that redneck slang for something, cowboy?"

Yeah, for the reason Heath was about to turn the kid into hamburger meat. He reeled it back. This was one of the times when he needed to use caution instead of letting his temper boil. Charli's trust in his ability to figure that out settled into his bones and he let that ride for a long minute.

"Where did you hide the heads?" Heath asked him, his voice evening out as the strangest sense of calm soothed his raised hackles.

Harvard edged back an inch, clearly confused by this

new, less violent Heath. "Man, I don't know what you're talking about."

Sure. It was a total coincidence that this kid had showed up at the exact time of the theft so he could deface Heath's truck. Maybe Harvard hadn't intended to steal the vehicle since he likely had another ride stashed somewhere. The vandalism represented an ultimate Screw You as Harvard rode off with his ten-million-dollar bounty.

"That's fine," Heath returned pleasantly. "The police can sort this out. Good thing they're already on site collecting evidence from your other crime. I'm sure they'll be quite thrilled I'm able to provide them a suspect to match the fingerprints taken from the scene. It'll cut down the investigation time exponentially."

"Wait. What?" Alarm flitted through Harvard's gaze as Heath watched calculations scroll through the kid's head. "You can't take fingerprints from skinned animals. You won't pin any of that on me."

Oh for the love of Pete. Heath bit back a curse. Pieces clicked into place instantly. The skinned animals had been *this* guy's calling card? Along with the vandalism, it fit. Random, petty acts of a desperately immature grad student who had suffered humiliation at the hands of someone twice his size with twice the intellect.

"Oh, we can and will," Heath promised him. "Plus the theft of the ancient, priceless artifacts that are currently missing. I'm sure everyone will appreciate it if you just return them."

Harvard sputtered. "I didn't take anything. I may have trashed some of the other students' research, but it's all garbage. They're analyzing bone fragments and sifting through beads like all that crap matters."

Bone fragments. A hint of a memory darted through

Heath's head. That's what No-Logo had mentioned he was researching outside the ransacked trailer. Harvard wasn't confessing to have broken into the guarded trailer containing the safe, but the research trailer. Intending to cause havoc. Not to steal anything.

That would explain why the kid didn't seem to have a clue what Heath was trying to goad him into confessing. Was that really the case? Harvard wasn't the thief? Then who was?

The entire world had gone off its axis.

"All right," Heath said dismissively. "We'll let the cops straighten this out."

With no warning—and thus no chance for Harvard to make a break for it—Heath grabbed him by the arm and hustled him back the way he and Charli had come. Straight to Gun Barrel City's finest, where he deposited his protesting detainee. Given that Heath had a measure of authority at the ranch, none of the police officers batted an eye when he told them to arrest the kid and throw theft charges at him.

They wouldn't stick. Harvard had convinced Heath that he wasn't the mastermind of the statue theft, but that left so many open questions, it wouldn't help to mention them to the local authorities.

"You know he didn't take the jaguar heads. Right?" Charli suggested as she dogged Heath's steps away from the general chaos of the police taking statements and attempting to organize the scene.

Heath had plenty enough of that experience to want to avoid being the keeper of the peace at a crime scene on this ranch.

"Yeah, I know," he told her with an eye roll. "It was meant to keep everyone busy."

"You think it was Karl." Charli chewed her lip. "And that he killed my father too."

This was so not the conversation he wanted to be having with her right now. Or ever. She was wearing a T-shirt that was too large for her, so it sat off to one side, exposing a bit of shoulder that he couldn't peel his eyes from all at once.

What kind of dog was he that he couldn't think of her as a friend? Margo should be the woman on his mind, but he couldn't force that, even if he wanted to. There was no comparison between the two—and he couldn't envision starting things back up with Margo at this point. It felt...wrong.

And Charli didn't seem to be at all interested in his feelings on the matter. He'd even tried to broach the subject before Margo had showed up. And after, forget it. Charli couldn't have pushed him away fast enough.

He got it. Heath was fine for practice but not for real. It was never real, not on her side. Not even the times when it had seemed like they were so in sync that they were practically reading each other's thoughts.

Heath was just her bodyguard.

"Go back to the house and I'll be in later," he mumbled, aware that the situation was indeed an indictment on his abilities to do his job. After all, the name of the security company employed by the ranch had his name on it.

"Yes, sir, Mr. Babysitter, sir."

She saluted and wheeled to do his bidding, but not before he caught a glint in her eye that sat funny in his gut. As if her smart-aleck response might have more to it than just Charli giving him regular grief.

Great. Had he hurt her feelings? There was no scenario where he had the time to chase after her and yank an explanation out of her as to what was wrong. That part of their relationship was over.

Groaning, he rounded the trailer, avoiding everyone with a uniform, as well as Madden, who was still riding point with all the locals.

Heath needed to end this thing. Now, not later. Not by sitting on his hands while less invested people took up the mantle. He still hadn't answered his own question about how the thief had gotten into the trailer, who was likely Karl, as Charli had surmised. Nothing Harvard had said pointed at him as the thief.

But Karl could be anywhere with those heads by now.

Careful not to disturb anything that might yield finger-prints, he checked the entire perimeter of the trailer for handholds that might allow someone with a bit of skill to scale the fiberglass siding and roll onto the roof.

There were a couple of spots that might be viable. The thief had surely worn gloves, but just in case, he opted not to press his own fingers into the crevices to check if they'd hold a man's weight.

Besides, going in through the roof would be like ask-ing to be spotted. Especially in daylight. A niggle in his gut shifted his gaze. If he'd been doing this job, he'd never pick *up* over *down*.

He dropped to the ground and peered at the undercar-riage. It took him a while to find what he was looking for, but eventually he spied the cleverly hidden square in the floor of the trailer. Just as he suspected. The thief had cut a hole in the floor. Just like Heath had done in an operation near Kandahar to extract a briefcase from a locked room.

Likely the thief had created the hole last night under cover of darkness, then accessed the brand-new entry point today. That's why none of the guards had seen the thief. Wouldn't shock him if the timing turned out to overlap with shift change.

The hole wasn't large either, which could explain Dr. Low not noticing the cut from the interior. He'd never seen a picture of Karl Davenport but if he measured in at an average male height and weight, Karl wouldn't fit through this hole. Neither would Heath, for that matter, a fact he knew for certain because the first time he'd practiced cutting a hole for Kandahar, it had been too small.

Margo had laughed at his poor judgment as she'd cataloged his progress on the mission, asking if he'd planned to invite her along to push *her* through the hole.

His pulse kicked up a notch due to the narrative forming in his head. The one where the thief wasn't Karl but someone with a much smaller stature. Someone who had established a perfectly legit reason to visit the trailer and spend as much time cataloging it as she wished to.

Margo.

She'd likely walked up and asked the guards when their shift change happened and they'd blithely told her, blinded by her smile and considerable charm as she stole the jaguar heads out from underneath them.

Heath let that wash over him as the truth burned a hole in his chest.

She'd played him. She hadn't taken this assignment to cozy up to him in hopes of rekindling something between them. She'd taken it to *distract* him.

And she had. He hadn't followed up on his suspicions about her orders from JSOC. Which likely didn't even exist. In retrospect, he should have asked a lot more questions about why Spec Ops would care about some Maya treasure.

What an idiot he was. Shame and not a little embarrassment coated his skin like shellac.

What he did not feel was heartbroken.

That told him everything he needed to know about why

the whole scene with Margo had felt…off. He wasn't in love with her anymore. If he ever had been in the first place.

She'd reevaluated during their time apart—so had he. With distance, he could see their relationship was dysfunctional at best. At worst, toxic. And she wasn't as pretty as he'd remembered. She wore entirely too much makeup, and you could feed a small village for what her diamond earrings cost.

Now he knew what it was like to be with a woman who not only encouraged him to be himself, but seemed to *like* him, too. As if Heath McKay unfiltered and unaltered worked for her in a million different ways.

It was heady, especially in comparison. A relief. He should have realized all this a long time ago, saved everyone a lot of grief, especially Charli. What if instead of trying to give Margo the benefit of the doubt, he'd just told Charli how he felt about her? Would she have thought about it and realized how good they were together?

He had to find out. As soon as possible.

Unfortunately, that had to come *after* he fixed this other mess. If Margo was the thief, he was the only one with a prayer of finding her. He was the only one with the skill set. The score he had to settle with her for stealing from the Langs and making a mockery of him? That was just a bonus.

Chapter 23

Heath texted Charli again at a rest stop and waited for a reply. Nada. Just like the last three times.

Her lack of response sat in his gut like a cocklebur, sharp and uncomfortable. And worrisome. Things between them were still strained, that much he knew, but come on. He'd gone out of his way to make sure they were okay, that Margo hadn't changed anything between them.

If nothing else, he and Charli were still friends.

Which he'd do everything in his power to change eventually. As soon as he could.

But no response could mean Charli had fallen down another well.

She better not have. He'd specifically instructed Pierce to stick to Charli like white on rice and he'd trusted his partner with his life on many occasions, so smart money said it was something else.

Was she ignoring him? He'd explained that he'd had to go in all three text messages, that he'd fill in the gaps as soon as he could. But he couldn't risk tipping off Margo, just in case she'd set up a tap on everything Lang-related. It would be her style.

With no time to waste, he pushed on, cranking the air conditioner in the SUV he'd rented. His truck was still at the body shop getting a new paint job to erase Harvard's artwork on the door panels. Too bad he couldn't have arranged a flight, or he'd have done it. His contacts in the military were suspect at this point, though—all the people he knew also knew Margo and there was no telling how many others had been turned.

Not to mention the fact that he wasn't 100 percent convinced he'd find Margo at her father's lake house in Austin. It was a gamble, but a good one given that she'd often spent time there when she'd had vacation from work.

If she wasn't there, he faced a long few days of trying to track her with a cold trail. He was trying not to think about that—but unfortunately his thoughts drifted to Charli the moment he let his guard down. The distraction alone made that a bad idea.

But he couldn't help it.

He missed her. Not for the first time, he wished he'd had the latitude to invite her along. She'd have made this trip a thousand times more interesting. It would have been a good chance to spend time together. Learn some things. Talk about their favorite movies. Whatever. He craved that kind of normalcy. He'd never had that before and wanted it desperately.

The roads in this area of Texas stretched for miles, long and winding and treacherous for someone who had been on the road for three hours already. He had to find Margo, had to confront her about the stolen jaguar heads and the lies.

The weight of her duplicity bore down on him. Who had turned her? And why? What was her end game?

When he finally reached the lake house after only one wrong turn, a chill washed over him. The structure itself stood up on a hill, a dark silhouette now that the sun had set. He parked the SUV a short distance from the house, rolling it into the heavy brush to avoid drawing attention.

As he exited the SUV, gravel crunched beneath his boots, ringing out in the still air. Heath froze. After a beat, he heel-toed it to the tree line, hoping there'd be enough ground cover to mask his steps.

The night air was heavy with humidity and the scent of sage from the bushes growing wild along the road. Hills rose behind the house, a majestic backdrop that he wished he had time to explore. It would be a lot more fun to have made this trip with the intent to hike. With Charli.

Was she thinking about him? Did she miss him?

That was one thing about being with someone like Margo. She was pretty self-sufficient, and she'd never once expressed a single personal thought about Heath being gone all the time when he'd been with the navy. She'd only cared whether he'd completed his missions or not and whether the team had been successful.

Honestly, sometimes he'd wondered if she'd have even missed him if he didn't come home. And not for the first time since he'd found the hole cut in the floor, he cross-examined himself on why he'd wanted her back so badly.

Pride. Probably. Which pretty much drove him now too.

With each step, his senses heightened. Crickets chirped, insects buzzed, and moonlight reflected off the giant picture windows overlooking the lake.

Slipping through the shadows, gratified that he hadn't lost his stealth skills, he crept through the row of hedges landscaped to the hilt, peering into the first window from a hidden vantage point. It was dark inside, but the front room led to a hallway and a single light shone from the back of the house.

Could be a security light programmed to switch on after dark. Or it could be Margo.

Heath circled the house, keeping to the darkest pockets as

surely Mr. Malloy had cameras around this property and possibly pressure sensors to warn of intruders. But he couldn't take the time to study the security logistics. Especially given that he planned to get inside in a matter of seconds.

At a window approximately three-quarters of the distance to the back of the house, he surveyed what he could see from this vantage point. There were fewer shadows here thanks to the floodlight affixed to the highest peak of the roofline, but as he tilted his head, he saw her.

Margo. She moved through the room with purpose, clearly outlined by the overhead lights. It was a bathroom of enormous size, with an ocean of white tile. Fortunately, he had zero qualms about spying on his former girlfriend while she took a bath.

Not that he'd stick around to enjoy the show. It would simply be a good distraction for her while he figured out his entrance logistics.

She didn't stay in the bathroom, though. In typical Margo fashion, she checked out her appearance in the full-length cheval mirror, straightening the straps of the black tank top she wore. Then she exited the room, flicking off the lights with her index finger.

Heath waited a millisecond to ensure she didn't backtrack, then quickly scouted for a good way inside. A lucky break—several of the windows were open on the second floor to let in the cooler night air. Which also meant Margo wasn't expecting him.

He couldn't wait to see her face when she realized he'd figured out her game so quickly.

A trellis near the screened-in porch made an excellent ladder, though it wasn't so easy to push the ropy vines aside with his boots. He made it to the roof of the porch after a minor brush with a startled lizard. With agonizing caution, he crept across the porch roof to one of the open windows, an old-fashioned kind with a turn handle. Margo had cranked it just enough that he could get his arm up through the crack and lever it open wide enough for an entire former SEAL to slip through.

Glad he hadn't lost his touch, he toed off his boots and stowed them in a shadowy corner in case Margo passed by this room. The downside of being out of the Teams—he had boots, not stealth footwear, and had never envisioned a scenario where running security on a ranch in Texas would require anything different.

Granted, none of this had anything to do with the ranch. Charli and her sisters were just the unlucky owners caught in the middle of whatever game this was.

Heath slid across the threshold of the bedroom and into the hall. A light shone at the far end. Margo stood underneath it, hands clasped in front of her. Waiting for him.

The hall light glinted off a long kitchen knife between her palms.

"Hello, darling," she purred. "So nice of you to join me."

Adrenaline coursed through his veins, cutting off his self-congratulatory spiel. She'd set this up. It was a trap, and he'd fallen right into it, a blind lion scenting fresh meat, then limping his way right into the lair of the hunter.

"It was good of you to leave such an easy trail to follow," he returned, schooling the expression on his face, though it was likely a lost cause. She knew she'd bested him. This was her gloating face.

She lifted a manicured brow. "Honestly, I expected you much earlier. Couldn't find a ride?"

"Obviously I can trust no one," he said with a shrug. "Plus, there was a little matter of a vandal I had to ensure the police arrested. I can do two jobs at once. Can you?"

She had no reason to answer him, but she didn't hesitate. "Quite well, apparently. It's amazing how much information comes across my computer screen that presents interesting opportunities. Only a fool wouldn't see the potential to profit."

"That's what this was? A paycheck?"

Margo lifted her shoulders. "What isn't about a paycheck? That's what we work for, isn't it?"

Maybe *she* did. But he worked with Madden and Pierce because they meant something to him. Because they believed in each other. They all cared about their clients and about ensuring people who couldn't protect themselves had someone in their corner who could. At least that had always been the case before.

Charli had been different from the first. Who knew the perfect woman for him preferred jeans and horses over couture and superficiality?

But he couldn't think about her. Not now. This situation needed his full attention, particularly given the hardware involved.

Did Margo know he'd tucked his gun into the waistband of his jeans? Or did she truly intend to stab an unarmed man?

"I need the heads back, Margo," he told her with far more calm than he'd expected. Than the situation called for.

She clued in on it, too, cocking her head and surveying him with a puzzled sweep. "Who are you and what did you do with Heath McKay? Did you take a Valium in the car?"

There was nothing funny about this showdown, but he couldn't help laugh at her question anyway. "I didn't have to. I'm a reformed hothead. Sorry I didn't send you an announcement."

"That's an egregious oversight." She tsked and brandished the knife. "I'm overdressed for the occasion, then. I was expecting a knockdown, drag-out fight."

He lifted a brow. "You against me? I've never been *that* much of a hothead."

"Well, that's debatable," she said delicately and sniffed. "And I didn't want to find out what your limits were."

That stuck him in the gut far deeper than any piece of steel could. She thought he might lose control one day and… what? Actually hit her? The thought made him green all the way to his toes.

Thankfully, Charli hadn't flinched at being front and center with Heath. Present in a way that he'd never had before. Or realized he'd want so deeply.

"That's okay," he said with a tiny smile. "Someone else helped me figure out what my limits are."

Granted, a lot of that had come about because Charli had tested them. But it still counted.

"Oh, yes, your country bumpkin." Margo nodded sagely. "I could tell something was going on between you. That'll last about another two seconds, until you get bored and start spoiling for a fight. She does know that you're not overly fond of roots, right?"

"My relationship with Charli is none of your concern," he told her with zero heat and enjoyed every second of it. Holding out his hand, he flipped his fingers in a gimme motion. "The heads, Margo. They belong to the people of Mexico, not your highest bidder."

She laughed. "I'm not selling them on the open market, are you insane? I'm the delivery girl. Half up-front, half upon transfer. You don't know the guy."

"Try me." He showed his teeth.

"Silver hair? About yay tall?" Margo made a shelf out of her hand at about the six-foot mark. "Name's George."

"George." Heath rolled his eyes. "Because that doesn't sound fake. We're not having a conversation here, Margo. This is my job and I'm not leaving without the statues. Don't get in my way or you will find out what I'm capable of."

She raised the knife, malice churning through her eyes. "Come and take them, Navy Boy. I've never been one to stay behind a desk. Might be a harder job than you anticipated."

Flashing her a smile that she didn't know what to do with—judging by the confusion floating around—he used the scant few seconds to catalog the hall, noting the window behind her, the staircase winding to the ground floor.

One second he was standing there, the next, he'd leaped forward, rolling into a crouch, then swept one leg in an arc to take out Margo's from underneath her.

She went down with a cry, but contorted midair and drove the knife downward. Straight into his leg.

White-hot agony lanced through his calf. He bit back a scream and rolled with the wave of nausea for a second. But he had to move. Couldn't just lie there and bleed.

Margo leaped to her feet, not the slightest bit dazed. They both glanced at the knife that had clattered to the wood floor near the wall. As she dove for it, Heath twisted and pulled the gun from his waistband, aiming it at her heart.

"Back away slowly," he rasped, and she threw up her hands. Good. She wasn't going to be stupid.

Fighting through the pain, Heath climbed to his feet, careful not to put weight on his sliced leg, and palmed the knife. Blood seeped into the fabric of his jeans, but he didn't have time to check how deep the cut was.

"Take me to the heads," he ordered her and jerked the

barrel of the gun to the left as he held the knife in her general direction. Hopefully she got the hint that he'd gladly use either on her.

"Not even if you shoot me," she said with a defiant toss of her hair and crossed her arms. "You can't fathom how much money I'm being paid to deliver these statues to my client."

"Is it worth the gamble that you might die in the process?" he asked her quietly, struck all at once that he'd imagined himself in love with this woman not that long ago. And she'd waltzed back into his life as an enemy—one who didn't seem that unhappy about the lot she'd chosen.

And she certainly didn't want him back. It was a relief to finally be shed of this woman forever.

She scoffed. "Please, you wouldn't kill me."

No, he wouldn't, not unless he had to defend Charli. Or himself. That was the thing she failed to realize. She'd meant something to him once, and still did, but not the way she seemed to assume. "I was talking about your client. Once he has the statues, there's no reason to keep you alive. And if you're dead, he doesn't have to pay you the second installment. You're dealing with criminals, Margo. They don't have to honor the rules of engagement."

Not that she was doing that either, but there was still a part of him who didn't want to see her suffer for the terrible choices she'd made.

"What would you have me do, darling?" she purred. "Hand them over to you in hopes my client will see the error of his ways? I don't think so."

Heath nodded. "Okay. We'll do this the hard way, then."

While they'd chatted about her descent into darkness, he'd maneuvered close enough to the side table near the stairs to pull the long runner free. Before Margo could formulate an escape plan, he flung the knife to the other end of the hall, out of reach, then snagged her wrist, twisting it behind her with his free hand.

Shoving the gun against her ribs, he forced her to walk. "Move. Heads. Now. Or you will have a bullet wound through multiple internal organs. Your choice."

Margo hesitated for so long, he started formulating plan B. Then she spat out a curse, testing his strength with a surprisingly strong yank against his grip on her wrist.

He'd been braced for that since moment one. So it didn't work. He jammed the gun deeper into her ribs. "Try again. See where that gets you. Or cooperate. Then this is over faster."

Finally, her spine relaxed a fraction. Which in turn allowed him to breathe a tad easier.

He held the runner with his teeth as she stalked down the stairs. It was dicey trying to keep up with her and not let on that the pain piercing his leg with each step nearly stole his breath. The trail of blood he left on the floor should probably concern him more, but unless he passed out, it couldn't be a factor.

Once they hit the ground floor, he'd lost enough blood that he needed to make things easier on himself, so he tied her wrists together with the runner instead of using it as a tourniquet, which had been his first plan.

"Keep going," he advised her as she shot him a black look.

Snarling low-level threats that amounted to nothing more than grumbling, she led him to into a well-appointed office. Behind an oil painting of a ship, she revealed a safe.

"Good luck with that," she taunted. "I'm not going to tell you how to open it."

Heath's head swam from stress and blood loss. There

was no guarantee that she'd even put the statues in the safe, but he had a feeling she'd wanted to see him sweat over this additional complexity or she wouldn't have led him to this room in the first place.

"You don't have to tell me," he informed her and unplugged a lamp from a side table next to a leather chair, then force-sat her in the chair, tying the cord around her legs with a sailor's knot that she no doubt recognized.

She could still likely get loose if he gave her long enough, so he scuttled from the room as quickly as he could in search of towels and water to clean up his leg. Losing more blood wouldn't help this situation.

In seconds, he'd found a bathroom and cleaned up the worst of the wound. It wasn't as deep as he'd feared and the knife hadn't cut anything critical other than his skin, so he tied a fluffy guest towel with the monogram AAM around his calf.

As he exited the bathroom, he spied Margo's handbag sitting on the island in the kitchen. Not one to look a gift horse in the mouth, he took precious seconds to go through it. She'd slid her phone into the front pocket, which he didn't dare hope he could get into unless she'd enabled facial recognition. No one in Special Ops would ever do that since an enemy could easily use it to gain access to important data, even if you were dead.

Something fluttered to the floor as he pulled out her phone. A slip of paper. Crouching, he picked it up, his eyes widening as he took in the sequence of numbers. They sure looked an awful lot like exactly what he was looking for. But really? Surely Margo hadn't *written down* the combination to the safe.

But this was her father's house. Not hers. There was no reason for her to know the combination. And no reason for him not to try it. Worst-case scenario, it didn't work and he moved on to plan C.

"Found it," he said as he clomped back into the home office and flicked the paper up between two fingers to show her.

Something flashed across her face, informing him instantly that it *was* the combination. He shut his eyes in disbelief. If she hadn't stabbed him, he'd never have pulled his gun and none of this would have unfolded. She might have run, and he might have chased her, never realizing the statues were in the house all along.

Within seconds, the safe popped open. Gold gleamed from its dark interior. The jaguar heads.

He scooped them out and shut the safe. "Nice doing business with you, Ms. Malloy. I hope I never see you again."

Heath exited the room, Margo muttering slurs on his character that got more inventive the further he trudged. The trip to the second floor to retrieve his boots nearly killed him but an eternity later, he had everything he'd come for. Once he got out of the house, he called the local police to come pick up Margo, and explained—very patiently—that they needed to coordinate with the Texas Rangers and Gun Barrel City PD.

Not his problem any longer. He'd spent far too long thinking he wasn't good enough for Margo, that he needed to change to make her happy, but the truth was that she wasn't good enough for him. The missing element in his life wasn't the ability for him to manage his temper, but the acceptance of it. Of him. Wholly and unaltered. He only needed Charli to be happy.

And she still hadn't responded to any of his text messages.

Chapter 24

Charli liked being babysat by Paxton even less than when Heath had been her shadow. Actually, it wasn't the same at all. With Heath, she'd felt like they were spending time together while he protected her from harm. Like they were connecting.

It was only when Paxton had materialized at her side and mumbled something about Heath asking him to fill in that she'd understood that Heath was gone. *He'd left.* As in flat out just walked out the door with Margo.

Well, of course he had. That's what she'd encouraged him to do. His commitment to Margo remained steadfast, ironically one of his best features.

But was it too much to have wished he'd said goodbye? That Charli had meant enough to him to take two minutes to call a time-out and pull her into his arms for the last time?

Clearly that wasn't a thing. Then he'd *texted* her.

Heath: I'm sorry, but I have to leave

Heath: Are you okay? I'm worried about you

Heath: I'll explain later. I just can't right now

Of course she'd ignored him. Oh, she'd read all the text messages, but what was there to say? To explain?

She'd known this was coming. What she hadn't anticipated was Heath still trying to maintain contact, like everything between them hadn't been torn up at the roots like a tree in a hurricane.

The missing jaguar heads provided an almost welcome distraction, tossing her into the middle of a mess that she and Sophia, along with Ace and Paxton, had to temper without Heath's help. Charli was just now coming to realize how much order he'd brought to the chaos. And not just on the ranch. He settled *her* in ways she hadn't honored nearly enough.

The local police had no leads but insisted on going over every inch of the ranch a second time. Keeping the dig nerds out of the way proved nearly impossible and Dr. Low kept trying to talk to Charli about insurance claims. By dinnertime, she just wanted Heath. And a bath. And to sleep for a million years.

None of those were going to happen.

Finally, she managed to roll into bed at midnight, exhausted but unable to sleep. Stupid cast. She couldn't get comfortable, and Heath wasn't here to soothe her with his heat and magical touch.

Fine. That was fine. She didn't need him.

The crunch of gravel outside made her bolt up and she dashed to the window to see a nondescript SUV rolling into the circular drive at the front of the house, then continue to the back. Just as she grabbed her phone to text Paxton that they had unwelcome company, Heath swung out of the driver's seat.

Heath.

Alone. Without Margo.

Oh, dear heavens. What was he doing here?

She watched him walk toward the kitchen door instead of the bunkhouse, hatless, his gait a funny one-two step. Was something wrong with one his boots?

More to the point, he had a lot of nerve showing back up here after not even bothering to say goodbye. Really, she should have realized that he'd come back to finish his assignment since his security company still had a contract with Sophia.

But still. She had a piece of her mind to give him.

She marched down the stairs without a single consideration for her Hello Kitty pajamas, meeting him at the door of the kitchen, arms crossed so she didn't reach out to touch him, just to assure herself that he was here and whole and real. This man didn't belong to her and for all she knew, Margo was waiting for him at a hotel somewhere while he picked up some of his things that he'd left behind.

"Look what the cat dragged in," she said.

The kitchen light threw his features in harsh relief, highlighting fatigue and stress. "I can't fight with you right now, Charli."

"I thought we were friends," she stressed, not because that's what she'd wanted them to be to each other, but she'd thought that part of their relationship was sacred.

He clomped past her into the room with that same one-two step. That's when she noticed the rust-colored stains caking the leg of his jeans, which had been sliced open to the knee. Her pulse shuddered to a halt in milliseconds.

"What's wrong with your leg?" she quavered as she forgot all the things she'd meant to lambast him with and rushed to his side to help maneuver him onto the bench seat at the table.

He didn't protest when she helped him ease off his boots.

When she saw the row of uneven stitches, the sound that came out of her mouth wasn't even human.

Not rust stains. Blood. *Heath's* blood and a lot of it.

"What happened?" she demanded and sucked in a hot breath, then asked a second time, but a little more calmly.

"I got the statues back."

Heath slumped without warning, nearly sliding to the floor, which left her with no choice but to slide over to him, cradling his head against her shoulder as best she could with the stupid cast.

"Of course you did," she murmured, smoothing his hair back from his forehead. Then what he'd said registered. "Wait. What?"

"The statues. I opened the safe. There they were."

He was slurring his words, which would have been alarming enough without his eyelashes sweeping up and down in exaggerated blinking motions, as if he couldn't quite focus on her.

"You went after the statues?" she repeated in the world's biggest duh moment. "Not Margo?"

"Both," Heath corrected, and his eyes closed for so long, she thought he'd gone to sleep, but then he pried his eyelids open with what appeared to be considerable effort. "Margo took them. Had to get them back. My leg hurts."

So many things crowded into Charli's chest she could scarcely breathe. "Margo took the statues. She stole them? From the safe?"

Heath nodded. "And then she stabbed me."

Charli's eyes widened so far that they started to ache. Nothing he was saying made any sense, but she did know one thing. He was scaring her. "I'm guessing you've lost a lot of blood."

"So much blood." His words slurred again.

Okay, two things. He needed to sleep for like twelve hours. And she needed to know that he was safe and that Margo couldn't touch him. There was a slight possibility that he'd mixed some things up, but she'd take Margo in the role of villain any day and twice on Sunday.

"We'll pick up this conversation later," she advised him and hefted one of his arms around her shoulders, trying to stand with Heath's dead weight leaning on her. "Okay, this is not going to work unless you help me. Let's get up, Heath. Come on now."

After three tries, he did it and then somehow, they managed to get up the stairs to her room with only one false start and a quick breather midway up. And they didn't wake anyone. A miracle.

As soon as he saw her bed, he whumped onto it and fell back crossways over the comforter.

"Not so fast." She crawled in after him and roused him enough to get him to scooch sideways so his head lay on the pillow. She'd sort out later what a colossally bad idea it was for him to be there.

Geez, he was so beautiful, even ashen-faced. The flutter low in her belly came hard and fast and she shoved it away. This was no time or place to be thinking like that, when Heath was practically catatonic. And still technically off-limits, at least until she heard the full story about Margo and the stitches. Probably not then either, dang it.

There was still too much unsaid between them.

It was harder to tear her gaze away from him than she'd like to admit, though.

What had happened? Never in five million years would she have guessed that Heath would be lying in her bed tonight. That was yet another miracle, one she didn't trust. At all.

The blanks in recent events were enough to get her moving—away from the temptation to forget all the questions and whatever unnamable things had started spreading through her chest, warm but confusing. Just as she started to roll from the bed, figuring it was better to let him sleep alone, he pulled her against his side, settling her in next to him with a soft sigh.

Oh, well, gee. Nothing she could do about it now. She snuggled into his body, careful of her cast and his stitches. The tide in her breastbone settled instantly and she might have melted into a puddle of Charli-goo.

Why had she done such a moronic thing as to fall in love with him?

"Missed you," Heath said into her hair, his breath stirring against her skin. "I texted you all those times. Is your phone broken?"

"Yep," she lied, figuring it was better to let him think that than to get into why she couldn't have responded. To make up for it, she drew little circles against his skin, wherever she could reach, hoping it would soothe him to sleep.

He shouldn't be talking. Not now, not ever. Especially if he was going to say sweet things that she immediately got busy misinterpreting.

"I'm not in love with Margo," he slurred and let that bombshell sit there between them as her fingers froze.

"Maybe we can talk about that in the morning too," she advised him. Man, he must have lost more blood than she'd realized. He was practically hallucinating now.

"Wanted to tell you as soon as possible. Drove very fast and far to get here."

With that pronouncement, he fell into the deepest slumber, leaving her to lie there replaying *not in love with Margo* over and over in her head until it lulled her to sleep.

* * *

In the morning, she opened her eyes to the sight of Heath's blue ones trained on her. They were much clearer than last night but still strained, with fine fatigue lines around them. Something else flitted through them that stole her breath.

And terrified her more than anything else ever had in her life.

"Hey," he murmured. "I don't know how I got here. Do I have a lot to apologize for or just a little?"

"You don't remember much of last night," she said. It wasn't a question because of course he didn't.

That would require him to recall the things he'd said without a reminder and her life didn't work like that.

"You don't have a single thing to apologize for. You basically passed out the second your head hit the pillow." She rolled from the bed despite it being the absolute last thing she wanted to do.

"Stop running away, Charli."

Heath's voice had gained a lot of strength too. That was the only reason she didn't flee to the bathroom after gathering up her clothes. Plus, she didn't like it when he read her mind. Or that he'd called it correctly.

She wasn't a coward and to prove it, she turned and stuck her non-cast hand on her hip. "For your information, you need a shower, and I was going to go downstairs to make you breakfast while you washed off all the blood and other...stuff."

Like Margo's fingerprints.

But saying that would require finishing their conversation from last night and she'd rather not. His presence here had so many land mines associated with it that she scarcely even knew how to talk to him.

If Margo had taken the statues and he wasn't in love with her any longer, what did that mean? That was the question she wanted to ask. Which was why making breakfast appealed so much more, because it was downstairs. Away from Heath. Who hadn't stopped watching her with that mixture of pure, unadulterated affection and slight exasperation.

"I can't take a shower with stitches," he informed her calmly. "Only a bath so I don't get them wet. And you're right, that's what I need, along with you in charge of the soap, washing the places I can't reach."

The implied intimacy in that nearly caught her hair on fire and she'd literally never wanted to do anything more in the history of time.

So instead, she made a face at him. "You'd like that, wouldn't you? To have me attending to your every need. Should I find a French maid uniform?"

Heath contemplated her. "What do you think is happening here, Charli?"

Oh, man, the million-dollar question. She sat on the very edge of the comforter, but only because her knees had buckled. "I don't know. You were here and then you left. Margo was gone too, so naturally I assumed you left together and that was that. I spent all day yesterday making my peace with that, and then...*this* happened."

She waved at the bed to encompass the enormity of his big body in it. The implications were clear. He'd come back to her once he didn't have any other options.

"Considering the fact that Margo's responsible for these stitches, I think it's safe to say she's no longer a factor in my life." The bed shrank as he locked her in his sights, his gaze heated and bubbling over. "I came home, which I should have realized much sooner was wherever you are."

"No." She sliced her hand at the air, blinking. "That's all wrong. You're in love with Margo and everything between us was just practice."

"It's not, Charli. It never felt like practice to me."

It had never felt like practice to her either. But hearing him say that, confirming that he'd been feeling the same way all along—it wrecked her. Last night, he'd said he wasn't in love with Margo. She desperately wanted to take that at face value.

But she couldn't. "And yet you still chose her. Not me."

The mournful last note made her sound pathetic. Heath reacted instantly, though, climbing to his knees and crawling to her. He was too close, and she didn't want him to sense how truly torn apart she felt inside. It was a lost cause, obviously, because he just tipped her chin up and drank in whatever he'd found in her expression.

"I'm sorry," he murmured. "It was a mistake from the first moment. I never should have put her between us."

Well, if there was anything sexier than a man who apologized and admitted he'd screwed up in the same breath, she'd never run across it. It weakened her and she didn't want to be weak. Not about this. "That's... I appreciate that, but it doesn't change the fact that whatever you think there is between us is only the result of the bet."

Heath shook his head, his mouth tightening. "We should have canceled the bet a long time ago."

"What?" She dragged out the word with exaggerated flourish to hide her genuine shock. "What is this thing you're saying to me?"

"There's no bet," he said with exaggerated enunciation, as if to make it perfectly clear he knew exactly what he was telling her. "Not anymore."

His thumbs came to rest on each side of her jaw and stars

exploded against her skin where he touched her. Deeper down. Behind her eyes. In her heart. With no bet and no Margo, what was she supposed to hide behind to ensure he didn't destroy her?

"You can't quit now. You're winning," she muttered, instantly sorry she'd blurted that out, but he'd beleaguered her senses from day one. Why should this be any different? "I don't know how to navigate all of this, Heath."

"What is there to know?" he asked, his thumb brushing across her cheek. "I'm here, you're here. Let's figure it out together."

She wanted that more than anything. Wanted to sink into him and know that it was real this time. But that would require her to take a step toward him too. To make herself vulnerable.

And she didn't know how to do that and survive if he left her again—if he didn't come back.

"Heath?" His thumb stilled. "It doesn't feel like practice to me either. I can't understand how that happened. How to trust this is real when it was never supposed to be."

"We came into this all wrong." He heaved a sigh. "But that doesn't seem to have made much of a difference in how I feel about you."

Her heart missed a few beats. "What way is that?"

"Like I stumbled into a wolverine–honey badger cage match honestly."

That almost made her smile. "Fair. I'm still mad at you."

Heath leaned into her, resting his forehead against hers. "Also fair. But I didn't know I had a choice, Charli. Be honest with me. With yourself. Did you give me one?"

"That's not the point," she protested and pushed back on his chest, a thread of panic chilling her. She wrapped her arms around herself for warmth. Protection. "It was always Margo for you. Until she turned out to be the bad guy. And then it was all Charli, all the way. I want to be picked first. I want to know that there's a man out there who sees my worth from the first and is like, *I want that*. No holds barred. No question."

To his credit, Heath didn't touch her again but the expression on his face sure did. It reached inside and squeezed her heart.

"Let me tell you what I thought was going to happen with Margo," he said, opting to slide off the bed in favor of pacing, though it was more of a one-two shuffle, as he ticked off his points. "I wanted to be different, the opposite of a man who is a self-confessed hothead. I thought if I did that, she'd see it and meet me in the middle. She'd be inspired to be different too. But I didn't know how to be that guy. I thought it was a failure on my part that I couldn't stop using my fists. Then you came along. You flipped that script on its head."

"Because it's stupid to want you to be someone different, Heath," she informed him crossly. "You're already perfect."

His quick grin faded. "That's exactly right. I'm perfect for you. Not Margo."

"But that's who you wanted the whole time," she countered, though his words were weaving a spell she feared she might not be able to break. "You never wanted it to be real. Every time things got a little intense, you threw down how it was practice."

"You jumped in to agree with that every time!" He sucked in a hot breath and exhaled, staring at her. "What in the blazes did you think the time-outs were for? Because I wanted it to be real, but I also didn't want you to accuse me of cheating. It's a fine line. One I wanted to honor and I did, but not solely because it was important to you, but it was important to me too. I needed to give my pride a chance with Margo, but that's all it ever was. Pride. A way to make myself feel better that she couldn't love me the way I am."

The sentiments winnowed underneath her skin, loosening her resolve. Dissolving her arguments.

He must have sensed he had the advantage, because he crossed back to the bed, halting directly in front of her so she couldn't look away, and pushed a finger to her chest. "You taught me that a relationship should make you better, not just different. You make me want to be the best version of myself. I'm only husband material when I'm with you."

Okay, that was going way, way too far. What was he saying, that he wanted to *marry* her? Panic licked through her blood as she slapped his finger away. "That's ridiculous. You're you, no matter what. What in the world could possibly be different with me that you can't—"

"Because I'm in love with you, Charli," he practically shouted.

Everything inside her exploded in a shower of confetti and fireworks as she stared at him. The moment shrank down, heavy with anticipation and meaning and a billion other things she couldn't sort fast enough. "Say that again."

"I'm in love with you." He squeezed his eyes shut for a blink. "Though this is not the way I would have liked to announce that."

Well, this was absolutely the way she would have liked to learn that. It changed everything.

Boosting herself up on her knees, she took his beautiful face between her palms, wholly unable to be anything other than honest in that moment. "I'm in love with you too. It's making me bananas."

Snorting, he pushed his cheek into her palm, his scraggly beard rough against her skin. "Obviously that's going around."

"Did I ruin this?" she asked in a small voice. "I don't know if you know this about me, but I'm neurotic and I tend to pull the trigger first, then ask questions later."

Heath's lips tilted. "I thought I was the one ruining it with my late declarations and ridiculous temper. Though it is par for the course with us to get around to saying how we really feel during a fight."

"I like fighting with you," she murmured, gratified when he nodded his agreement. "You're my safe place. The only person I can trust when I'm Hurricane Charlotte."

And he hadn't given up, moving on to easier, greener pastures. Even when she pushed him away. He wasn't like Toby. Or her father, for that matter. *She* was the one like her father, running from the best thing that had ever happened to her.

This man was everything. So much more than husband material. So much more than a man tasked with keeping her safe.

He was her match.

The only man who could stick with her through everything she could throw at him. Whether he considered it practice or the cold, hard reality of being hit in the face with the brute force of Hurricane Charlotte, he took it all. And kept on ticking.

She couldn't fight this any longer.

"Heath," she murmured and nuzzled his face with hers, which turned into a kiss in the space of a heartbeat.

Their lips fused together, the sensation of finally, finally falling into this moment sliding through her with so much silk that she sighed. This wasn't the heightened, electric kiss she'd expected. It was far sweeter, far deeper, as if every thread in the universe coalesced into this meeting of souls. The way their bodies fit together felt like reuniting missing pieces.

His fingers threaded through her hair as he cupped the back of her head, tilting her neck to deepen the kiss and she let herself go, let herself open to the experience of being wholly consumed by Heath McKay.

This was not a kiss. It was a surrender. On both sides. He held nothing back, pouring himself into the kiss, stamping his signature over every cell in her body, and she accepted everything he was giving her eagerly.

He quite literally overwhelmed her. She loved him so much.

"There's no bet." He slid his lips into her palm, kissing it as he hooked her with his stormy gaze that was now full of something else, something hot and hungry. "No Margo. This is not practice. It's the real thing, no excuses. If you're scared, that's fine. There's a lot of that going around too. But talk to me instead of running. Or pushing. From now on."

She *was* scared. It was unreal how he could read her, how he continually made everything better by virtue of just being Heath. He had the power to destroy her, but she trusted that he wouldn't. That he'd be there for her always. "That's a deal. Now tell me again."

"That I'm questioning my sanity? Done." His smile lit her up inside. "But despite all of that, I love you, Charlotte."

"You know what this means, right?" She brushed a finger over his lips. "You won the bet."

"Oh no, my darling. We both won."

Epilogue

The day of the memorial service brought with it a cold front that required Charli to pull out her fall jacket to guard against the brisk wind. She buttoned up and joined Heath, gripping his hand tightly as they took their seats next to Sophia and Ace.

Veronica sat on Sophia's other side, Paxton next to her. Probably in his role as her newly appointed bodyguard, though—please God—there soon wouldn't be much to threaten any of the Lang sisters. The university people had their stupid jaguar heads back and as far as she knew, they'd found no evidence that Pakal had commissioned baby jaguar statues.

Their mother, Patricia, sat ramrod straight, dry-eyed, next to an empty seat. Symbolic? She'd lost her husband years ago when he'd abandoned them all in search of treasure. Thankfully, Charli had figured out that she didn't have nearly the same sense of wanderlust as her father. And that nothing could compare to the love of a good man.

Heath spread his arm behind her, his fingers warm on her shoulder.

The service began, a pastor Charli had never met walking up to speak about her father. The guy had never met David Lang either, opting to make benign comments about his work and the discoveries he'd made that contributed to the world's knowledge of Maya history and culture. But she knew there was so much more to him than that, layers upon layers she and her sisters had no opportunity to uncover now that he was dead.

She'd almost missed how like her father she was. She'd been so busy trying to paint Heath with the wrong brush that she'd never realized how David Lang's abandonment had shaped his family into people who could easily repeat his mistakes.

But she wasn't going to. Heath deserved 110 percent and she would give it to him as long as he would accept it.

As the pastor invited anyone who wished to share memories to come up, Veronica was the only one to stand. Ironic since she couldn't possibly remember their father too well. He'd left when she'd still been pretty young. Her bold, brilliant sister had the knack for words, though. That's how she'd won all those cases, not because of her fancy degrees.

Paxton watched her sister with careful attention, but he did that with everything. Charli hoped he would provide a lovely distraction for Veronica while she was in town, but the odds of lightning striking three times for the Lang sisters didn't seem very high. Especially not since Veronica still seemed to have unresolved feelings for Jeremy—otherwise, she would have blown off their breakup a long time ago.

The pastor closed the service soon after, leaving the family to receive the condolences of David's acquaintances from when he'd lived at the ranch and probably some people who had known Charli's grandpa.

Heath leaned down to kiss her temple, pulling her tighter into his side via the arm he'd kept slung around her waist the entire time. "You doing okay?"

She nodded. "I'll be a lot better when you can put your hat back on. It's weird to see you without it."

Grinning, he ran his free hand through the ridiculous curls at his neck. "You love my hair."

She did. It was her favorite thing to wake up with her fingers tangled up in his hair. He had a new scar on his leg, a near match to the one near his throat that he'd earned during an operation in Kandahar, but she got to fall asleep against his very lived-in body every night. She liked to think that the sheer force of her love had gone a long way toward healing all the hurts inside him.

He'd certainly made up for lost time loving her hurts away.

Some two hours later, Charli got sick of playing hostess. There were only so many times you could smile and nod when people talked about a man you'd never known. She retreated to Sophia's office, which was apparently her office too since her sister had bought her a desk and her own chair. Charli half sat, half fell into it, a different kind of chair than the one Sophia used, and it wasn't too bad. More comfortable for sure.

Veronica followed her into the office and Sophia poked her head in a moment later.

"Is this where we're hanging out to avoid all the mourners?" Sophia asked and slipped inside, shutting the door to lean against it. "Man, I love Mom, but she owes us for this."

"It's been interesting seeing how many people had good things to say about Dad after all this time," Charli allowed and jerked her chin in Veronica's direction. "At least we got to spend some quality time together. Have you decided what you're doing next?"

Her younger sister shrugged. "I don't know. I was thinking I might stick around for a little while, if you don't think I'll be in the way."

"No, not at all," Sophia said at the same time Charli said, "Yes, you'll absolutely be in the way."

But then she grinned. "I'm just kidding. We all know 'stick around' is code for 'I'd like to make kissy faces with Paxton.'"

Veronica didn't laugh. "I'm not sure that's going anywhere. I was thinking about writing a book, though. About the treasure and Dad's role in finding it. I was really inspired by what the pastor said at the service. And I don't remember him at all. It feels like a nice way to connect with him."

Biting back the negative comments instantly forming, Charli just raised her brows. "That sounds great."

Sophia's phone pinged and she glanced at it, then up at Charli, her expression puzzled. "Uh, Ace says you should go to the window."

What in the world? Charli jumped to her feet and strode over to the big picture window that overlooked the yard, Veronica and Sophia scarcely a half inch behind her. Heath stood there, obviously waiting for her. And wearing his battered Stetson, which he pointed to and flashed her a thumbs-up.

What an adorable goof. She nearly opened the window to yell out something about how it would be more of an improvement if he'd turn around so she could appreciate the rear view, when Paxton appeared with something wide and white in his hand. He handed it to Heath, who turned the card to the window.

It said:

This is my shame sign video.

Paxton pulled out his phone to start recording it, which felt silly when Charli was standing here watching the whole thing, but the fact that he'd held himself to the letter of their bet put a strange lump in her throat.

That alone propelled her toward the latch. She threw up the sash and called out, "We already established that we both won. What are you doing?"

He held his fingers to his lips and pulled the lead card away from the stack to shuffle it to the back. The second one read:

I made a bet with Charli Lang that I could change her mind about men. Except she changed my mind about everything.

The third one read:

The bet was never about winning but about Charli putting me through my paces so I could become husband material.

Oh, man, he was going to make her cry. She shoved a palm against her lips as Sophia grabbed her arm and held on. The fourth one read:

Charli told me I didn't need the practice, but that's only because she makes it easy to love her.

The fifth one read:

And honestly, I never dreamed about being anyone's husband but hers. Charlotte Lang, will you marry me?

Aw, dang it. That broke the dam, and she laughed through her tears as he got down on one knee and held up a ring box. She didn't bother to go around, just vaulted through the open window to the yard, and sprinted to the man she loved. Who caught her easily when she flung herself into his arms, despite being off-center.

"I like the way you do shame videos," she told him and held on to the brim of his hat as she kissed him with every ounce of the gale force winds inside her.

"Is that a yes?" he asked between kisses. "Because I have to send this video to my mom and she's going to want to know the answer."

"I don't know. Maybe we should practice some more so we can be sure I'm wife material."

"I already know," he growled. "You're everything I want and then some."

A few more tears fell to her cheeks as she nodded and held up her finger so he could slide on the ring. "You know a wedding counts as a date, right?"

And then they were both laughing, though Heath had a shiny glint in his eyes as well.

The Cowboy Experience represented a chance to change her fate, to find a place to belong, and that's exactly what had happened, just not the way she'd imagined it. Thank God. She'd found Heath. A cowboy who definitely had to be experienced to be believed. He was exactly what she'd needed but never dreamed would be possible.

* * * * *